controlled
BURN

ERIN
MCLELLAN

RIPTIDE
PUBLISHING

Riptide Publishing
PO Box 1537
Burnsville, NC 28714
www.riptidepublishing.com

Controlled Burn

Cover art: Natasha Snow, natashasnowdesigns.com
Editor: Carole-ann Galloway
Layout: L.C. Chase, lcchase.com/design.htm

ISBN: 978-1-62649-577-7

First edition
August, 2017

Also available in ebook:
ISBN: 978-1-62649-576-0

controlled
BURN

ERIN
MCLELLAN

RIPTIDE
PUBLISHING

To Megan, for helping those who are lost find their way.

table of
CONTENTS

chapter one

Sweat prickled on my neck as soon as I walked into the auditorium classroom. Why was it always hot as balls in here? It was going to make it hard to stay awake today.

I slunk to my normal seat at the very back. I would gladly skip Ethics in News and Media if I could. It was a huge class, so it wasn't like Dr. Milner would notice—it wasn't like he even knew my fucking name. But his snooty TA, Jacob, took attendance, and it was something like fifteen percent of our grade.

"Well, hello, Joel Smith!" I looked up blearily at the owner of the purring voice, only to be confronted by my obnoxiously perky classmate Paulie McPherson. "Rough night?" he asked with a chuckle.

Paulie was this cute, swishy guy who had claimed me as a class buddy because he'd recognized me from the local gay bar. His name, he told me before the first class, was Paul, but everyone who was anyone called him Paulie. That first day, he grabbed a seat next to me, told me he had a 4.0 GPA, and always found a responsible person to befriend in case the world ended and he had to miss class. *Then I'll be able to borrow your notes, and you can borrow mine if you miss,* he'd said. *"You take good notes, right?"* After a mumbled reply from me, he'd smiled and asked, *"You're not dumb, are you? I could go find someone else."* I assured him I was not dumb and would take excellent notes on days he was absent. Besides that exchange, we'd hardly spoken.

Or, well, I'd hardly spoken. Paulie always tried to draw me into conversation.

Good luck with that.

"I'm okay," I told Paulie. He shrugged, settled into his seat beside me, and arranged his pile of sticky notes and different-colored highlighters.

This was definitely my least-favorite class. Journalism was *not* my thing. But my advisor had "advised" me to take it since I still needed my mandatory ethics credit, and the class was notorious for being easy. Which was what I wanted in my general education courses. *Easy.*

The class clatter quieted as Dr. Milner approached the podium, and his TA dimmed the lights. The projector flicked on. *Can I sleep without anyone noticing?* I'd stayed out at the Lumberyard way too late yesterday, especially for a Wednesday night. And the evening had been a complete bust: not only had I gone home alone, but Travis, my best friend and housemate, had gotten lucky and kept me up even later. Loud bastard.

I laid my head on the little tablet desk and closed my eyes.

Dr. Milner cleared his throat. "As most of you know from the syllabus, today we're focusing on the treatment of minors in the press, and we'll continue to evaluate what constitutes private versus public matters." Dr. Milner plodded on for a couple of minutes, and I tried to ignore the scratching of Paulie's pen as he took notes.

I pulled my jacket off the back of my chair and folded it up under my head as a pillow. The hot room and the hum of the professor's voice were going to lull me to sleep.

"Our case study is from a little-known incident in a small town in Nebraska, in which a young man died in a car accident while reading a text message from his alleged boyfriend. After his death, he and his boyfriend, both minors at the time, were outed by the press. Jacob is passing around a packet of the articles we'll look at today, the first of which is titled 'Online Exclusive: Local Baseball Star Dies Reading Sext from Boyfriend.'"

I jerked my head up and almost tumbled from the chair. The newspaper article on the projector at the front of the class caught my eye.

Horror climbed my esophagus like bile. *No, wait.* That was actual bile.

"Please take a few minutes to read the article," Dr. Milner continued. "Make sure to consider . . ."

Dr. Milner droned on, and I swallowed convulsively so as not to blow chunks. The girl next to me handed me a stack of packets, and I took one and passed them on to Paulie.

Diego stared at me from the front page of the packet. It was his senior picture, and even though the copy was black-and-white, I knew his sweater was green and his eyes light brown. I knew he hadn't liked this picture as much as the one in his letter jacket.

This couldn't be happening. I'd outrun this.

Everyone in the room was rustling around, trying to find the article in their packet, but I didn't need to read it to know what it said. The article quoted a source from the local police department that claimed Diego and his boyfriend had been sexting at the time of his death. It had the contents of one message: *I love your mouth. You have the sweetest mouth in the world, D.*

My hands shook as I reached for my backpack. I couldn't be here. I couldn't do this. I knocked my packet onto the floor, and it flopped open to another article: "Sweet Mouth Texter Incident May Lead to New Driving Legislation."

The room spun sickly. For some reason, *that* news article always hurt the worst. Probably because it proved the depth of Diego's parents' hate. They hated me so much that they started a pointless vendetta with a slimy politician from their church to penalize people if they texted someone they knew was driving. It hadn't worked, but it still hurt.

Dr. Milner's voice filtered in through my panic as I shoved everything into my backpack. "Jared Smith's name wasn't released in the press until he turned eighteen, a couple weeks after Diego died, but a substantial amount of personal information about him had already been exposed by one journalist in particular. She was eventually fired due to . . ."

Three years and two states between my past and me; I'd changed everything to escape it. Even my name was different. Dr. Milner had no way of knowing that I had any connection to that boy in the news article with the perfect lips and killer smile.

Acid rose in my throat, and thick saliva filled my mouth. I stood up, ready to flee. Which was what I always did. *Run.* A weight clamped on my elbow, holding me steady.

From very far away I heard, "Joel, honey, you okay?" The room was tunneling to fuzzy gray, but I recognized Paulie's sweet, lilting voice. I felt like the ground had turned to mush, and it was only affecting me.

"Joel, you look like you're going to be sick. You gonna ralph?"

I nodded. My perpetually weak stomach lurched a little. He scrambled over his backpack and rushed me out of the classroom with surprising efficiency.

By the time we made it down the long hallway to the bathroom, my dizziness had cleared, but blood still pumped in my temples. I told Paulie I was fine, and instead of retreating to one of the bathroom stalls "to ralph," I slid down the wall to sit on the floor across from the urinals, bathroom germs be damned. Paulie wrinkled his nose before crouching beside me.

"If you're going to puke, you better warn me so I can move," he murmured before his soft hand landed on my forehead. Hysterical laughter tried to escape my chest, but I pushed it down and closed my eyes.

My God, I was *not* well. If seeing those articles for the first time in years could undo me so completely, I was obviously still a big fucking mess, which really shouldn't come as a surprise to me. I lived in my head every day. It wasn't pretty.

After a couple of minutes of deep breathing on my part and endless questions on Paulie's—"Is it food poisoning? Are you hungover? Do you have the flu? How do you feel? I'm the worst nursemaid ever. I need you to tell me if you're gonna ralph"—I finally opened my eyes.

"It's fine. *I'm* fine. I'm not going to *ralph*, but I can't . . . I don't think I should go back to class."

"Well, let me drive you home, honey. You look positively green," Paulie said.

"I live right across the street. It's one of the reasons I took this class," I said.

"Well then, I'll walk you home. It'll be a pleasure," he said with a sassy laugh. "Let me just go grab our stuff and tell the TA."

Paulie was on his feet so quickly and gracefully that the room spun again. As he left the bathroom, I called after him weakly, "But then no one will be here to take notes for you." He either didn't hear me, or didn't care about class notes today, because he didn't react at all.

He also didn't question me on the walk to my house, which was a relief. I didn't want to delve into the pain of losing Diego without either the ability to sleep it off or a lot of liquid courage, and I simply did not feel strong enough to dredge up a lie for Paulie's sake. The last thirty minutes, from the moment class had begun to the whole walk with Paulie, was almost like a dream—one where all of a sudden you're naked in public or the nice guy next to you has a knife to your ribs. A bad dream. The type that makes you sweat through your pajamas and grind your teeth so hard your jaw aches for days. But *nope*. This sweat was purely the waking kind.

So I shut down. Clicked my brain off like a light switch, something I was rather adept at, and guided Paulie to my home, which was an ancient, crappy two-bedroom house that was a five-minute walk from the campus cutoff. Paulie's silence left me little to do but distract myself by staring at him. I'd never really given him more than a passing glance before. He was unfairly pretty in a slightly androgynous way. He made my skin prickle, but I didn't find him attractive, exactly. Sure, he was attractive from a purely objective definition of beauty, but he wasn't really my type. Short for a man, probably only about five foot seven, with dark hair shaved close to his scalp and a square jaw. He was already fighting a five-o'clock shadow, even this early in the afternoon, and his skull trim left his face exposed and open. Yeah, *pretty*.

I stared, and he must have felt it because he glanced over at me and smiled. His lips looked plump and wet, and I was struck by the slight gap between his two front teeth.

"You have a gap," I said because I was a dork who wasn't coping well at all. "I've never noticed it."

He side-eyed me like I was losing my nut, which was obviously the case. "I don't think you've ever looked at me before today, Joel. It's been quite the hit to my ego. Must be losing my charm." He glanced at me through eyelashes so black and thick I thought he might be wearing makeup. There was teasing in his voice, and it made my stomach dip.

He smiled again and skipped ahead of me. At least for a two-minute space of time, I hadn't thought of Diego.

The two men couldn't have been more different.

I let Paulie in through our front door, and we were immediately confronted with Travis, in his underwear, lying on the couch playing the ukulele. *Poorly*. He played every instrument poorly.

Paulie gasped out, "Well, hello, Hot Pants!" in his musical baritone.

Travis was seriously smoking. A six-foot-three black guy with long muscles and a spanking fetish—which, like his near-nakedness and bad musical ability, I was used to—Travis turned heads everywhere he went.

"Hey! I know you," Travis said. "Paulie, right? I've seen you at the Yard. You're a good dancer."

"See, at least some people notice me, honey," Paulie whispered to me darkly before wandering over to the other side of the living room, where some of Travis's weird avant-garde decorations covered the wall.

When Paulie turned his back, Travis swiveled to me, and his eyes bulged like they were going to pop out of his head. Travis and I both had men over frequently enough, but not usually before 10 p.m., and he had certainly never seen me with anyone like Paulie.

Travis's brow furrowed. "You all right, man? You look terrible."

I felt terrible but didn't exactly relish hearing that it was so obvious.

"He got sick in class today. That's why I walked him home," Paulie piped in from across the room. He swiveled back to me. "You're still a little pale. Maybe you should get something to drink."

"You're probably right. Want anything? We have beer, Dr Pepper, and water." I headed for the kitchen. Was it too early for beer? Some days I wished for an IV drip. The thought of drinking anything, even water, made my stomach flop, but I'd gladly take the buzz of beer over the ringing in my ears.

"Milk is fine," Paulie called after me. I hadn't mentioned milk, but he sounded distracted. Travis had that effect on people.

After stealing some of Travis's expensive organic chocolate milk, for which I would surely owe him later, and downing a huge glass of water, not beer, I was less nauseous, but it still felt like a weight was pressing down on my chest.

I led Paulie to my bedroom, and he plopped down on my bed.

"Oh! This is nice," he said and patted the mattress next to him. "Comfy too. So much room for activities." He smiled up at me, and I wasn't sure if he was flirting or if that was just how he talked to everyone. And, well . . . shit. He was *so* not my type—he wasn't quite anonymous enough for me—and I didn't want to give him the wrong impression. I sat in my desk chair on the other side of the room.

"Your boyfriend is pretty hot," he said slyly.

I narrowed my eyes slightly. Travis and I did *not* give off boyfriend vibes.

"He is, but he's not my boyfriend."

"Oh, good. Think he'd want to be mine?" He grinned at me. A twinge of something—disappointment that I'd read his interest wrong, that he was interested in Travis, maybe?—echoed through my gut. That pang made me more honest than I probably had a right to be.

"That depends, Paulie. Trav is a bottom, and he likes it rough. You think you could do that for him?"

Paulie blew a big raspberry, which made me laugh and his cheeks pink. "He wants a bossy top? That's definitely not me." He sipped the chocolate milk demurely, both hands wrapped around the cup like a child.

"Why not?" I wanted to hear him say it, to hear him say he wasn't into the things Travis was.

"Well, you have eyes, sweetheart. Everyone assumes I'm a femme-y bottom. I know what I look like, and I don't fight it anymore."

I flinched. I'd goaded those words from him. And I wanted to apologize, to tell Paulie that appearance wasn't everything, and that no one should ever make him feel like he had to be a certain way in bed because of how he looked or spoke or walked. But then he threw a proverbial bucket of ice water on my head, and all those nice, conciliatory words I wanted to say disappeared.

"The TA said we could complete the class assignment together and turn it in next Tuesday before class. We just have to create a list of all of the ethical issues in those texting articles, and then write a couple of paragraphs in support of the journalist's decision to write the articles and the choices she made."

All the muscles in my body clenched up and bile burned my throat again. *Fuck no.* Absolutely not. "I'll take the zero," I gasped. Then, before Paulie could catch on to my weird behavior, I said, "A zero on a class assignment won't hurt too bad, and I have a lot going on this weekend. You'll get a better grade without having to work with me on it."

I felt pretty proud of how normal that excuse sounded, until Paulie's eyes narrowed. He stood up slowly, sat the half-gone milk on my bedside table, and walked toward me. He touched my forehead again and sighed. "You still feel clammy. You should get some rest. I'll take notes for you if you're not better by class on Tuesday." Then he grabbed his backpack and left.

Low voices reached me from the living room and then Travis's booming laugh. The front door shut a couple of seconds later. Something terrible and unwanted—like loneliness—rushed through me. I clenched my eyes shut until the wave of emotions dissipated, but I couldn't deny, couldn't ignore that I wished Paulie had run his fingers through my hair. I couldn't remember the last time someone had done that to me.

chapter two

The Lumberyard was the only gay bar in western Oklahoma, and it was within walking distance of the Farm College campus and our house. When Travis and I slipped through the entrance, the dance floor was already pulsing with music and the sway of bodies. The beat of each song sang through my blood, much like the two shots Travis pushed on me as soon as we reached the bar. I was *not* a tequila guy. Unless I was eager to get shit-faced, and let's be honest, I was. But 8 p.m. was a little too early to get trashed, and I needed to make it to midnight. The memories of Diego were always worse after midnight.

I tried to tell Travis I was still sick from yesterday, when he pushed a third shot on me, but he hadn't believed I was sick in the first place. He'd accused me of an "afternoon delight gone wrong."

And, thank God, a big guy in a leather jacket caught Trav's eye about ten minutes in, so I'd get a temporary reprieve to let the alcohol catch up with me. Sure enough, within minutes, he abandoned me at the bar without even a good-bye.

A rowdy pack of men and women came through the front door with a gust of night-chilled air. I sized all of them up out of habit as they filed past me. Paulie was toward the back of the group, his arm around the shoulders of a petite woman with short black hair. They looked striking, like twin anime characters, all big eyes and delicate features.

My heartbeat sped up as he got closer. I wasn't sure I was happy to see him. My main goal for the night was to get fucked or drunk until the Diego in my head disappeared. I wasn't going to fool around with Paulie, and I wasn't getting drunk with him either, so it shouldn't matter one bit to me if he was at the Yard or not. But now, with the recollection of Paulie's irrepressible kindness fresh in my mind, it was impossible not to be drawn to him at least a little.

Paulie didn't appear to see me sitting at the bar, until he was ordering. I leaned over to tell the bartender that Paulie's first drink was on me and bought one for the woman as well. Paulie grinned at me and sauntered over until we were side-by-side. The music beat so loudly we couldn't hear each other speak without getting really close—closer than I wanted—so I just smiled back at him. Thankfully, he didn't ask me if I was still sick. I didn't want to think about that right now. Soon, when I could no longer keep the memories of Diego at bay, I would get trashed or find someone to blow. But I wasn't there yet.

His friend shotgunned her drink—a gin and tonic, which you were probably not supposed to shotgun—and then grabbed my hand, passed my beer to Paulie, and shouted at me, "I wanna dance, and you'll do."

I only resisted a bit. I wasn't used to women pulling me anywhere, and I was worried I'd screw this whole dancing thing up. She probably didn't want to bump and grind, which was really all I was good for.

Thankfully, a pop song with a catchy chorus flared up just as we made it to the middle of the dance floor. In the space of a few seconds, the dancers around us quit dirty dancing and began jumping to the beat. When the chorus started, the entire club shouted the words, and it was ridiculous and perfect and a rush of giddiness bubbled through me.

"I'm Angie," Paulie's friend yelled after a spin that put her right in my personal space. I shouted my name in her ear, and she hip bumped me in acknowledgment.

"Are you Paulie's sister?"

She stopped dancing, so I stopped jumping, even though I was finally getting the hang of it.

"No. We're not related. Thank God. His family is a shit show." She rolled her eyes and resumed bouncing and twirling around me.

After several songs, Angie grabbed my hand. "Come on, I need another drink."

Paulie smirked at us as we approached. I leaned against the bar beside him and scanned the room for Travis, who was still talking to the guy in the leather jacket. Without another word, Angie kissed Paulie on the cheek and flounced off to the rest of their group, where a bucket of Coors Light awaited.

"Enjoy dancing with a girl?" Paulie asked in my ear. His breath was warm, and it tickled my neck.

I couldn't help but smile because I *had* enjoyed it—the whisper of his breath *and* dancing with Angie.

"It was a first for me. I never even danced with a girl at prom," I admitted.

Diego and I had gone to prom our junior year with a big group of friends. We'd spent the night getting drunk on the cheap liquor he'd smuggled inside in his cowboy-boot flask. Afterward, I'd nursed him as he got sick on the side of the road. I could still see the glisten of sweat on the back of his neck and hear the tremble in his voice as he apologized over and over.

I hadn't gone to senior prom. Diego had no longer been there, and I just couldn't.

"Dancing with women is the best. There's no pressure or expectation," Paulie said.

"There would be no pressure or expectation if you wanted to dance with me either."

I didn't know where that came from, because I used dancing almost *solely* as a means for hooking up, and suddenly, I was offering Paulie the opposite. But I understood why he'd want to dance without the weight of casual hookups pressing in on him. It was hard to let loose and enjoy dancing when it was only about sex, when you knew your partner was judging you and trying to decide how fuckable you were. It could suck the joy right out of it. But dancing had never been about joy for me. And I had never wanted to dance just for the fun of it. Until now.

His dark eyes held mine, and I wondered again if his sooty lashes were the product of mascara or if he really was that pretty. But before I could ask about his makeup habits, he downed his beer, handed me mine, and waited while I did the same.

Then we danced.

Travis had said that Paulie was a good dancer, and he was. He blew me away. His chest and stomach, visible under his tight shirt, flexed and twisted with the music, and his hips rolled in a hypnotic rhythm. He moved like oil over water, fluid and sexy. *Everyone* noticed him, and I couldn't believe I never had. After a couple of minutes, another guy stepped up behind him and put his hands on Paulie's hips. Paulie's shoulder immediately clenched under my hand.

I pulled Paulie flush against me and spun him away from the touchy bastard. We ended up with my back to the other dancer and Paulie's back against my chest. I had one arm across his torso, like a wrestling hold, and the other hand on his hip. He soon relaxed and fell liquid again. The tendon on the side of his neck caught my eye, and I followed its path to the smooth, delicate skin behind his ear.

Paulie turned in my arms and grinned up at me, his face flushed and his adorable gap fully on display. He said, "Thank you," and I shrugged it off.

We danced for three more songs, and I just had fun—*actual* fun—and I placed myself between every dancing interloper and Paulie because I wanted to be that guy for once. I wanted to be a friend that he could dance with and not have to worry about being groped or humped.

After we stopped for another drink, a guy I had screwed around with the year before stopped to say hi. Alex Oleastro, all pierced and tatted and hot as sin, was also incredibly nice and one of my best lays ever. Plus he'd never expected our hookups to lead to a relationship, so in a way, he'd been perfect for me. He asked Paulie to dance, and before I could blink, they were off to the dance floor, Alex leading Paulie by his hand. Right on the edge of the crowd, Paulie turned around to look at me and mouthed, *Oh my God!* before pretending to grip Alex's ass. I laughed wildly, too loud and all alone.

While they were dancing, Travis resurfaced from a hot and heavy make out session with Leather Jacket to tell me they were going back to our place, and it was nice of him to warn me. The sound of spanking could be jarring if you didn't expect it.

Paulie and Alex danced for another song—this one slow and sexy. I got hot watching it. Both of them could move, and they weren't being moderate with the touching. By the end of the song, Paulie had his head tilted back on Alex's shoulder, and Alex had one hand splayed across Paulie's stomach under his shirt. With every sway, there was a flash of Paulie's pale waist. They were both flushed and smiling, Alex whispering in Paulie's ear.

As the music crescendoed and cut off, Paulie tipped his head off Alex's shoulder, and his eyes met mine from across the bar. Shame rushed through me; I felt like I'd been caught watching porn. I forced a smile to cover my discomfort, and then I waved to let him know I was leaving. He turned back and said something to Alex before squeezing through the edge of the crowd to reach me.

I laughed at the excitement radiating off of him. He seemed like a kid about to open Christmas presents.

"That dude is fucking hot!" he said, fanning himself.

I leaned forward and whispered in his ear, "And he knows how to use that tongue piercing, let me tell you." Paulie made a strangled noise full of heavy consonants, and I laughed at him again. "You be a good boy tonight, Paulie, and have fun."

He smiled up at me, but it was a different grin than the wide-open one he flashed around without censor. It was soft and shy, and my stomach clenched at the vulnerability there.

Then he leaned forward and kissed me.

The kiss surprised me so much I was still thinking about it hours later while I lay in bed waiting for sleep to take me. It had been a friend-kiss. Just a quick cling of dry lips, no tongue, no breath. But I wasn't used to getting friend-kisses. I didn't have the type of friends who kissed me in a nonsexual way. I didn't really have friends, period, besides Travis, which should probably bother me but didn't.

I had friends once. They were ephemera.

I was half tempted to go ask Travis why we didn't ever platonically kiss. I'd seen him greet countless friends that way, but never me. He and Leather Jacket were pretty quiet now, so I probably wouldn't be interrupting much.

But I was too scared. Scared because I knew the answer Travis would give if he were totally honest.

You're cold. You cut yourself off. You don't put yourself out there.

As if being open was the ultimate expression of being a good person. Well, fuck that.

I didn't want to fall into the dark, oppressive hole that held every reason why I kept people at a distance. I didn't want to fall asleep thinking about Diego again, not when he was so close to the surface already, pushing against my lungs until I couldn't breathe without imagining the smell of his teenybopper cologne. Not when I could so clearly see the bliss in his eyes as I'd taken his virginity, or worse, the agony I imagined had flitted across his features as he was impaled on a fence post.

So instead I imagined Paulie and Alex together, which made me feel dirty, but so what? They would have fun, and Paulie deserved that. He so generously gave other people fun, gave *me* fun.

And, frankly, I didn't deserve that sort of gift.

chapter three

the Tuesday after my meltdown in class and our friend-kiss at the Yard, I asked Paulie if he wanted to come over to do homework. I didn't know why I asked. We were saying good-bye, and then the words were suddenly out there and I couldn't exactly take them back. Yet, as the weeks tripped by and he kept walking home with me after class, I was thankful I'd extended the invite.

Paulie and Travis developed a fast friendship, even though—I couldn't help but notice—they weren't kissing friends. Travis liked that Paulie was a bit of a natural diva, so Paulie vamped it up around him. They could banter back and forth so quickly my head would spin. And suddenly I found myself in possession of *two* friends.

Paulie and I never went to the Lumberyard together. He had a standing date on Fridays with his wild group of friends, who were evidently all accounting majors like him. But if we were both there, we always danced several songs together, and he always kissed me good-bye.

By the end of September, we were hanging out several times a week and eating lunch together after class on Tuesdays and Thursdays. At lunch one Thursday, Paulie told me he would see me at the Yard on Friday, but he didn't show up with his buddies. I snagged Angie and asked if he was sick.

"He had a family issue come up. He didn't tell you?" she said with a weird smile. I liked Angie, but I always felt off-footed when we spoke, like she was in on a joke I couldn't fathom. "You need to ask him about it, Joel. I can't believe he hasn't told you about his family! It's totally nutty, and he's normally super open about it."

I never asked about Paulie's family because then he would ask about mine. And I wasn't going there unless forced. Anytime he brought up the past or high school or boyfriends, I simply maneuvered the conversation away from me. He never seemed to notice.

I didn't see Paulie until a week later, right before our Thursday class. He had even missed class on Tuesday, and I'd actually paid attention and taken excellent notes for him. I figured he would tell me why he was gone all weekend. Instead, he asked, "Miss me?" and then launched into a story about a drunk booty call from a guy he was friends with freshman year. By the time I caught up with his story, he was almost done.

"He was so drunk and only about every other word made sense. And it seemed like the ones that did make sense were all 'cock and balls.' At last, I get it through his thick head that I am not going to leave my apartment at 2 a.m. on a weeknight to bend over for him, and he responds, clear as day, 'Jesus, Paulie, you tease. You could have just told me you weren't interested.'" Paulie giggled at his own story, and I tried to laugh too, but it came out brittle.

Finally, I blurted, "Where were you last week? Are you okay?"

He stopped laughing so abruptly it made me feel bad. No one should ever stop his laughter. It was a crime.

"I had a family thing, but you don't want to hear about my messed-up family."

"I *do* want to hear about your family." And I found it was the truth, even if it meant navigating the land mines of my past. "Why would you think I wouldn't?"

He waited a beat before answering—long enough for me to see guardedness in his eyes for the first time. "Because you don't talk about yours."

Shit. Evidently he *had* noticed that I didn't respond. I took a step back, putting more distance between Paulie and me, and locked down my expression out of habit.

He sighed. "Come on, honey. Class is about to start." He grinned up at me, trying to lighten the mood. "I'll tell you all about the McPherson clan if you buy me a drink after class. If ever there were a group of people that could push me to day drinking, it would be my family."

The class dragged on even more than usual, and by the time the TA turned the lights back on, I was half-asleep and irritated.

While Paulie gathered up his notes and textbook, I asked if he wanted to go to happy hour at Ropers, a country college dive about a block away from the Yard. They had the best happy-hour deals in Elkville.

"*You* go to Ropers?" he asked.

And as I championed the merits of the Ropers' happy-hour margarita, exasperation wafted off of Paulie like heat waves.

"No, Joel. I should have said, 'You feel comfortable going into that hick hellhole?' I mean, Elkville might be this liberal college town in the Middle of Nowhere, Oklahoma, but it's still the Middle of Nowhere, Oklahoma. And Ropers is the epitome of redneck."

"*Oh*. Travis and I go sometimes, and no one has ever bothered us."

Paulie raked his eyes over me, and then fiddled with the forest-green scarf wrapped around his neck. And it hit me like an uppercut. Both Travis and I could pass as straight if we wanted, but Paulie—wearing skinny jeans, a pale-yellow blazer with a feminine cut and floral lining, and a sheer scarf that was not for the purpose of keeping him warm—couldn't.

His clothes weren't the only reason he might have trouble passing. He had a deep voice but spoke in lilting tones and used endearments like *sweetheart* and *honey* all the time. Plus, he moved in a soft manner, not timid exactly, but with grace. Even the way he was standing, with his hip cocked and his long neck stretched in a seductive, open curve, broadcast that Paulie was sassy and different.

I wanted that cheap margarita, though.

"Could you maybe tone it down a tad?"

I wanted to choke the words back down the moment they left my mouth. This was why I didn't have friends. I was such an asshole.

He lifted his gaze slowly from his scarf, and disbelief washed over his face, vicious and ugly.

"I'm going to pretend you didn't ask me to do that, Joel," he said softly, his voice flat. All the musicality with which he normally spoke had vanished, and it scared me. "I have tried, for my entire life, to, as you say, 'tone it down.' If I couldn't do it for my parents, I certainly won't do it for you. Now are you going to buy me a fucking drink or not?"

I was disgusted with myself. The frightening reality that I was about to screw up this whole thing—this *friendship*—practically knocked the breath out of me.

"I'm sorry," I said, because, God, I was an idiot.

I wanted to hug him but was too self-conscious. I had always been able to hide being gay, and for so long, hiding had been necessary. Diego had depended on our secrecy because it kept him safe. I had been safe to him because I could pass. Would he have wanted me if I were swishy? A resounding *no* practically cracked in my vision like a comic-book bubble.

Paulie sighed loudly, snapping me out of the past. "At least let me take off this damn scarf."

"No!" I said, sick that I'd made him question himself in the first place. "I like the scarf."

He'd already begun to unwrap it from his neck, and I stilled his hands. I rearranged the gauzy fabric, but couldn't get it to lie as artfully around his neck as it had been. When I was done, the tails of the scarf hung loosely against his chest and his throat and collarbones were exposed.

Paulie's dark five-o'clock shadow contrasted sharply with the pale skin of his neck, and I was struck with the sudden urge to run my thumb along the line of stubble. I moved my gaze away from Paulie's throat and dropped my hands before I did something stupid.

"Keep the scarf," I said. "If you want. It looks good on you."

He was breathing a little hard, probably from anger, but he nodded and shot me a small smile.

"Let's go, cowboy," I said. "It'll be like going to the zoo."

Peanut shells littered the floor and antique oil and gas signs lined the walls of Ropers. Old horse tack hung from the ceiling and pool tables crowded what would have been a dance floor in the other college bars. Cheap drinks drew the masses, though the redneck regulars made their presence known through the music.

I ordered us a super cheap pitcher of strawberry margaritas, and we found a booth away from the crowd. After several minutes, Paulie began to relax. I asked him what happened with his family, and he looked into his drink.

"Have you ever heard of the Quiverfull Movement?"

"Like a quiver of arrows?"

"Yes, arrows for God," he said bitterly. "Did you grow up religious?"

"No. Not at all," I answered warily.

Besides the stray wedding and Diego's funeral, I'd only been to church once. I'd been fifteen, and it had been almost a year before Diego and I had crossed the line from friends to fucking. My parents had been fighting worse than normal, so I'd spent the night with Diego and gone with his family to church the next morning. Diego's parents had fed me, given me a bed, and ensured I did not have to listen to my screaming parents or my mother's inevitable crying. But I'd known they would never accept me if they knew how much I wanted their son.

And I'd been right.

"Long story short," Paulie explained. "Quiverfull is an evangelical movement where big, strong Christian fathers don't believe in wrapping their tools, and faithful mothers don't take birth control. So everyone has a shit-ton of kids. I'm the second oldest of eleven."

"God!" I gasped. "Wasn't that expensive?"

Paulie laughed low in his throat. "Yeah, it was. My dad's an engineer. My mom homeschooled us, which is common in Quiverfull. I loved having a big family when I was little. There were always babies to play with, and every day seemed like a Christmas card. Like, we had homemade bread all the time. But I didn't realize how much we struggled financially until I got older. God always provides—that's what they say."

"What happened?" I asked.

"I'm gay. That's the first major problem, but maybe not the biggest." Paulie paused for a second, like he was shoring up his reserves before letting the floodgates open. "I have eight sisters, and then the youngest are twin boys. So it was a very female-centric house for a very long time, and my sisters are so warped. They were all taught that they should follow the path of their husbands, and that a strong man will lead them from temptation. And that it is their duty to have as many kids as they can pop out, and to do otherwise is against God's will. As far as the church and my parents are concerned, it's their preordained role to be the helpmeet. It's sick.

"Daria, who is a year younger than me, ran away when she was seventeen because she wanted to go to college but my parents didn't think she needed it. Their neighbor's son was courting her, and that was going to be her life: the baby maker. Now my parents won't speak to her, and she's in therapy to deal with the constant guilt. That's the thing about growing up that way. You're, like, indoctrinated to feel guilty over every action or thought. It turns my stomach to think about how my other siblings deal with sex and desire and intimacy. They're probably all perfect robots. Daria and I got out, but the guilt is still an ugly thing. It's not easy to kick."

"You don't see your family at all?" I didn't want to see my mother very often, but I liked knowing I *could*.

"No, not besides Daria. My aunt took me in when I was fourteen, and Daria when she ran away four years later. See, I always knew it was total bullshit. I was one of those little boys who wanted to wear dresses and play with my sisters' Easy-Bake Oven. I knew I was different, but never tried very hard to change. Like, God made me the way I am, and my parents were obviously wrong. Why couldn't I be more into dolls than trucks, you know? When I hit puberty, there was no going back. My parents hated everything about me, and I stopped trying. I was grounded all the time because of the way I wore my clothes, or spoke, or because they had found my stashes of teen magazines.

"When I was thirteen, I called my dad's sister, Ruth. I'd never met her. She was the only one of my dad's siblings to leave the fold, and I had to use the computer at the library to find her number. I think I said to her, 'I'm so gay it's not even funny.' And she told me that eventually I might want to leave, and she would take me. That's exactly what happened."

"I can't believe your parents didn't put you in one of those reparative therapy camps, that they just let you go live with your aunt."

That had always been Diego's fear, and it could have been legitimate. We never found out. Diego never had to experience the heartbreak of his parents' rejection and contempt. Though, in the end, they had no issue turning it on me.

"I expected that too, and was sure my family was five seconds from a pray-the-gay-away intervention. So I never outwardly admitted it to them. In fact, the first time I said it out loud was to my aunt that day on the phone, and the second time was when I told my parents and asked to move out. They felt like I was old enough to choose to leave. They drove me to my aunt Ruth's house and helped us with all of the legal stuff. Maybe they just saw me as a lost cause, which was pretty much the truth. Whatever they thought, they just shut down, and I became nothing to them."

Paulie stalled out and downed his margarita. The pink drink stained his mouth a little at the edges like Kool-Aid.

I had no idea what to say. It wasn't only that he'd been rejected by his parents. It was that they'd delivered him to his aunt wrapped up with a bow and never spoken to him again.

He spilled his story, his past, so easily, but I didn't tell anyone, not even my closest friends, where I was from or about my past. I closed myself up tight and not only protected my emotions but also hid away those memories that were tainted and ugly.

Paulie had no idea how courageous I thought he was in that moment. How much I envied his strength. How much I liked him.

"In the past, I've enjoyed telling that story," Paulie said, watching me closely. "I felt like it made me interesting or something. But I didn't really want to tell you. I didn't want you to think I'm a freak. And you never talk about your family, so I figure they're either fucked up like mine or abnormally normal."

I hesitated, because I hated repaying Paulie with a lie after he'd been so forthcoming, but I couldn't risk telling the truth. I didn't want to open myself up, no matter how much I appreciated Paulie's honesty.

"They're not fucked up like yours. I think I'd be hard-pressed to find one that is. I'm an only child. My dad won't speak to me because I'm gay. So it's just me and my mom." I spewed the words like a line in a play, well-rehearsed and smooth.

I couldn't tell Paulie about the day Dad had backhanded me and called me a faggot. I didn't mention that my rather explosive outing ripped apart my parents' already tenuous marriage, and ultimately, my relationship with my mom had suffered almost as much as the one with my dad.

Paulie nodded in understanding, even though he couldn't possibly understand at all.

"But I was older when all that happened, you know?" I said. "A senior in high school. You were what? An eighth-grader? A freshman? Fourteen is really young to lose your family." Mine had imploded at eighteen, and most days I didn't care. Most days I tried not to care about anything.

Paulie's eyes flashed with pain. "I don't think I realized what I was doing. I don't regret it. Not *now*. But it's impossible for a sheltered fourteen-year-old to fully understand the consequences of that type of action. I wasn't thinking about not seeing my siblings or parents again. I just thought about myself and wanting to be happy."

I was fully aware of the teenager's capacity to not comprehend consequences.

I finished my drink and looked around. The sky had darkened, and the happy-hour patrons were dwindling. A group of farm boys fired up a redneck song on the jukebox, and everyone cheered. That was probably our cue to exit stage left. "So you still haven't told me why you were gone last week."

"Daria's sick," Paulie explained. "She was always sensitive, and she always took everything so hard. I don't think she's had a day since she ran away where she wasn't completely overwhelmed. She's depressed, and she sleeps around a lot. It's like she's fetishized the guilt or something, so she feels awful about screwing around with random guys but can't stop, which is actually pretty normal for people who leave Quiverfull. Anyway, some days she does great, and some days she can't get out of bed."

"Did something happen last week? Is she gonna be okay?"

"Well, two weeks ago, she cheated on her boyfriend, and he broke up with her. She's been struggling since then. I went home to help her move out of her dorm room at Emporia State University and back in with our aunt because Daria's therapist thinks a more controlled environment will help her. Aunt Ruth lives in Emporia too, so Daria will be able to keep going to school. And I do think she'll be okay. She's really strong."

I reached across the sticky linoleum table and grabbed his hand before I considered how it would look. I didn't care. His eyes were really bright, and, oh God, it hurt. I would have done anything in the world at that moment to see his gap-toothed smile. I had nothing to offer, though. I knew what it meant to lose someone, but had no practice in offering reassurance.

"Let me buy you dinner, Paulie. Anything you want." I had so little else to give.

He did smile then, and I was shocked by how that smile could turn me inside out when no one, no one since Diego, had been able to come close. I didn't like it at all.

"You're turning out to be a very good date, sweetheart. You've protected me from all of the big, scary rednecks, and now you're buying me sushi."

chapter four

ravis and I squeezed through the crowded entrance of the
Lumberyard, and the low, familiar hum of excitement raced
through my body. The Yard was holding its monthly rave night, which
meant a bigger and wilder crowd from all over western Oklahoma.
Strobes pounded to the electric beat, and glow-in-the-dark sticks
and necklaces flashed around like lightning rolling through storm
clouds.

A group of five young guys stumbled right in front of us.
They were trying to hold one of their buddies upright. The sight
of them, so fresh off the bus and yet completely fucked up before
10 p.m., snapped something in me. I remembered being that green
and trying so desperately to be an adult—to drink like one, look like
one, fuck like one.

What if I never actually managed it?

We slipped by them, and Travis said, "God save me from drunk
newbies," in my ear before snagging a space at the bar.

I gripped Travis's biceps. Everything was too bright, too loud,
and too desperate. *I* was too desperate, and I didn't know why.
Didn't know why suddenly Diego's voice and scent and laugh was
drowning me.

"I want to get laid. Shots. On me."

Travis raised one of his eyebrows at me, and his white teeth
flashed in the black lights. "Consider me your best wingman. Paulie
has nothing on me."

"Paulie's not my wingman," I said, rejecting that without thinking.

"If Paulie isn't your wingman, what is he?"

Fucking hell, now he wasn't going to leave it alone.

"Well, he's my friend, but it's not like he helps me get laid." I threw back the first shot. Travis followed with his.

"Why not? You have similar tastes. You both like clean-cut, boring tops. What's the problem?"

"Not *boring*. And it's not like we're always around each other when we want to find a hookup."

"That's bullshit," he said, and downed his second shot. "You hang out with Paulie *here* all the time. You know, the gay bar, which is where *you* meet guys, almost exclusively, since you don't like Grindr."

I took my second shot and filled with fire. "I don't know what you're trying to say. I just haven't been—" I stopped when a slow smile spread across Travis's face. *Irritating prick.*

"Haven't been *horny* since you started hanging out with Paulie?" he said with a calculated leer. "Or *interested*?"

This conversation needed to be over, like right now.

I signaled to the bartender for another round.

"I do believe you're trying to get me drunk," Travis said when I handed him the third shot. I gulped mine, but Travis simply rotated his glass on the bar. "So . . . since Paulie has come into our lives, you haven't *wanted* to get laid? Is that what you're telling me?"

"Why's it matter? I'm interested now."

I assessed the crowd and started toward an opening in the sea of writhing people on the dance floor, savoring the way the alcohol and lighting made my vision swimmy.

Travis grabbed my shoulders and wheeled me around. "Whoa, I didn't mean anything by that." He smoothed his hands up and down my arms, which was a sure sign he was feeling the music. "I only noticed you haven't been fooling around with anyone lately, and I personally think there's a reason for that. I'm not sure what that reason is, but I don't think it's a bad thing. In fact, I think it's probably a good one. Not my business though, huh?"

I brushed off his words. Didn't want to think about how long it had been, or why. I couldn't think about that now, not when the need to get laid, to stop thinking for five fucking minutes, was so strong. I let Travis lead me toward the dancers.

Before the crush of people could pull us apart, he shouted in my ear, "Your type at ten o'clock with the goatee, three o'clock with the blond Kennedy hair, and red shirt just coming through the door, since you *are* interested and horny."

The guy with the goatee and the blond were both dancing in my line of vision, and they were promising. Before I could turn toward the entrance, which was behind me, Travis smacked a kiss on the side of my head and said, "See ya later, sweetheart. Practice safe sex." He waltzed off toward the DJ. His kiss shocked me so much—*evidently, we were kissing friends*—I almost forgot to look at the door.

When I turned, there was only one red shirt at the front of the club, and the man wearing it was Paulie.

Paulie scanned the area by the bar, and I could tell he was looking for me. My stomach jumped in happiness or fear. Travis thought Paulie and I had something going, or at least that I wanted to. But I didn't. Paulie and I were friends. That was all.

But with Paulie, the vise around my emotions loosened and allowed all of his brightness and silliness and fun to slip inside. Maybe that wasn't a good thing. If spending time with him truly loosened the latch on my feelings, it also left me exposed.

My heart pounded in my eardrums, and my chest bumped into the back of a tall, muscular guy wearing Day-Glo yellow. He turned and grinned at me. He wasn't the goatee or Kennedy hair, but he hit all my normal buttons. Cocky. *Check*. Beefy. *Check*. Mostly sober. *Check*.

I placed a palm on one of his pecs, rubbed in a little circle, and he grabbed my ass. *Check*.

"I'm David." His breath hit my ear. "David McDavid." The last name shocked me. Not because it was ridiculous—which it was—but because he'd given me one at all. Random hookups did not require surnames. That was what condoms were for.

"You should own a used car lot. Come on down to David McDavid Chevrolet."

His eyes widened, and he grinned again. "Oh good. You're funny. I like funny," he said, as if I had met one of *his* requirements. I stole my arms around his neck. He'd do.

Once David McDavid realized I'd give him full control, he took it. I let him maneuver me into a dirty grind, one of his hands clenched in my hair, and closed my eyes to the glaring lights and this man I didn't actually want.

I wanted the release, sure. I wanted to forget. I wanted to escape the mess of my fucked-up existence. But no, I didn't want David, like I hadn't wanted any of the men before him. Not for a long time.

Then a hand slipped over my shoulder blades and down my spine. It wasn't David's, and I turned to the newcomer. At first, I could only make out red and a glow-in-the dark necklace, but with each flash of the strobe, more appeared. Dark eyes and stubbled jaw. Cropped black hair. Wide cheekbones. Wet lips. *Paulie*. David dropped his fist from my hair and opened himself up so Paulie could almost slip between us, and as Paulie turned toward David, different parts of him were exposed to me. The tight knob at the top of his spine. The whorl of his ear. The strong line between his shoulder blades. The curve of his neck that got me every fucking time. He ran his hands up David's pecs, much like I had when I first met him.

Then Paulie's hand snaked behind his back, found mine, and pulled my arm across his middle. He kept his fingers twined over mine, so I could feel nothing except his palm and the heat of his body. My heart pounded against my rib cage and confusion rushed through me. I didn't want to like his hands on me, but I couldn't deny that I did. He shimmied against me a little. I was already hard, and he could surely tell. That was new for us. When we danced, neither of us got hard-ons, or if we did, we certainly didn't touch each other with them. I wasn't sure how to feel about this, and part of me wanted to have a messy meltdown about changing the rules before I was ready. But instead, I sunk into the sensation of Paulie's hot little body in front of me. As the beat picked up, Paulie gripped David's hip and dragged him forward, riding his thigh. David groaned and extended his arm over Paulie's shoulder and wrapped his fist back into my hair.

In no time at all, Paulie had us rocking to the electro-pop beat, and the sight of him and David pressed together in front of me pulsed behind my eyelids every time I closed my eyes. The tension in Paulie's abdomen rippled against my palm as he leaned in and sucked David's bottom lip into his mouth.

I flinched away to give them room even as it hit me that Paulie had totally swooped in on my catch for the night. But Paulie's hand, which was still pinning my palm against his stomach, gripped me hard. The kiss lasted around five seconds—fifteen strokes of the strobe lights.

Paulie released my hand, spun, and looked up at me. "You normally wait for me to start dancing."

His hands slid along my jaw and into my hair, knocking David's away. I let Paulie lead me, not sure how we ended up *here*, erections pressed together and heat ripping through me. He yanked my face down hard, and my mouth landed on his. My mouth was slack with surprise, like a sloppy adolescent, but then Paulie slipped his tongue inside. He never friend-kissed me with tongue! It felt amazing, like his tongue, hot and slick and suggestive, was the urgent answer to everything I needed *right then*. I sucked on it before skating my tongue past his lips and into his mouth. Paulie's body melted against mine. I was only vaguely aware of David's hand on my hip and the three of us still moving to the beat. Paulie began to draw away, but as our mouths slid apart, I skimmed my tongue over his front teeth because more than anything I needed to feel that little gap and know who it was that I was kissing.

After Paulie pulled away from me, his face was still close enough for me to see sweat beading along his hairline. I wanted to lick it off. Both of my hands were clamped in the back of his shirt. He tilted his head up, gave me that crazy, open grin, and winked. The song surged to its ending, and he turned in my arms to face David.

Paulie thanked David for the dance, but I barely tracked their words. And then suddenly, Paulie stepped away from us. As he walked behind me, he ran his hand down my spine again, and I shivered.

David's hands landed on my shoulders like claws, digging in and trapping me. "Oh my God, that was hot. I want you so bad," he said. The next song swelled into the chorus, and his mouth crashed into mine. The music and the pressure of David McDavid's mouth washed away the taste of Paulie, and I wished I could snap my teeth shut and stop the loss.

Thirty minutes later, I couldn't shake the memory of Paulie's tongue in my mouth, and David was still all over me. He had me pressed against my closet door, his groin grinding into mine, his hands roaming through the hair on my chest.

"What is it that you want to do exactly?" I asked. I liked to know limits. It made the dismount smoother.

He paused, his mouth open against my collarbone. "I don't really want to fuck," he said, and relief almost weakened my knees.

And that scared the shit out of me.

Travis teased me that I was always "down to fuck," but that sentiment wasn't quite true. I was always "down to forget" or "ready to screw the memory of my dead boyfriend out of my head." Sex did that for me. It rocketed me outside myself for a short moment of time. And then it put me to sleep, so it was perfect.

And fucking was so impersonal, not at all like some of those other acts—the fingering, the caressing, the kissing—that involved tenderness and eye contact.

"Blowjob?" I asked, and David nodded. I hit my knees, pulled his cock out of his pants, and rolled a condom down his length. And— thank the God of Cocky Tops—he didn't fight me on the rubber.

Still, unease prickled down my spine, and I swallowed him down quickly. It would go faster if I deep-throated him, even though that always made me gag. He clenched his hands in my hair, like he had been doing all night, and whispered, "Holy shit."

My vision blurred from the raw burn in my throat and the tang of the latex. I swallowed him again. He smelled good, but it wasn't enough to stop the distress creeping in on me. I suddenly wanted it to be over so badly my eyes filled with tears.

What the fuck was happening to me? Why didn't I want this? I needed to get him off and get him gone before I cracked.

I fumbled with the zipper on my too-tight club jeans and managed to pull myself out. I was still hard. My body still wanted the release, and maybe if I came now, I wouldn't have to worry about David wanting to reciprocate. I pumped myself a few times, which helped clear my head. David groaned above me, and I glanced up to see him watching me jack off. The eye contact obviously ratcheted him higher but left me cold.

I sucked hard on his tip before pushing him to the back of my throat. His body tightened, so I swallowed over and over. My vision started to tunnel from lack of air, and I pumped myself faster and harder, focusing right on my crown. I wanted to go over at the same time as him. I wanted it to be done. I drew a fast breath and dove again. My back clenched as my orgasm rose from the base of my spine.

I moaned, not because it really felt that good, but to trigger David's orgasm. He doubled over and pumped harder into my throat as he came.

Seconds later, my body spit out a pathetic, sticky little mess in my hand. Less than an instant's rush of euphoria before my muscles relaxed, and it was over.

chapter five

After David McDavid caught his breath, I asked him if he wanted me to walk him back to the Lumberyard. Confusion and hurt flashed across his handsome face, and guilt sunk my stomach because I normally didn't kick a man out the minute we both came. But I needed to be alone. I needed to breathe.

David could clearly tell I wasn't quite right, the wariness obvious in his eyes. He stripped the condom, dropped it in the trash can by my desk, tucked himself back in, and crouched down next to me on the floor. He cupped my cheek and asked, "Are you okay?"

He was *nice*. They were always fucking nice, and I couldn't, just couldn't, for the life of me, figure out how I always seemed to end up in bed with the nice ones.

I tried to smile at David—this super nice, super-hot person in Day-Glow yellow—and said, "I'm fine. I just need to crash."

So he left.

I scooted around to get my back against the wall. My breath was coming easier, but my arms and legs still trembled. I didn't know why I was upset.

Sex normally made me happy. I liked the evisceration of it. Even when the power of it wasn't enough to wash the memory of Diego from my mind, I had never been distressed by it. I banged my head in frustration on the wall behind me. The memory of Paulie's hands stroking my hair flashed, unwanted, through my mind.

A gasp tore out of me. It was *Paulie*. This shame and guilt and nausea, this *trembling*, was because of him. I didn't want him, but I was drawn to him. Even more so now that I knew about his family.

But he wasn't the type of guy I needed. He was beautiful, but he wasn't *faceless* enough to eviscerate me.

The front door slammed, and I froze. I couldn't let Travis find me like this, sans David McDavid, and obviously a hot mess. Fuck, he had probably passed David on his walk home! I jumped to my feet and changed into my pajamas, hoping that if he came looking for me, he would think I was getting ready for bed. Then I heard voices.

"Why'd ya bring me here, Trav? I'm fine. And don'tcha go get that dickhead, either. He's with Mr. Pectoral and would never forgive you for cockblocking him." Paulie's voice was slurred but resonant in our old house.

I moved to the hallway, still out of sight, and listened.

"You're not fine, Paulie. You're trashed. And why do you think Joel's a dickhead?" Travis asked. *Don't answer,* I wanted to tell Paulie. *It's a trap.*

"He's not a dickhead," Paulie sighed. "He's Mr. Perfect. And he'll have adorable babies with Mr. Pecs. They'll hyphenate their names to be Joel and What's-His-Name Perfect hyphen Pecs. And I'm not drunk. I don't get drunk."

It was true. In fact, Paulie hardly drank at all. The shock of hearing him slurred and unfiltered was making me lightheaded.

"That cute little scenario would have to assume Joel gets serious with people. But he doesn't. He'll hardly ever sleep with the same guy twice. Also, he's not perfect. He snores. Hella loud."

"I do not!" I said without thinking. Realizing they surely heard me, I moved around the corner. Paulie moaned and flung his head back. It bounced off the top of the couch.

"You alone?" Travis asked.

"Yes. He's gone. Paulie, I'm astounded that you're drunk." I sat down next to him.

He whimpered softly before slinging his arms around my neck and tucking his face against my shoulder. I wrapped my arms around him reflexively, and he burrowed deeper into my chest. My heart raced as I looked at Travis over Paulie's head, and he grinned.

"I'm not drunk," Paulie whined. "And I don't like it."

"You don't like *not* being drunk?" Travis asked.

Paulie scoffed, and his breath brushed across my collarbone. "No. I don't like the way I feel."

"That's because you're drunk, buttercup, and evidently a cuddler," Travis replied with a laugh. I rubbed Paulie's back in what I hoped were soothing circles. Holding him like this after my earlier shame was maybe a little too much for me to handle in one night. Emotions, ones I couldn't begin to place or put to words, bubbled under the surface, threatening my disaffected façade.

"Buttercup!" Paulie sat up abruptly and swayed so hard Travis and I had to catch him. "That's what I'll call you, Joel. Buttercup." He whispered the last word with a smile, and then slumped back into me.

"You already call me 'honey,' 'sweetie,' and 'sweetheart' all the time. Why can't we stick to that?"

"Because it matches your hair. You're a buttercup." Paulie's eyelashes flitted across the sensitive skin of my neck, and he sighed as if he were falling asleep. Then he groaned, and Travis and I both recognized that sound.

"Buttercup, I think I'm gonna ralph," Paulie said, but Travis and I already had him moving to the bathroom.

We leaned him against the bathroom wall after he lost the contents of his stomach, and he mumbled something about accounting spreadsheets.

"That shit wouldn't make sense to me even if he were sober," Travis said.

"He has a test on Monday. I think that's what he's talking about."

Paulie nodded as if to say, *Duh. What else would I talk about?*

When we were pretty sure he wasn't going to throw up again, Travis hauled him to his feet.

"Your bed?" he asked.

"Yeah, I can keep an eye on him."

"Where's your guy from earlier?" Travis peered at me, like he was trying to see through foggy glass, and I feared I had given too much away. Maybe he could see how drained I was, or could tell the idea of being in bed with Paulie left me feeling raw.

"He had to go home. Just wanted a quickie."

"Do we need to change your sheets?" God love him, but Travis managed to say that without a sneer, smirk, or judgment. I shook my head.

Travis grunted in response, and Paulie muttered about pivot tables.

We got Paulie's jacket and jeans off of him, neither of which he gave up easily. When he was down to nothing but a pair of briefs and a shirt, both bright red, we convinced him to crawl beneath the covers where he fell asleep almost immediately. He looked vulnerable like that, in my bed and helpless, and I was so thankful he hadn't gone home with anyone else.

"I'm going to get him some water," Travis whispered.

"Maybe some aspirin, too?"

"Of course."

Travis slipped out of the room to retrieve the supplies, and I moved my trash can to the side of the bed in case Paulie needed it, lay down on top of the bedspread, and wrapped myself in a spare blanket. When Travis returned with the hangover cure, I reluctantly pulled my eyes away from the shape of Paulie's hairline on the back of his neck. It came to an off-center little point, and I had to stop myself from tracing it with a finger.

"Good night, lover boy," Travis whispered as he left my room again.

"Fuck you," I said drily, and a bark of laughter followed him down the hallway.

Paulie sat up abruptly, which, in turn, jolted me awake, and I almost fell out of bed. He steadied me with a hand against my side, and I took a deep breath, trying to slow the sudden pounding of my heart. I'd forgotten he was in my bed, and waking up next to him was a shock. He seemed disoriented too, like he'd also just woken up, but his eyes were bright and alert. He was probably a fucking morning person. I grabbed my phone to check the time.

"Six forty-five," I said. He blinked at me and then scanned my room quickly. I could see him assessing the situation—me lying on top of the bedspread in pajamas, him in his underwear, and the trash can on the floor next to him.

"I'm going to go throw up and then shower." When he stood up, he didn't even waver.

"Sure you're okay? I'll find you some clothes that don't smell like the bar, and we have a couple spare towels under the bathroom sink. Also, extra toothbrushes in the drawer."

He nodded at me grimly and walked out of my room. I fell back against my pillow and could smell him in my bed: light sweat and liquor and an undertone of the soap he used. *Oranges.* The scent turned my normal morning wood into something a little more insistent, which was too much if Paulie was going to walk back in here wearing just a towel.

I jumped out of bed and rushed to find him a pair of my sweatpants and a sweatshirt. They would swamp him, but at least he wouldn't have to walk around half-naked. I *really* didn't want him to walk around half-naked.

I left the clothes, plus a pair of clean boxers, in a neat pile outside the bathroom door.

When Paulie slipped back into my room, still slightly wet from the shower and blushing, I tried to stifle my smile. I liked the way he looked in my clothes—comfy and small. He had rolled the sleeves of the sweatshirt a couple of times, but the neck exposed the notch of his throat and part of his collarbones. The bottom of the sweats dragged on the ground.

"Thanks for the undies," he said, plopping down on the bed. He snatched the water off the bedside table and took several big swallows. I had to rip my gaze away from the rippling of his throat and the bob of his Adam's apple. What was wrong with me this morning? I was like a teenager. He smiled at me and lay back down on my bed.

"You feeling okay?" I asked.

"I feel good actually. Just tired. I think puking last night helped."

"Guess you can't say you don't get drunk."

He chuckled. "Drat! And it was such a banner of superiority! I liked to throw it in people's faces."

"Well, Travis and I won't tell. Your secret's safe with us."

"Oh, sweetie, that whole club saw me. I'm pretty sure at one point I yelled, 'Let's get shwasted!' And everyone cheered. Then Travis told me he would take me home, which obviously did not mean what I thought it meant because I assumed I would wake up in my own bed."

"Yeah, sorry about that, but you needed to be taken care of. Not a big deal, and I'm glad you weren't alone. Did you throw up again this morning?"

"Nope! But thanks for the toothbrush. Why do you guys have a drawer *full* of toothbrushes? There's literally nothing else in that drawer." He patted the bed next to him, so I lay down too. We were on our sides facing each other, and we were probably closer than my queen-sized bed required.

"My mom's a dental hygienist," I said. She always had boo-koos of dental care paraphernalia, but I didn't really want to tell Paulie that I stole her stash so Travis and I would have extras for late-night company.

"You never talk about your family or where you grew up. I told you all about my childhood, but sometimes I feel like I don't know anything about you." He spoke softly, and our intimate little scene threatened to overwhelm me.

"I don't like talking about my family," I admitted. "Please don't make me." It was one of the most honest things I'd said to anyone since coming to college. Heat rushed to my cheeks, and I looked down to avoid his eyes.

"Sometimes, Joel, I feel like the way I grew up stunted me a little. Like it made me younger than I really am because I didn't grow up knowing stuff that other teenagers knew, and I didn't get the chance to develop social skills with anyone outside the church. So I don't feel twenty-three." At the question in my eyes—I had assumed he was twenty-one like me since we were both juniors—he said, "I was held back a year in middle school after moving in with my aunt, and I haven't taken a full course load every semester." He smiled wryly. "So yeah, I'm stunted. But there are times when you seem so young to me, and I think, 'Thank God, I'm not the only one who's still figuring shit out, still learning how to be okay.'"

I bristled, but I got what he was trying to say. I wasn't alone. He knew what it was like to be rejected by his parents. But he didn't know, *couldn't know*, just how truly stunted I was.

Still, it was nice that he'd let me off the hook and hadn't pushed me to talk about my parents, so I reached out and squeezed his hand.

"Okay, enough of that, buttercup! If we're going to lie in bed all day, let's talk about something fun."

"Like what?" I laughed. I had hoped he wouldn't remember the nickname.

"Sex."

"What? Why?"

He glanced at me slyly. "I had no idea your type was brawny chic until I saw you dancing last night. Then Travis told me that you always go for that type of guy."

"'Brawny chic'? That's cute. Travis says my type is 'boring top.'"

"You always bottom?" he asked, and I blushed again. I looked down at his sweatshirt, *my sweatshirt*, which gaped at the neck.

It wasn't that I didn't like to top, but when I bottomed, I could just let everything happen to me. Could stop thinking so hard. Feeling so hard.

"Normally."

"And you like being manhandled."

It was true that I let men manhandle me, and I didn't *dislike* it. I just wasn't sure how Paulie could tell all of this from seeing me dance with one guy. "How do you know that? Me and that guy last night—"

"No, it was me. I could tell you liked it when I manhandled you."

I flushed hot and cold. When Paulie had hauled my mouth down to his, I hadn't thought of it as manhandling. Maybe because he was small and swishy and adorable, but I had never seen him as a top.

One thing was for sure, though: when he'd kissed me, I'd loved it.

Rather than responding to his statement, I asked, "Why don't you top? Do you not like it?"

"I have no idea if I'd like it. I've never had the chance." His tone wasn't really bitter, just matter-of-fact. "I've always figured I would get to switch if I were in a relationship, but that's like a unicorn. Paulie's boyfriend—a mystical being that lurks in the magical woods of a faraway kingdom . . . not called college."

He grinned at me, but I couldn't smile back. Memories of Diego assaulted me suddenly. We'd been in a relationship, but I'd still been too scared to switch.

"You shouldn't have to bottom all of the time, Paulie. Not if you don't want to." It was something I wished I could have said to a different beautiful, dark-headed boy once. I would forever regret missing that chance.

"I know," he said with a mournful sigh and eye roll. "And bottoming is such an imposition. I just don't know how I'll ever survive!" We both laughed at his sarcasm, and the cloud of pain and guilt cleared from my mind.

After a thoughtful silence, Paulie said, "Sex is one of the things I feel stunted about, actually. I never even watched porn until I had my own dorm room. I literally didn't know how it worked when guys had sex with other guys. I just knew that I wanted it. I had so little understanding of the dynamics of sex and hooking up and just the gay scene in general. And I still find myself making all these assumptions, and I feel bad for putting everyone in boxes, for putting myself in a box. Like I'm a bottom because I'm a nellie queen, and yeah, *I like it*, but I have never once in a hookup scenario questioned who would top or bottom. I've never asked to top. And maybe that's because I'm attracted to guys that I think of as stereotypical tops, like you, Mr. Brawny Chic. But then I learn that you mostly bottom, and it blows my mind. And Travis, who also seems like a top to me, not only prefers to bottom, but is kinky."

Paulie rolled onto his back and stared up at the popcorn ceiling of my bedroom. "I feel stupid and small-minded," he finally said. "After getting to college, it was like I had something to prove. I left my family so I could be gay, and I somehow convinced myself that I wasn't truly gay until I did, you know, gay things. So I fucked around a lot, and often it was with guys who treated me like complete shit. But I don't want to be like that anymore. Sex makes me—I don't know—unsure, maybe? So I decided a while back that I would slow down. I've fooled around with a couple guys in the last year, like Alex, but didn't have anal with any of them." He worried his bottom lip with his teeth. "Do I sound totally insane? Do other guys worry about stuff like that?"

My nerves unwound, like pulling a loose string that unravels a whole shirt. I could do this. I could be there for Paulie. I could be a good friend. I didn't have to close myself off all the time.

I couldn't tell him everything. I couldn't tell Paulie that sex helped me lose myself in something other than thoughts of my dead high school boyfriend or how much it had hurt when said boyfriend's parents had stood up on a stage with that politician and blamed me for his death. I couldn't tell him about my name change or my fucked-up parents.

But I could give him a story—it was even a true one.

"I met Travis during my second week at college. He was pretty much my first friend, you know? See, I had a fake ID, so I went to the Yard because I wanted to get fucked, but I didn't have much experience picking up guys." I hadn't had *any* experience picking up guys. I hadn't picked Diego up. Diego and I had fallen together naturally—so naturally, every hookup since had hurt. "So I walked into a bar for the first time in my life with this plan to hit on the first top I could spot. And there was Travis—this tall, hot black guy. So I walked straight up to him and said, 'I'll let you fuck me if you buy me a drink. But you have to be good at it.' I kid you not. Worst pickup line in all of history."

Paulie gasped, then began to giggle, and I waited for him to finish before continuing.

"Travis was actually super nice about it, but I know it about killed him. He bought me a drink anyway, and then told me he would help me get laid if that was what I wanted, but if I wanted a top, I would have to look elsewhere. I spent half the night just shooting the shit with him, and he did in fact help me get fucked. He's a great wingman. So you're right. Not everyone has it figured out. I certainly didn't. Don't. I certainly *don't*. I muddle my way through and hope no one notices."

Paulie didn't say anything in reply. He just looked at me, his gaze skimming over my face. His eyes were so dark, almost black, but this close I could see the color striations in the irises. The mix of browns and greens. They were beautiful. Time slowed, and I savored this quiet minute; I hadn't allowed myself very many moments of connection and understanding and friendship.

Paulie ran the rough pad of his thumb over my cheekbone, and my eyes fluttered closed, my breath catching when his thumb traveled up and over one of my eyebrows.

"You're a good friend," he whispered, and I wanted to open my eyes and trace his face, to see if he felt as overwhelmed as I did over something as simple as a touch. But I wanted another second of this. Of being touched by him.

Then my bedroom door banged open, and I jumped. Paulie dropped his hand and turned to grin at Travis.

"Wake up, sleepyheads," Travis said. He stared at me a beat too long, taking in everything, like the flush I could feel spreading over my cheeks and the too-small space between Paulie and me.

Paulie sat up and casually scooted away from me. "Thanks for holding my hair last night, sweet pea. Why don't I run to the corner and get donuts. Then can we watch a movie? Like, in bed, without moving for the rest of the day?"

So that's what we did, all in a row on my bed, my laptop on Paulie's stomach, with the sound of car chases and explosions breaking up the silence.

chapter six

On Sunday, Paulie, Travis, and I did homework together all afternoon and into the evening. Travis was writing a paper in Spanish for his Latin American Literature class, Paulie was studying for his Managerial Accounting test, and I was working on a research proposal I had put off for far too long. Dr. Yamato, my favorite history professor, thought I could win one of the undergraduate research fellowships with my work on the effects of the railroad on the settlers in the Great Plains. I hoped the fellowship would look good when I applied to graduate school. Winning it was a long shot though. The history of the Great Plains wasn't as glamorous as studying the Renaissance or as noteworthy as researching war, which were some of my classmates' topics.

Paulie and Travis finished first and then tried to distract me by throwing popcorn at each other. I was stuck and had been for about an hour at that point. I needed access to primary source material that I couldn't get without an Interlibrary Loan. Copies of journal entries from Kansas and Oklahoma settlers littered the table in front of me, but the words had ceased to make sense. I closed my eyes, hoping a few minutes of rest would clear the fuzziness from my head, and jumped when Paulie leaned against my back. The citrusy tang of his aftershave or soap or *something* tingled my sinuses. I inhaled deeply. He dug his chin into my shoulder.

"That's pretty." He pointed to one of the pages in front of me.

It was simply a photocopy, so his comment made no sense. Then he started reading. "'My favorite thing about wintertime is the sky at night. It stretches big and black above us but for the stars. Papa likes to listen to the wind whistle across the fields at night, but the sound frightens me. The coyotes cry, but Papa says they will not hurt us. Even with the noises, I like looking up at the night sky. I imagine the Lord wiping His big hand over the earth until the sky was this perfect shade of black.'"

"That's from a seventeen-year-old preacher's daughter. She lived in the Flint Hills in Kansas. Actually, it was close to where your aunt and sister live in Emporia. A couple pages after that excerpt, she mentions seeing a train for the first time," I explained.

"I've never heard coyotes."

And suddenly, I knew I wanted to show them to him. I wasn't only stuck on my proposal. The walls were closing in on me, and I needed to see the sky like this long-ago teenager. I needed to see the look on Paulie's face when he heard the yips of coyotes float through the night.

"I can take you." He looked at me like I had lost my mind. "Seriously, let's do that. Trav and I have driven out to this place like ten miles out of town and heard them. They're really common in this area. What do you say?" I turned to include Travis, hoping he could convince Paulie.

Travis's gaze traveled from Paulie to me. He normally liked to drive out into the boonies. It was novel to him because he had grown up in the suburbs, but he was going to say no. I could tell he had a very sly reason for it too.

He cocked that stupid eyebrow and said, "Oh, I can't. I'm meeting a new *friend* soon."

Of course Paulie jumped all over the insinuation in Travis's voice and had him spilling all of the dirty details on his "friend"—a guy from Grindr Travis was hoping to blow. I could almost guarantee it was made up. Not that there wasn't a guy from Grindr—Travis wasn't exactly in short supply of hookups—but I could tell from his crafty smile that he was too pleased I would be getting alone time with Paulie.

Within an hour, Travis had vacated the premises, and I was so pissed at him. He kept pushing Paulie and me together with innuendos and calculating smirks. I feared that the pressure cooker of our friendship would eventually boil over, and if that happened, I had no idea which way I would fall.

Paulie cranked the window down in my truck and closed his eyes as the wind hit his face. The shadow of his eyelashes fanned out along his cheekbones, visible only because of the glow from my radio display. I jerked my eyes back to the narrow road. In the distance, a huge wind farm with white-winged giants marred the flat horizon, but at night you could only see their red blinking lights.

I spotted the landmark I'd been waiting for—the bunch of evergreen trees—and slowed down. I pulled onto a dirt road directly after them and parked beside the turnabout for an oft forgotten historical marker.

"What's the marker?" Paulie asked.

"Something to do with the Great Western Trail. This was a cattle trail route."

I jumped out of my old truck and grabbed a couple of blankets and the pillows Paulie thought we would need. He said we could only stargaze if we were comfortable. My eyes adjusted to the near-black as Paulie scrabbled into the bed of my truck, brushed the red dirt off of his sweats, and spread out one of the blankets. He threw down a pillow and flopped onto his back. When I didn't immediately join him, he lifted into a sit-up and smiled at me.

It wasn't his usual wide grin full of those perfect white teeth and adorable gap. No, this smile was soft, and his face was full of some emotion I couldn't read, was scared to read. I was scared it was tenderness, and I wanted it to be tenderness. He tilted his head to the side and furrowed his brow as if to ask me what was wrong, and I had the sudden urge to tell him *everything*. I wanted to so badly I could practically see the words in the space between us. But I would break apart like gravel the moment he knew about Diego and my humiliation and my guilt. I was terrified to let go of my secrets.

I crawled into the truck bed and lay down beside him but not touching him. The sky was clear and deep navy with stars winking down at us. The smell of grass and dirt wafted over me, and I closed my eyes. All the restlessness and anxiety stilled in me. I loved being out here like this without the light pollution or noise of cars or people. Every few minutes I opened my eyes to see the night sky or look at the moon, but mostly I just floated and let myself feel okay.

Suddenly, the call of a single coyote drifted over the field, and Paulie clutched my forearm.

"Wait for it," I whispered.

The chorus of a large band of coyotes began to reach us from far away. The yips rising and falling like the gentle roll of the prairie. They weren't close to us. In fact, I could barely make out the different vocalizations, but Paulie closed his eyes and parted his lips like it was the most wonderful thing he had ever heard. He was still gripping my forearm, down close to my wrist, and I watched the emotions play over his expressive face.

I want him.

I couldn't fight it anymore. And it wasn't the punch to my stomach like I thought it would be. It simply *was*. It didn't matter that I was so fucked up over Diego. It didn't matter that I hadn't wanted anyone except Diego before, not truly, not ever—I definitely wanted Paulie. It didn't matter that the thought of letting someone in was terrifying. Or that Paulie and I were mismatched sexually. Or that losing someone else would absolutely wreck me. I wanted him, and I couldn't contest such a losing battle anymore.

The coyotes' cries rose up louder, and Paulie smiled, delight shaping his expression into something innocent and beautiful. Then he noticed I was watching him, and his eyes widened. They were dark and fathomless in that moment. I slid my hand into his and turned my body toward him. He froze.

"Joel?" he whispered. His uncertainty gutted me.

I couldn't hear the coyotes over the blood rushing in my ears, but I felt Paulie draw a shuddering breath when my lips brushed his.

Shyness swamped me. If Paulie wanted me, he would surely have made a move already. He certainly hadn't been shy in pursuing Alex at the Yard. I fought the urge to jerk away from him, hoping to save face by playing it cool and pretending that this was just another friendly kiss in the saga of our friendship. After a long, loaded moment, I pulled back slowly.

He gripped my hand harder. "Joel," he breathed. "What was that?"

"It's whatever you want it to be," I said honestly.

"Oh, good answer, buttercup." His voice was suddenly deep and throaty.

His soft lips rubbed over mine, and an ache reverberated through me from my fingertips to the top of my thighs. His kiss was tentative and sweet, just barely a whisper of tongue across my bottom lip. I groaned raggedly, and the sound echoed around us in the empty air. Paulie drew back, and I apologized. I'd forgotten how to kiss like this, to kiss someone I actually liked.

"Don't apologize."

He rearranged us so he was on his back with my face above his. Then he lifted up and kissed me. This time I'd get it right. This time I wouldn't moan like a horny virgin. His hands gripped my biceps, and I cupped the back of his skull and his neck.

I kissed him softly, just a tease of lips and breath and stubble. I sucked on his upper lip and he whimpered, a quiet sound in the back of his throat. I kissed his chin and ran my lips over the tender skin of his throat and the bump of his Adam's apple. He arched into me, and I had to get my hands on more of him, so I fell onto my side and tugged him closer to me. He tangled his legs with mine, and I couldn't help but trace the planes of his face, much as he had touched mine the morning after he'd gotten drunk. The morning after David McDavid.

Was that only two days ago? One day? It felt like a lifetime. I followed the line of his jaw and thumbed his plump bottom lip. His eyes, rimmed with those smoky eyelashes, fell closed, so I touched the lashes. They were soft. No makeup after all. He leaned forward, eyes still shut, lips seeking mine and trusting that I would be there. I licked the seam of his lips, and they parted on a gasp, so I slipped my tongue inside. A moan escaped me again, but Paulie quieted it with his warm, willing mouth and lips that pressed and clung so sweetly to mine.

Eventually, Paulie stole one hand inside my shirt, palm rubbing the muscles along my spine. His other hand slid into my hair, but he didn't fist it, just ran his fingers through it, untangling the mess of waves. He whined a little desperately in the back of his throat, and I kissed him harder. I trapped his jaw in both of my hands and tilted his head until it was at the perfect angle for my tongue to sweep in deeply. This time, when Paulie arched into me, we both groaned as our erections rubbed together.

Paulie pulled off my mouth with a gasp. "I don't want this to end."

I wasn't sure what he meant, but I didn't want to stop kissing him in my truck bed with the stars shining above us and the coyote calls as our soundtrack. I didn't want to push us until we both came and this moment was over. The thought of it being over terrified me.

I slowed the kiss until it was only small nips and sucks along his swollen, red lips, but the change in pace only seemed to excite him more. He rolled against me like a steam engine—slow, hard, and insistent—so I stopped him with a hand on his hip. His hip bone cut into my palm, and I almost gave in completely. I wanted to suck on it.

"Paulie, slow down. Please," I begged, and he settled back onto the truck bed. When his eyes met mine, his pupils were blown wide with need, but there was insecurity there too. "This isn't a one-off, okay? At least not for me."

"Me either," he whispered.

"I like this, finally kissing you and it meaning something. I don't want *this* to end. We'll get to the rest of it eventually."

He nodded, and I rubbed my thumbs along the stubble on his cheeks.

"I've wanted this from the beginning," Paulie said against my lips when I leaned back in to taste him. "I've wanted you from the moment I saw you in class on that first day, but I didn't want you to be just another guy I let fuck me."

Oh . . . Oh God. Vulnerable and cute and needy—Paulie was everything I'd ever wanted in that moment.

I smiled against his mouth. "Well, you still don't need to worry about that particular scenario. I don't want to be just another guy who fucks you. I want you to fuck me." The heat from his blush warmed my palms, but he smiled back.

And my heart lurched like it was free-falling from the top of a rollercoaster. I had fought these feelings for Paulie because I had known it would be different with him. I'd have to be different with him. I couldn't simply get fucked and move on. I couldn't do that to him.

But I couldn't be honest either. Couldn't tell him about Diego. Or the coming-out circus in the press. Or the truth of my parents' marriage. I didn't even want to tell him my original name. Was it fair to take this step with him? To lie so spectacularly? To hide the fact that my heart belonged to another and always would?

It wasn't fair to Paulie, but parts of my past needed to stay in the past. I couldn't dredge it all up—that would rip me apart and probably hurt him in the process too.

But while I wasn't going to tell him about Diego, I did need to warn him that I had very little relationship experience. "I've been having sex exclusively with strangers and fuck buddies for three years," I said. He stiffened beside me, so I caressed his cheek. "Hear me out. It's pretty scary to move beyond that, but I *want* to move beyond that with you. I don't want to fight this connection anymore."

I can't anymore.

Paulie burrowed into my arms, resting his head on my chest. He grabbed the extra blanket and pulled it over us. We listened to the coyotes call to each other, and I tried to slow my breathing as the heat from his body seeped into mine. Cuddling with Paulie was better than some of the best sex I'd had in the last year.

Out of nowhere, Paulie said, "I got drunk because you went home with that guy."

Embarrassment flooded me. That had been a fuckup if ever there was one. I rubbed my cheek on the top of his bristly head.

"I'm so sorry, Paulie."

"I think I can take a little bit of responsibility for how that night turned out. But I'm tired of fighting it too."

That night would probably have ended with David and me fooling around, even if Paulie hadn't given us foreplay at the Yard, but I wouldn't have reacted so poorly to the blowjob if Paulie hadn't put his tongue in my mouth not an hour before David's cock filled it. Still, I was equally positive that without my post-BJ epiphany, Paulie and I wouldn't be here now.

A supped-up truck turned onto the gravel road, slowing down as it passed us and making Paulie tense. It kept moving, but I could tell the threat of discovery had shaken him.

He kept shifting around, like he couldn't get comfortable, and freezing at the smallest noises, until eventually he said, "Let's get out of here before some redneck finds us neckin' and wants to do something about it."

chapter seven

I didn't know what to expect when we got back to my house. Paulie might gather up his homework and kiss me good night. Or we could pretend our gravel turnabout confession never happened. But Paulie was full of courage, so I shouldn't have been surprised when he grabbed my hand and led me into my living room like a mother duck steering her duckling. But, *God*, I was surprised because he led me with tenderness, and I didn't know how to take that.

Travis was lounging on his back in the middle of the living room, in his underwear again, reading a book. He lifted his head to watch us walk in, and as soon as he spotted our hands, he sat up. He was about to say something, the shape of the words visible on his lips, but Paulie kept pulling me through the living room toward the hallway. Right before we were out of sight, Paulie said, "Good night, Travis," and Travis's face transformed with glee. He fist-pumped the air, but then we were in the hallway and I couldn't see him anymore.

I started to say that Travis was too invested in our love lives, to be flip and pretend like this wasn't a huge deal. But then Paulie directed me into my bedroom, and pressed me against the door. He stretched onto his tippy-toes to reach my mouth, arms around my neck, and the slide of his lithe body against me almost brought me to my knees.

He flat-out seduced me with his mouth, every suck and tease suggestive of sex, while his fluid body rolled against mine. I touched him because I was finally freaking allowing myself to touch someone I *wanted*—from the gentle slope of his waist to the sculpt of his spine to his perfect, pert little butt. Paulie brushed his erection against mine, and the sensation made me moan and my balls hitch up next to my body. He did it again, and I was scared I was going to come from nothing but his tongue in my mouth and a little rubbing, so I grabbed his hips and pushed him back. At the last second, he sucked my bottom lip into his mouth and let it go with a *smack*.

"What's wrong?" he asked with a full-faced grin. When I did nothing except try to catch my breath, he dropped to his knees. Just the sight of him down there made it harder to think. "Take your shirt off for me, Joel."

I stripped off my jacket and shirt. I needed him to want me. To want to do this again. To not leave me vulnerable and alone once the dust settled.

Paulie made fast work of my shoes, socks, and jeans, and before I could catch up, I was naked and Paulie was still fully clothed at my feet.

He peered up at me with lust-soaked eyes. "You're so hot."

Warmth spread through me, and I barely contained a pleased smile. I managed muscles and definition with very little effort and a fast metabolism, and my legs and chest were hairy, which some guys liked and some didn't. But Paulie's praise made me happy in a way no other man's ever had. *He* thought I was hot when he was sex on legs.

My cock pointed right at his face, an obscene and obvious compass. Paulie leaned forward and kissed the pre-come leaking from my cap. My knees wobbled a little, and I slipped farther down the wall. Paulie ran his hands up my thighs, grasped my hip bones, and sucked me in. So wet and hot with those sweet eyelashes fluttering on his cheeks as he took me to the back of his throat and swallowed. He undid me. *Weak.* He made me so fucking weak.

My hands landed on either side of his head, and I yanked him off.

"Baby, you're going to make me come," I said. His eyes widened at the term of endearment, and my body temperature tipped achingly higher. I wasn't sure where it had come from, because I had never called anyone *baby* in my life.

Not even Diego.

Don't go there. Not now, not fucking ever. Pain slammed into my gut.

"Well maybe, *baby*, that is exactly what I want," Paulie said, clearly oblivious to my impending freak-out. He languidly lapped at another pearl of pre-come. It was amazing what a tongue could do. What it could make me forget.

"Want to taste you." Another lick, this one down the vein, and I loosened my hands on his head. How easy it was to lose sight of him. Of Diego. "And hear what you sound like when you let go."

Now I wasn't holding Paulie back but urging him forward as he sucked hard on that little harp string of nerves under my head. Urging him to take me there. Take me to oblivion, where no one existed except him and me.

"And know—" a swipe of his tongue along the base "—that I'm the one driving you crazy." He dipped down and drew one of my balls into his mouth and let it pop back out. *Crazy*, he'd said. And I was crazy and undone and so, so ready to let go. To chase the high of being with Paulie. Being with this sweet, beautiful boy. "Know that I'm going to get you hard again." A soft suck on my tip. "And then we'll come together."

He pulled me into his mouth until the press of his soft palate squeezed me. The sight of him down there, petal-soft mouth and dirty words and black-rimmed eyes, pushed me right up to the edge.

"Gonna—" I choked out, and his hand snapped up and squeezed my penis at its base, aborting the spiral of my orgasm. A groan ripped from my belly.

"Gonna what, buttercup?" he said, my tip painting pre-come on his lips.

"Please," I whispered. "Baby, please." *Lost. Please let me be lost with only you as a guide.*

He smiled at the endearment, and if he hadn't already been holding off my orgasm, the visual of my cock against his cute little gap would have made me bust. A porn image I wanted to relive and relive and relive on a loop forever.

He loosened his grip, jacked me once slowly with his hand, and I did bust, my first rope of come hitting his smiling lips. I made an inhuman sound, and his mouth closed around me. Then his throat, which milked me through the rest of my orgasm until my vision grayed and I could see nothing, feel nothing but the strong thumping of my heart and Paulie's hair under my fingers. When I opened my eyes, I was on the floor, still leaning against my bedroom door. Paulie was kneeling in front of me, his hands whispering across my face.

His lips were pouty and shiny with come, and it was smeared across one cheek. It blew my mind. I kissed him softly, sucking the bitter taste from his lips. Then I turned his face, kissed the come off his cheek, and ran my lips over his ear. A delicious shudder rippled through him.

"Come on. Let's get in bed," I said, and helped him to his feet.

He practically skipped to the bed and bounced to the middle, sprawled out on his back, his joy vibrant in the dark of my room.

"You need to lose these clothes." I ripped his sweats down. He was wearing bright-green briefs, and the color only highlighted the enticing bulge. *Oh yeah.* I wanted to take a bite of it. He wasn't ripped like a gym rat, but his body was supple and smooth and perfect. And he smelled good, like oranges and spice. When I got the sweatshirt pushed to his rib cage, he pressed up into a sit-up and raised his hands over his head. I whipped the shirt off of him, and he fell back onto the bed. I scooted up to kiss his mouth again, but a glint of silver distracted me. One of his nipples had a delicate silver barbell through it, and the sight made all of the blood in my body rush south.

"Holy fuck, Paulie." I ran a finger around the dark-pink nipple, and it tightened.

"Surprise," he whispered.

"How long have you had this?" I fell forward to swipe a tongue over it.

His voice was deep and tense as he said, "My high school girlfriend convinced me to get it." I jerked my face up to look at him. He just laughed and then moaned, "Oh God, lick me again." So I did, until he strained underneath me and each breath sounded like a small cry. Finally, I eased back and pulled his briefs off, and even if I hadn't known what I wanted before, I certainly did now.

"Paulie, has anyone ever told you that you are seriously hung? What the fuck!"

He rolled his head on the pillow. His cock was pillar straight and incredibly out of proportion to the rest of his compact body. I cuffed it lightly with one hand and laved his nipple again, enjoying the bite of metal. Paulie's hands strayed to my face. So gentle and kind.

"What do you want, Joel?" he whispered. "I'll give you whatever you want."

I kissed him. I wanted so much from him, and all of it was asking too much, too soon. After nipping his plump bottom lip, because it was juicy and red and right *there*, I said, "Fuck me, Paulie. Top me."

His groan wavered around us, almost like a sob. Excitement and desire washed over his face as he flipped me onto my back and straddled my hips. Our cocks batted together.

"Oh God. Oh my God. Oh shit," he whispered as I reached beside me for the lube and a condom from my bedside table. His litany of profanity continued as he ran his hands all over my chest and abs. "Holy fuck," he finished when I tossed the supplies on the bed beside us.

I grinned up at him. Then I placed my hand on his cheek, and he pressed it into my palm and closed his eyes. So *sweet*. My heart turned over with an emotion much bigger than lust.

I pushed the bottle of lube into his hand. He drew a shaky breath and popped the top. I ripped the condom wrapper open with my teeth and slid it slowly down his cock. "Don't want to have to worry about it later," I said. He nodded, suddenly so serious that I laughed, but then he slithered between my legs and anticipation choked me. Paulie drizzled lube on one hand, and grasped one of my thighs to pin me open with the other, unexpectedly aggressive and forceful.

Maybe he *could* eviscerate me. Maybe he was strong enough to flip that switch to off, make the Diego in my head disappear, and fill me with pleasure and the good kind of pain.

"Oh God, tight," Paulie groaned, as his slick finger slid right inside. He finger-fucked me hard, his eyes trained on where he plugged me.

Heat curled in my belly, and I needed more—more stretch and burn and *him*. Paulie, his lissome body rippling with movement and his lips parted in awe, lit me up. Like a match igniting a line of gasoline. He crooked his finger, rubbed over that sweet, spongy bundle of nerves, and a flush of heat consumed me.

"You're really good at this," I gasped. His eyes never left mine as he leaned down to suck on my hip bone before gently rolling me over. *Intensity—damn, did he bring it.*

"I've had a lot of practice. You know, on myself." His lips whispered against my shoulder blades as he thrust his finger back in, and then he licked the knob at the top of my spine. He pulled my ass cheeks apart with his free hand before sliding a second finger inside. The deep stretch made me fuck back onto his hand.

"God, you're so sexy," he said against my neck. "So tall. I love seeing you laid out like this, all gold skin and muscle." He moaned again when I started shaking, but didn't lighten up on that insistent press inside, the pad of one of his fingers flicking against my prostate with each stroke. "I love your muscles. You're hard all over."

"Brawny chic," I managed to choke out. The compliments didn't do much for me. I knew what I was. A coward. And guilty. And full of ugliness and pain. And lies. But that tap against my prostrate helped me forget all my sins.

He chuckled and bit my shoulder. The sharp sting made my balls tingle, and we needed to get this show on the road before it was too late.

"Paulie," I cried. "Please, Paul. God, please, fuck me. I'm going to come if you don't start fucking me."

He stopped mouthing my shoulder, and his fingers froze so abruptly I almost shook apart—the pressure inside too unrelenting without the push and pull. Paulie rested his forehead on my shoulder and drew a deep breath.

"I like that. I like you calling me Paul," he growled. Suddenly his fingers were gone. My legs were splayed apart, and I was already so close I wasn't coordinated enough to lift myself to my knees. Paulie shoved a pillow under my groin and gripped my hips until he had me at the perfect angle.

I was open and sloppy with lube, but the stretch of his head popping past my tight ring of muscle was still too much. Too much stretch, too much cock, too much, *absolutely* too much of him. But not nearly enough to blank my mind. He let the flared rim of his cap pin me open, not thrusting in, and each of his shuddering breaths echoed through me. It felt like forever before he finally slid forward in one long glide. The sound he made as he bottomed out was all liquid consonants and sexy kitten noises.

Nothing could have prepared me for how I would feel the moment Paulie was inside me. I had never let someone I actually *liked* fuck me, and it was mind-bogglingly different. I felt him. All of him. And I wanted *him*, not some half-baked idea or a distraction from bad memories. It stunned me stupid.

All my nerves had lit up, and my blood throbbed everywhere—my heart, my fingertips, my neck, my ass—like I was one giant pulse. He had stopped moving again, his breath thundering from him like he was running a race. I felt so alive and hot, everything too bright, too sharp, too good. I wasn't sure I could withstand real fucking.

"I can't—" He whimpered urgently, but then yanked my ass higher off the bed until my spine was almost impossibly arched. He slipped even deeper, and my eyes rolled back. "I'm scared to move. I'm scared I'll come."

"Please," I whispered. "Need you to move, Paulie."

But he didn't, except to run a hard hand from my tailbone up my spine. I wiggled my hips, and for half a second the relentless fullness eased, but the shift pushed his cock directly across my prostate. I screamed into the mattress.

"Paul," I gasped, pleading. "Paulie!" I tried to rock my hips again because I was so close to coming. All I needed was a little more pressure on those nerves, even though I'd never come just from a dick in my ass. But Paulie wouldn't let me. He pushed deep and hard until I had no leverage, his cock so far in my gut I could taste him. He smacked a hand between my shoulder blades and held me down.

I didn't try to fight his hold. Giving up control to him was irresistible, and I couldn't believe that I was his first. That I was this lucky. I was incoherent with it—the euphoria, the stretch, and the need for him to fucking move. Finally, he pulled almost all the way out, and tentatively stroked back in to the root. The tremor of restraint in his body as he settled into his role as the fucker rather than the fucked undid me. I could have turned over, bared my stomach like a puppy, and begged for whatever he wanted to give.

My hips sunk down into the pillow, and the friction of my cock against the soft padding tipped me closer to orgasm, until I could feel my release, just hovering, waiting to flip from controlled to uncontrollable. But then Paulie hitched my hips up off the pillow, his thumbs digging hard into my butt cheeks, the growl in his voice making my head spin. His slow stroke detonated something deep inside me. Struck my fuse, and I was on fire. White heat blinded me, shaking all of my atoms loose until I spilled over again and again. Choked by the overwhelming joy of hitting the edge and falling, as Paulie pulsed and shivered and sobbed out the curse words of his own fireworks.

And then it was all over but the soft, throbbing aftershocks and Paulie's moan when he pulled out.

Sleep threatened me immediately, and I didn't care that come tangled in the hair on my stomach or that I had collapsed on top of a wet pillow. But I did want to see Paulie's face, kiss him, and know that he was okay. And that was a desire I hadn't had in a *very* long time. It almost made me shut down completely.

Paulie tied off the condom and threw it in the trash can by my desk. "I should clean you up," he said. "That's the etiquette, right? A warm washrag."

"It doesn't matter. Come here." I pulled him down to my side so I could kiss him, trying to sink the panic that threatened to drown my post-come high.

"Roll onto your back," he said against my lips, and I flopped over. He pulled the soaked pillow out from under me and tossed it off the bed. I closed my eyes, fighting the pain of the Diego memories creeping up on me, so the rasp of Paulie's tongue in my belly button surprised me. He cleaned me like a cat, eating the semen off my stomach and humming against my tingling skin. I looked down into his dark eyes and traced the sharp line of his jaw with my thumbs, completely in awe of him.

When he was done, he crawled up the bed and curled into my arms. His fingers twined into my chest hair, and sleep tugged at me again.

"That was the hottest thing I've ever done. I loved it," Paulie whispered.

It was different than any sex I'd ever had before too. Different than sex with Diego, who had been moody and cheerless. Different than the men who usually fucked me, who were perfunctory and polite and interchangeable.

"I loved it too," I said, my lips seeking his. He made a yummy-yummy noise, and I laughed. It wasn't even faked.

"What time's your test tomorrow? I'll drive you home in the morning." We had some logistics to work out, but I refused to consider the possibility of Paulie not sleeping in my bed.

He groaned. "It's at eight thirty."

"You can shower and stuff here. Do you need to go home before going to class?"

He nodded against my chest, his short hair scrubbing under my chin. "You splooged on the clothes I wore today, buttercup. And I need to grab batteries for my scientific calculator."

"Okay, nerd," I laughed. "How's seven thirty sound?"

"Like it's too early. Do you only have one pillow?"

We were pressed chest to chest. His head rested on my biceps and mine rested on my pillow. I was perfectly comfortable.

"No. I have two. But you fucked me until I *splooged* all over the other."

He giggled, and his breath puffed against my neck. "That's right. I guess this is okay, then."

I kissed his forehead. *This* was way better than *okay*.

chapter eight

Paulie spent the next night at my house, even bringing a change of clothes so he wouldn't have to go home before our class together. I was so pleased by that little pile of clean underwear, socks, and a T-shirt that I let him fuck my mouth, me on my back and him straddling my face.

After he came, he brushed his thumb over my bottom lip, which felt swollen, and worry built in his face. He hadn't held back, or hadn't been able to, and I could tell my puffy lips bothered him. I, on the other hand, had needed to know he felt even a hint of the swirling, crazy, restless desire I did. I needed him to show it so I didn't feel so exposed.

Before he could ask me if I was okay, I said, "You make the sexiest noises when you come."

"It sounds like I'm crying," he said.

There had been times in my life where coming was just a pitch away from crying, either from sadness or pain or happiness. I cried the first time I came with another man after Diego died. I'd let this random guy top me—my first. When it was happening, I hadn't felt Diego's loss so hard, so acutely, and it had felt so good to let go of him for those quick, rushed, and painful moments. I couldn't remember the guy's name, but he had been the first in a long line of men I let use me up.

So maybe that degree of separation between euphoria and heartbreak *was* miniscule. It felt like it now, with Paulie's dazed eyes looking down at me with concern. And last night when he had taken me so sweetly and then licked me clean so I didn't fall asleep sticky, it had felt like he'd held my heart in his hands and could so easily have dropped it like a hot potato and covered it with bruises.

"Your lips ... Did I go too hard?" he asked.

"I'll tell you if it's too rough. I promise. I loved it."

"Sometimes people don't give you the chance to say something's wrong. I don't want to do that to you."

My fingers clenched on his hips. Who had treated Paulie like that? Who would willingly hurt him?

Paulie licked my mouth. "Don't get your panties in a twist, Joel. I was speaking figuratively." He moved down to my chest. He was deflecting—I was certain of it—but when his lips skated across my ribs and found erogenous zones that hadn't existed before his mouth discovered them, I decided that Paulie deserved the right to deflect if he wanted to as well. After all, I deflected all the time. Which, I guessed, was *me* willingly hurting him.

Afterward, with Paulie fast asleep in my arms, it hit me that if we kept doing this, whatever *this* was, he might find out about Diego—there were enough clues about my past littered around if he knew where to look—and I definitely did not want that to happen. Sure, I wanted to be with Paulie. But did having him require me to give up my secrets? Give up the modicum of control I was finally exerting over my life?

I just wanted Paulie. I had chosen. But if I told Paulie about Diego and my fucked-up past, I knew, just knew, that nothing else would matter, and our relationship would fall apart.

It took less than two weeks for Travis to highlight all the ways I was ruining the best thing that had happened to me in a very long time. Travis had been dying for the details, but Paulie and I had been practically inseparable, so he hadn't been able to question me. Tonight, though, Paulie, the *traitor*, had a study group with some of his accounting friends, so Travis was cooking me dinner. He'd insisted.

Inexplicably, Travis had on an honest-to-God blue gingham apron and boxers. Nothing else. I sat on the counter to watch him cook a stir-fry. He was a vegetarian this week.

"You look adorable in that, but you should wear a shirt. Grease or something is going to pop up and burn you."

He scoffed. Once he had worked some magic on the veggies that he assured me would make them taste good without meat, he slammed a lid on the skillet and set it to simmer.

"You've been avoiding me," he said.

"I have not! You see me all the fucking time."

"Well, you've been using your new boyfriend as a shield. I want to hear everything, but I can't gossip about him with you if he's right there!"

"I don't know if I'd use the word 'boyfriend.'"

So far we'd pretty much just fucked like bunnies. But I liked thinking of Paulie that way. Liked using *boyfriend* in my head. Paulie and I hadn't talked about it, though, and I didn't want to push it.

Travis laughed until he had tears streaming down his face. "You think you're not boyfriends?" he practically choked. "That's so cute."

"Oh, shut up." I threw a rag at him. "What do you want to know? Ask your questions, and then we're going to eat that tofu thingy and watch football or something because I don't think I can handle that much girl talk."

"Come on, buttercup," he crowed, his use of Paulie's crazy pet name making my cheeks hot. "It's not girl talk if there are no girls involved. And we've talked about guys we've slept with before."

True. My friendship with Travis began because he helped me get laid. We weren't exactly shy about sex.

"This isn't just us talking about some guy I picked up at the Yard, and you know it. So go."

Travis rubbed his hands together in glee and paced the kitchen a couple of times. I immediately regretted giving him even a sliver of control. Travis was what my mom called *people smart*.

"Okay, so Paulie has pretty much looked at you like you're ice cream and he's starving from the beginning. You were oblivious. And I was a little worried about that, you know, because Paulie is not at all like the big, boring tops you normally go home with, and he's so sweet. I didn't want him to get hurt. So that night at the bar, he saw you gettin' it with that guy—"

"David McDavid," I cut in, mostly because Travis would think it was hilarious, and I wanted a distraction from the way guilt sliced through me. Paulie had wanted me, and I hadn't noticed at all.

"Okay, that's *awesome*. But don't distract me. So you're dancing with *David McDavid* and Paulie comes up to me to say hi, and I can tell he's surprised. So I tell him you always choose guys like that, and you prefer to bottom."

"This is starting to feel like a story and not a question, Trav."

"I'll get there. You know the rest anyway. Paulie goes out to dance with you, and he makes about every bitch in that place wet with his little show. *Including me*. Then you leave, and Paulie gets trashed. It took him no time at all since he's such a lightweight. There were guys all over him. And it freaked me out because he doesn't get like that very often, and I didn't want him to go home with anyone if he wasn't in control. So I brought him here. I completely expected to have to take care of him and hope he was too far gone to realize that David Mc-fucking-David was fucking you in the other room. But David was gone. So what really happened that night?"

"That doesn't have anything to do with Paulie and me." Sweat bloomed under my clothes. I was sure Travis would see more than I wanted him to.

"I suspect it has at least a little something to do with Paulie. So tell me."

I narrowed my eyes at him. "I blew him and jacked myself off, and then I made him leave. And, unfortunately, David was super nice, so I actually feel bad about that. But we didn't fuck, and I didn't want to fuck." I paused because this part was hard. "I felt guilty about Paulie, like I was cheating, even though it didn't make a lick of sense. Paulie practically shoved David and me together, but all I could think about was him."

"That's the most romantic thing I've ever heard."

"Fuck you," I laughed. "You know what happened next. Voila. Here we are." It was so much more than that, but I prayed Travis would let me off the hook.

"Okay, now, don't take this the wrong way. I love you. You're the best housemate ever. You don't care if I have loud sex, and you make sure that we never need the shower at the same time. But you can be a little . . . uh . . . let's say, *reserved* when it comes to information about yourself. In fact, I'm totally fucking shocked you're having this conversation with me. So . . . are you going to close yourself off to Paulie?"

And this was exactly what I'd feared when Travis started this question-and-answer game: his perception.

"I'll try not to," I said, but it was a lie.

Travis peered at me, his dark eyes sharp like a predator's.

"I don't get you sometimes, Joel."

"Okay."

My response was obviously not the one Travis wanted. "Look, I don't know what happened to you, but I'm not stupid. I have eyes. And it's okay if you never tell me. But I have to be honest: I suspect my imagination is ten times worse than the reality."

I stared at him in shock, and my whole body ran hot. I thought I'd hidden everything so well. Thought I had started over. That I'd fucking outrun this shit! And I absolutely did not want to know how deep and dark Trav's imagination was. I couldn't tell him the truth.

"It's okay if you never tell me, but, baby, I watch you shut down. It's a physical thing, the way your eyes shutter and your body stills, and it is heartbreaking. But at least think about telling Paulie. He deserves your full self, you know? Even the bad or hard stuff."

My gut rebelled at that thought. Paulie and I had *just* started dating. It had been less than a month. I couldn't betray Diego for something so new, so unformed. And, yes, I selfishly couldn't handle anyone knowing the truth. The lies kept me safe, kept me in control.

"I like Paulie a lot, Trav."

"That's a good thing. You say it like someone died."

I flinched, but Travis didn't notice. He was stirring the vegetables again, so his back was turned. My heart hammered through me, like it would pop out of my mouth the second I opened it. Someone *had* died, and that was the only reason I was here, talking to Travis about Paulie, and not following Diego around like I'd done for years.

chapter nine

the screen of my computer blurred white and gray, and it didn't seem to matter how many times I reread my proposal, I found mistakes and typos every fucking time. It was almost 10:30 p.m., the research proposal was due in the morning, and I needed to just call it and head over to Paulie's. But it wasn't my best work. I knew it, and Dr. Yamato would know it too. Not to mention the judging committee.

It felt like so much hinged on whether I could pull this proposal off. If I could get the fellowship, maybe my mom wouldn't feel like I was wasting myself on academia. Maybe I could prove that this whole thing—moving to Oklahoma, changing my name, choosing a major I loved—had been worth it.

I had to admit I didn't want to fuck tonight. In fact, the thought of sex made me *so* tired. But Paulie and I had fooled around every night we'd been together since that wonderful first night months ago. We hung out during the day too. Sometimes we went to the Lumberyard with Travis or Angie, and once we chilled with all of his accounting friends. And, every now and then, Paulie held my hand when we were walking back from class, and I felt so incredibly special. But not once, not ever, had we skipped the orgasms at the end of the night.

I was exhausted, disappointed, and so scared Paulie wouldn't want me there just to *cuddle*, so I called him to cancel.

"Are you sick?"

"Well, not really. I'm just tired and stressed. I won't be any fun." Maybe he would read the euphemism in *fun*, and I wouldn't have to spell it out.

"Okay," he said, his voice fragile and hesitant. "We could just sleep, you know. We don't have to have sex. I would love to get to see you." Those words had cost him, the strain evident in his voice. He hurried on, "But it's up to you. I'll see you tomorrow either way."

My gut clenched with want. I *wanted* to have his warm body lull me into sleep, and I *wanted* to kiss him good night.

"You're sure?"

"Please, Joel. Come over."

He greeted me at his door in plaid pajama bottoms with a mug of tea. He looked like home, and nothing had looked like home in a very long time. Even as a child, my fighting parents made *home* a burden.

Paulie insisted I drink the tea. He drank it all the time—he said it made him hip—but I'd never had hot tea until we started dating. The tea was sweet, and he rubbed the tightness in my neck while I drank it.

When I finished, he led me to his bedroom, which I'd loved from the first time he'd brought me into his home. It was bright and colorful and full of old stuff he found at antique stores, and I much preferred it to the impersonal, utilitarian space of my bedroom.

We lay down, and rather than letting Paulie curl under my chin like normal, I moved into his arms. Needy. *Please don't turn me away* needy. I couldn't deny how much it would hurt to learn we had nothing more than hopped-up hormones and chemistry between us.

My ear rested directly over his heart, which was pounding loud and strong. He continued to rub my neck and scalp, and the tension poured out of my body. Made me pliant and weak.

"Tell me about it," he whispered.

Tears stung my eyes because it almost felt like he was asking about Diego. And, again, I could picture myself telling him everything. Could picture purging it all and being clean for the first time in years. Travis's words from weeks ago repeated in my head, and I imagined being strong and open, like Travis wanted. I imagined giving Paulie the honesty he deserved.

I was almost weak enough to relent and let Paulie see the real me.

Instead, I told Paulie about my project. About the diaries and journals I'd read and the way the railroad had simultaneously cleaved apart the fabric of the settlers' lives and opened up a new world to them. I talked about how the railroad had affected the Native American tribes and the buffalo. How it had affected the land around us, around Farm College even. And I talked about the characters I couldn't stop thinking about—the preacher's daughter who'd written about the sky, and the old cowhand who'd written about horses like they were people, and the young missionary who'd questioned whether converting Native Americans was really the right thing to do. I told Paulie why I loved history so much. How I liked getting swept up in the people of the past. How it helped me make sense of life.

By the end of it, I could barely keep my eyes open, and Paulie was still running his hands through my hair. I looked up into his eyes, and they were all lit up with some infinite emotion that was begging to be noticed for the first time. How much of *that* had he been hiding from me? The thought woke me right the fuck up.

"I don't think you've ever looked at me before today," I whispered into the quiet space between us, and he smiled at the words he'd said himself, the day I freaked out in class.

"I'm a little scared by how much I like you right now." He ran his thumb over my lips and chin.

I closed my eyes and fought tears again, because it hurt. Like falling off the bed of a truck and having the wind knocked out of you or wrenching an old injury that time hadn't fully healed. These feelings that Paulie pulled to the surface were so unexpected . . . and *unwanted* because it hurt falling in love again. It hurt knowing that someone else was filling that broken chasm that Diego had left behind. It hurt to care for someone and want someone like I had once cared for and wanted him. I wasn't ready to replace or lose Diego and didn't know if I'd ever be.

I hoped Paulie couldn't see how hard those emotions flared up and choked me. But he kissed my closed eyelids, and I knew he could feel the moisture there.

His lips found mine, salty and soft. I kissed him hard and clutched him to me, not because I wanted to move us toward sex but because I needed him to know that I felt it too. That I was scared, and it hurt, and I loved him, even if I couldn't say it yet.

Perhaps I would never be able to. The first time I told Diego I loved him, we had been having sex in my pickup out on some old country road, which was pretty normal since we had been too scared to do it at our respective homes. Diego had been on his back across my bench seat, one leg thrown over the top of the seat and the other planted on the floorboard. Once we were done, I had looked down at him and blurted it out. I just couldn't believe how lucky I was, and I had wanted him to know I didn't take it for granted.

Diego had laughed and tilted his head back and away from my gaze. He'd never said it back. Not then. Not ever. I had stripped the chance from both of us with a dumb text message.

Diego's laugh haunted me. Paulie wouldn't laugh if I told him I loved him. He would be gentle and kind. But I wasn't sure I could be any of those things for him. I wasn't sure I wanted to hear those words from anyone when I had never heard them from Diego.

Maybe love was just an illusion anyway, like jigsaw puzzles that looked like a picture or a painting from a distance. But the closer you got, the more visible the cracks. Wasn't until you shined a light on it that the illusion fell apart.

The next morning in Dr. Yamato's office, which was full of weird Ikea-like concept furniture, I sat down on an uncomfortable yellow plastic chair and handed over my proposal.

"So, this is about the effect of the railroad, right?" Dr. Yamato said, lightly tapping my proposal packet against her desk. She was tall and willowy with dyed red hair, wore gray almost every day, and her office was scary clean.

"Yeah."

She smiled and stared at me a beat too long, like she expected me to say more, but I sucked at conversing like a normal person. "I'm glad you followed through on this. I'm looking forward to reading it."

"Thank you," I replied, and then scrambled around for something else to say. "I'm hoping to turn it into a larger body of work for graduate school. Like a thesis."

"That's wonderful. I didn't know you were interested in graduate school."

"Uh. Yeah. That's the plan at least."

"I'll write you a reference letter when you apply, if you'd like."

"That'd be nice," I said, hoping this meeting could be over soon.

"How's everything been going lately? Life treating you okay?"

Dr. Yamato was an excellent professor, but she had never, in almost two and a half years, asked me a personal question.

That dark, secretive cloud, the one that unfurled when my past came too close to the surface, pressed in on me, and I stammered that I was fine.

"That's good! You've seemed happy recently," she said with a smile, and proceeded to thumb through my proposal. "I look forward to reading this. I think your ideas have a lot of potential, and I'm not just saying that. I'm eager to pass it along to the committee."

I mumbled, "Thank you," and rather inelegantly escaped. When I made it home, I got straight back in bed to sleep the rest of my morning away.

Paulie kissed me awake a couple of hours later, and I slapped a hand over the drool on my cheek. I tried to pull him down on top of me, but he slipped out of my hands.

"Dr. Milner posted the instructions online for our final paper in Ethics in News and Media today. I'm sure he'll talk about it tomorrow in class." Paulie grinned, his eyes bright, and skipped over to my desk and sat down. I didn't respond. Everything about that class made me cringe now. "He wants us to choose any article that he's used as a case study and then write an analytical paper on one of the ethical issues in it. Half the paper is a literature review, and that's basically history, so you'll like that. The other half is explaining the ethical issue in your article and creating a recommendation for handling that issue in the future."

"Sounds great," I lied.

"Yeah, no. It totally sucks. The paper is supposed to be between ten and twelve pages! I don't think I've ever written a paper that long."

My proposal was over twenty pages, and I wrote long papers in my history classes all the time. Travis would be equally unimpressed by Paulie's dismay. He was an English lit. major.

"I'll proofread it for you," I said, mostly because I knew he would respond like a diva.

"I have a better grade in that class than you, thank you very much, Joel Smith. I can proofread my own damn paper."

I held my arms out to him, and he rolled his eyes and hopped back into bed with me.

"I'm kind of excited about it though," he said. "Remember those articles about the kids who got outed because they were sexting, and one of them died while driving and reading a message? You might not have read the articles. It was the day you got sick, and you, *sweet thang*, refused to do the assignment with me."

The choking metallic tang of horror filled my mouth, and sweat sprouted in my armpits and along my spine. I flinched away from him, but Paulie didn't seem to notice.

"I want to write about the press outing people against their wills. It happens often on those gossip sites with celebrities and politicians, but these were just normal guys, kids even, and evidently someone in the police department leaked the contents of the messages to a reporter, and that's how everyone found out. Isn't that crazy? Then, get this. A local politician who was running for some state office made it a campaign issue because supposedly the boyfriend of the boy who died knew the kid was driving and sent him the text anyway. So this politician vowed to pass legislation to make people liable if they—"

"I read the articles, Paulie. I don't need your commentary," I snapped. He stopped talking, and I was so relieved I thought I would faint.

And why the fuck couldn't I handle this? It had been years now! But I couldn't. Not yet. And . . . oh God . . . the politician. Fucking Robert "Bobby" Lankford, the Martinezes' conservative Baptist butt buddy. I wished I could pin the whole freaking circus in the press on Bobby Lankford. But I couldn't. It was all my fault. One of his campaign speeches rushed up on me like heartburn. He'd blamed me. Said responsibility needed to be laid to bare.

And the journalist had been almost as bad. She'd recently graduated from college, and everyone had said she didn't know any better. But I didn't buy that.

When that woman had outed Diego, he'd already been dead. He hadn't deserved to have his secrets spewed all over the newspapers *postmortem*. No one had needed to know what he liked in his sexts or in bed. He was *dead*. No one had known the real him except me, and it should have stayed that way.

Only I knew that Diego had liked tenderness and romance. He'd found dirty talk garish, which was why our sexts had almost always been G-rated. And that's how I became the Sweet Mouth Texter. Diego had had the most beautiful lips and this cocky smile that could have been dropping every pair of panties with daddy issues in our little country high school—and daddy issues weren't exactly thin on the ground. *Hell*, I'd had daddy issues. But he'd chosen *me*. He'd kissed *me*. And, for that privilege, I'd told him he was beautiful and sent him the text message that killed him.

My words had been revealing, and that was what I regretted the most. When the message contents had been leaked to the press, they hadn't just revealed that the catcher and first baseman on the high school team had been banging. They hadn't just outed Diego to his religious family and me to my small, broken one. That text message had provided everyone a glimpse into this sweet and innocent thing that had been secret and hidden and fragile. *Diego* had been secret and hidden and fragile. And I had exposed him. I became the Sweet Mouth Texter, and Diego became the boy who liked it.

"Hey, where'd you go?" Paulie said, bringing my attention back to him.

"Just spaced out. I'm half-asleep," I lied, but concern burned in his dark eyes. Still, I couldn't talk to him right now, couldn't handle this. And I absolutely did not want Paulie to write a paper about Diego, journalistic ethics, and *me*.

Paulie talked about his other finals, and I followed the rest of our conversation half-heartedly until he suggested working on homework in the living room with Travis.

My relationship with Paulie made me happy. It was precious, full of something so close to love, but so tenuous we couldn't speak of it. But now, with suspicion in his eyes and panic soaking me in flop sweat, I couldn't ignore the cracks.

chapter ten

The rest of the semester flew by in a blur of laughter and easy camaraderie that lifted me outside myself, like I was living someone else's life, someone who was lucky and wasn't hiding a huge, scary secret. Paulie and I were each immersed in each other, in our schoolwork, and in our easy college jobs—his at the Registrar's Office and mine tutoring for the History Department. And I was happy.

But these moments would hit me, moments where I realized how little of myself I'd divulged to him, and I would feel so ashamed. One day, he asked me what my high school's team name had been in Salina, Kansas. He knew that was where my mother lived now, and I had let him believe it was my hometown, worried he would piece together too much if he found out I was from the same town in Nebraska as the boys in the newspaper articles. I had told him the Lions, but found out later, after searching online, that they were the Mustangs.

Holidays came and went. At Thanksgiving, I lied to Paulie and Travis by telling them I was visiting my mom, but after they both drove away—Paulie to Emporia and Travis to Oklahoma City to catch a flight—I stayed.

During the second week of December, the day before my first final, my mom called.

"Hey, Mom. What's up?" I saved my paper, and leaned back in my desk chair.

"Hi, Joel. I was checking to see if you're still coming up for Christmas."

I paused because she'd actually called me *Joel*, and that meant she wanted something. Her question was warranted though. I'd bailed often enough.

"Yeah, same plans that we talked about last week. I'll drive up to Salina on the twenty-third and head back to Elkville the day after Christmas. That okay?"

"I wish you were staying longer, is all. What are you going to do in Elkville besides freeze to death?"

I rolled my eyes, thankful she couldn't see me. It would be cold in Kansas too, and I would rather be alone in frigid Elkville than spend too many excruciating days with my mom, who did not get me at all.

"I'm going to work on some internship applications, so I'll stay busy." An internship would give me a fallback if the fellowship didn't pan out. It was hard focusing on my finals, much less thinking about internships or fellowships, when I'd rather be curled up with Paulie in bed. He'd been finishing the final paper in Ethics in News and Media over the weekend, and I'd avoided him, terrified he would look at me and somehow see the truth.

A soft knock sounded on my door, and Paulie slipped inside a moment later. I liked that he did that—just came and went from my room like he owned it. Snow dusted his hair, his cheeks were rosy, and I wanted to tackle him. He plopped down on my lap and kissed the side of my neck opposite the phone. His breath tickled when he whispered, "Who is it?" in my ear.

I mouthed, *My mom.*

Mom sighed like she could tell I wasn't paying attention. Paulie snuggled deeper into my lap, his head tucked against my neck.

"Harlan's coming down for Christmas," she said, her voice resigned. I jackknifed out of my chair like a puppet with someone pulling the strings, and Paulie spilled onto the floor.

"Oh shit! Paulie, I'm sorry!" I gasped. "Are you all right?" I crouched next to him, but my head spun. *My father?* At my mom's for Christmas? I *couldn't*— I didn't know if I could—

"I'm okay," Paulie mumbled. His face was creased with alarm, and he clutched my shoulders to steady me.

"Who's Paulie? Whose voice was that?" my mom said, her tone brittle.

"It's no one," I said without thinking. Paulie snatched his hands back and closed his eyes.

"It's obviously *someone* if you're talking to him when you're on the phone with me."

"Mom, it's—" I hesitated. She didn't need to know anything about my personal life. "Just a friend. Don't change the subject." Paulie's lips quirked up into a self-deprecating smile. He laughed a little, stood, ruffled my hair, and rambled out of my bedroom. *Good. One thing at a time.* I couldn't juggle him *and* my mom. "Mom, I can't come if he's going to be there."

"He's family, and he wants to see you, Jared—*shit*—he wants to see you, *Joel.* He'll be there Christmas day, but isn't staying at my house. He's got a motel room. Listen, I know this is going to be hard, but I think it's time that we all forgave each other, don't you?"

I didn't know what to say to that. I loved Mom, and I was in awe of the sacrifice she had made to get me out of Townsend. But I didn't want to forgive my father. I didn't want to see him or hear his cold, flat, Midwesterner voice. I didn't want to remember that sting across my cheek.

"Do this for me, Joel. If it goes poorly, I'll never ask you again."

"Are you back together?" The thought made me want to punch something.

She made a noncommittal noise. "Marriage is complicated."

"So is divorce, evidently," I snapped.

"Your father loves you, and I love you, and Christmas is a day to spend with loved ones."

My first thought was of Paulie, and how he was the loved one I most wanted to spend the holidays with, but I couldn't abandon her for Christmas. Not after everything she'd given up for me. I owed her.

"Fine. But I'll leave if he's an asshole." Silence stretched between us like a taut wire. If one of us pulled any harder, it would break, and who knew what would spill out then?

"I love you, baby boy," she finally whispered, her voice thick with tears.

"You too, Mom."

She hung up, and I hung my head, still sitting in an awkward crouch on the floor. I didn't move until Paulie stepped back into my room with two beers in his hands and said, "Sounded like you need this."

"Paulie. I'm sorry. I don't know why—" *I called you no one.* I'd done it with little thought from some residual impulse I'd honed as a teenager.

"Shhh," he purred, his lips sliding over mine. "It's okay, buttercup." He kissed me soundly again, and then took a swallow of his beer. His Adam's apple bobbed deliciously, and I slid my gaze to his jugular notch.

"I want you," I admitted. I didn't deserve him though. He smiled and lifted an eyebrow, lips still wrapped around the bottle. After another long drink, he set both of our beers aside.

With an easy push, he toppled me onto my back on the floor. He climbed up my body, smooth as a jungle cat, and I tried to touch him everywhere at once.

"You can have me," he said, still full of cockiness. "You can have me if you promise to do one thing."

"Anything." I gasped when he bit down on my earlobe.

"Come home with me before Christmas. We'll carpool. Stay with me a couple days and drive from there to your mom's. Then pick me up on your way to Elkville, and we can come back to this drafty, old house and bang in the living room."

"I caught Travis doing that once."

A grin flashed across Paulie's face, and he slid his long fingers into my hair and tilted my head until my throat was exposed. He held me steady and sure, captured me and controlled me, and I wanted to thank him. He slipped his tongue past my lips and stroked it deep into my mouth. Then, as all of my brain waves were beginning to fray, he pulled back. "Travis will be wasting away in suburbia for all of break, so it's our turn. What do you say, buttercup? Come home with me?"

I wrapped my arms around his lithe, strong body and kissed him. "I would love to, baby."

The five-hour drive to Emporia from Elkville was like a dream, all soft and alight and perfect. I had read about the Flint Hills and seen pictures, but nothing prepared me for the moment the flatlands dropped off into limestone-soaked prairie hills. Farmhouses littered the landscape like reminders of the past permanently painted on the land, and a train rumbled by, going much faster than we could on the curvy road. The bluestem and wheatgrass lining the winding roads was brown and dry and spotted with tufts of snow that had yet to melt. I could only imagine the impact the rolling plains would have when the land was lush and green.

Here, nostalgia persisted as if the twenty-first century was a myth, but the region seemed to suffer from living in the past. Wood-paneled farmhouses had fallen to rubble and junk lots overflowed with old cars and rusted farm equipment. The cattle grazing the prairies were thin, and each little township we sped through was untouched by corporations and industry. Every once in a while, we would pass a Hardee's or a Pizza Hut, but they appeared sad and hardscrabble.

Yet, I could see myself here with the hills rising high around me and a creek tattooing my backyard. The landscape allowed for hunkering down, for settling in, and escaping the wide-open exposure of flat prairie.

We were about fifteen minutes from Paulie's aunt's house on the outskirts of Emporia when a doe with two fawns streaked beside my truck. I braked hard and settled the car slowly to a stop on a narrow shoulder.

The deer ran for another twenty feet before timidly crossing the road. They got to the other side, loped up the gentle hill and over the train tracks, and disappeared down a bank.

Paulie grabbed my hand. His breath hitched as he stared after the deer, and when he turned toward me with a soft smile, the one I thought of as mine, I hoped he was as thankful as me to share the moment with someone else. Maybe someone he loved.

I almost said it then. Almost said, *I love you*. But I couldn't love him. Not yet. I wasn't ready. The pain I carried about Diego was too near and present all the time.

Eventually, we arrived at his aunt's home, a small blue cottage-style house with a huge cottonwood tree in the front yard and a clothesline in the back.

Ruth and Daria met us in the front yard. They both seemed kind: Ruth immediately asked if I was hungry and informed me that she'd made cookies, and Daria smiled shyly and didn't say much.

His aunt grinned when Paulie interlaced our fingers and led me into the house.

The living room was dated, with dark-wood-paneled walls, but portraits of Daria and Paulie brightened it up. There were no pictures of them as children, and I imagined that their parents still had those. It was as if those days as Quiverfull children never existed, and the absence seemed palpable, literally written on the walls.

"I'm making your favorite for dinner tonight, Paul," Ruth said, and it shocked me to hear him called Paul. It sounded wrong, since I'd taken to saying it when I wanted him to fuck me harder. But it also sounded off in the same way it was wrong when my mom slipped and called me *Jared*. Paulie wasn't *Paul*. He'd made that choice.

"Tater tot casserole?" he asked, excitement lacing his voice. And that surprised me too. I'd thought his favorite food was sushi. Maybe he was a different person here, like I was a different person with my mom. Not unrecognizable, but differently patterned. In Elkville, he could be the swishy, happy man who loved sushi and drank a shit-ton of tea. And here he could be that same person, except perhaps he could relax and eat tater tots and ground beef. I felt oddly touched he trusted me to see this side of him.

"You betcha," Ruth said.

Paulie whooped and turned to me with unrestrained glee. "You're in for a treat, buttercup!"

"Yeah, he's in for something," Daria muttered, and Paulie stuck his tongue out at her.

"Here, I'll show you my room, so you can put your bags up," Paulie said to me.

I hadn't put much thought into where I would be sleeping, but I hadn't figured it would be Paulie's room.

As if reading my discomfort, Paulie's aunt said, "I had planned to pull the trundle bed out from under Daria's daybed and put it in Paul's room for you to sleep on, Joel, but that was because I'd assumed you two were just friends. Daria informed me otherwise, and there's no point in moving the trundle in there if you're only going to pretend to sleep on it."

My cheeks and ears flushed with embarrassment, but I was also a little hurt Paulie hadn't told her we were more than friends, even if neither of us ever used the words.

Did he bring buddies around often? Maybe she'd thought I was some charity case, which, *God*, was kind of the truth.

Paulie laughed, and Daria made a sly, obscene hand gesture behind their aunt's back at him. *Maybe not so shy*, I realized, charmed by her. With a bouncy little skip, Paulie pressed a kiss on his aunt's cheek and said, "Aunt Ruth, when you're right, you're right." Daria giggled, and then Paulie pulled me away from their teasing.

Paulie's bedroom was different than his room at school. His apartment at school was full of quirky antiques and bright comforts. His teenage bedroom was like walking into a jewel-toned, smoky bar. It had low lights, lamps with dark covers, and gauzy purple and blue fabrics covering the walls and windows. Concert posters from old punk and electronic-pop bands peeked out from behind the draped panels. It was a trip. He even had a beaded curtain hanging from the doorjamb of his closet.

My teenage bedroom had been painfully generic: posters of sports cars and women, baseball trophies, and a bedspread with sailboats, even though I lived in land-locked Nebraska. It had been nothing like this.

I walked to the closet and ran my hands through the strands of beads. "I like this."

"Yeah, I do too. No door."

"I guess you don't really need a door for your closet."

"Exactly," he said, and I smiled.

"Your room is . . . atmospheric. It really tells a story, Paulie."

He groaned a little, and then we both laughed.

"I wasn't allowed to decorate my room at my parents' house. They had controlled everything, so when I moved here and had this newfound freedom, I went a little overboard." Paulie fell back onto his queen-sized bed and gazed up at the ceiling, which was covered in glow-in-the-dark stars. "Aunt Ruth let me hang posters of men wearing makeup and staple sparkly fabric to my walls. I could be myself here.

I didn't have to worry about my parents' disgust because I liked the color purple, or whatever it was they hated about me."

"I'm so sorry that happened to you," I whispered.

Before he could respond, a knock startled us. Daria said through the door, "Can I come in, Paul? Are you naked?"

"Get in here, Peanut," Paulie called to her.

I settled into a deep-red pouf chair in the corner as Daria slipped into the room and sat down on the bed. She was tall and willowy thin with long, straight blonde hair that she twisted around her fingers almost constantly, and I was struck by how she didn't resemble Paulie at all.

"So how did your finals go?" Paulie asked her.

She shrugged and messed with a loose string on the bedspread. "Okay, I guess. Mostly *B*s."

"That's good. Why are you acting like it's not?"

"Because I know that I could have done better. I'm probably going to be a terrible nurse. I can't even make it through one semester without having to drop classes because of my own melodrama."

Her eyes got suspiciously shiny, which made me want to comfort her, but Paulie just watched her closely.

"First off, don't trash yourself. You're going to be an awesome nurse. You have so much empathy and understanding for other people, and you're good at thinking on your feet. And secondly, dropping classes doesn't make you a failure. I've had to drop my fair share, and I'm sure Joel has too. It's normal."

I nodded. I'd been forced to drop classes during my first two semesters in college. I'd fallen behind, and it'd been impossible to catch up.

Daria huffed a little but smiled too.

"How did your clinicals go this semester? Any interesting stories?" he asked.

Daria launched into a story about witnessing her first C-section, and then abruptly stopped talking.

After a couple of seconds, Paulie said, "What's up?"

"Oh, uh, nothing." She shook her head a little. "I was just thinking about how one of my teachers hated me."

"How so?"

"She always called on me in class when I didn't know the answer. It's like she *knew*. And then once, she used one of my assignments as an example to show the right and wrong way fill to out a medical chart. She blacked out my name, so no one knew it was mine, but still."

"Wait, was she using your assignment as a good example or a bad one?"

Daria crossed her arms over her chest and frowned. "I don't know. I got an *A* on the assignment, but she talked about the parts I'd gotten wrong forever. Like, she hammered them. I know I'd done a lousy job, but geez. She didn't need to show the whole class."

"But you hadn't done lousy. You got an *A* on the assignment."

She shrugged and curled a lock of hair around one of her fingers until it turned red.

"What about the theater?" he asked. Then he turned to me to explain. "She volunteers at the community theater here in Emporia."

"Oh my gosh, Paul. You would not believe the drama this season." She was suddenly much more animated, and a bright smile stretched across her face. "There's this crazy love pentagon between the two Brittanys, Dante, Roger, and Will. Everyone is sleeping with each other, and throwing subs on social media. It's like a reality television show. And people say *I'm* histrionic," she scoffed.

"Hey, who says you're histrionic?" Paulie demanded.

"My counselor," she bantered back, obviously joking. A bark of laughter shot out of Paulie, and my head spun. Their repartee was hard to keep up with, especially with the sudden shift from serious to jocular.

Paulie ruffled the top of her head. "What else? Any other news?"

"I met someone in one of my classes. A guy."

Paulie clucked his tongue like a disapproving mother.

"Oh, screw you," she laughed. "He's hot. Let me show you." She whipped out her phone and pulled up a picture of him from Facebook. In the photo, he was wearing an Affliction T-shirt, a trucker hat, and had a really fake tan. I was not particularly impressed. Paulie and I glanced at each other, and he quickly changed the subject to Christmas shopping.

After talking about what they wanted to get Ruth for a couple of minutes, Daria said, "I saw Timothy the other day." She glanced at me and said, "That's my ex."

Paulie's body snapped to attention, as if not all of his brain waves had been tuned in but they were now.

"He was with another girl. I tried to find out about it on Facebook, but he blocked me, so I can't see his profile."

Paulie made a "go on" noise in his throat.

"It hurt seeing him again, you know? *I* cheated. *I* ruined it, but it hurts," she said, her voice cracking a little. Paulie wrapped his arms around her, like the epitome of a good older brother, and it made me angry, suddenly, that he only got to support one of his siblings when he had nine others who might need him. Daria leaned her head against his shoulder and sniffled. "God, I'm dumb. I don't know why I always screw everything up." A fat tear clung to her eyelashes before darkening Paulie's shirt.

"It's okay, Daria. You're not dumb," he said, and she buried her head against his neck. I stood up slowly. Paulie's eyes followed me, but Daria didn't seem to notice. I jerked my head toward the door, and Paulie nodded and mouthed, *Thank you.*

Once I hit the kitchen, awkwardness swamped me. Ruth was sitting at the table working on a crossword puzzle. She glanced up at me. "Wanna help?"

"Yes, ma'am," I mumbled, and she smiled. When Paulie had talked about his aunt, I had pictured this bohemian artist type, but she was dressed in a pantsuit, even though she was retired, and wore her light hair in a short, severe bob.

"You can call me Aunt Ruth. I know I'm not *your* aunt, but I like the name. I never thought I'd hear it, so now it makes me happy."

I was, again, struck by the oddness of Paulie, Ruth, and Daria's little bubble. They had this huge family, but were completely separate, completely estranged, and dealing with the day-to-day fallout of that estrangement.

"Where's this from?" I asked, gesturing to the crossword. It was a photocopy, and I couldn't identify the source.

"Oh, every morning I walk to the library and make a copy of the crossword from the *USA Today*. Got to love retirement. Paulie used to help me with it, when I still got all the papers delivered to the door. He likes *The New York Times* crossword better, but it's a little too intellectual for me. Here, four across: American Western writer. Eight spaces."

"Zane Grey?" I said, too eagerly.

She smiled at me. Her eyes were dark like Paulie's, and it was the first identifiable *something* I recognized to link him to either of these women. "I've been saving that one for you. Paul told me you like the West." Before I could reply, Aunt Ruth said, "Daria will be okay in a couple minutes. When she sees Paul for the first time after a long absence, it normally all leaks out."

"How did you know she—" I hesitated as it hit me: Paulie, Daria, and Aunt Ruth—this amazing little family—they held themselves together through love and shared experiences. They supported each other through struggles and illness and pain. This was routine for them.

It was the way a family should function.

"Where are you from?"

"Nebraska," I said, still lost in my thoughts. As my answer caught up with me, I froze, and panic rattled through my brain. I had kept that a secret from Paulie for months and then blabbed it out to his aunt in five seconds. *God, hopefully she never mentions that to him.*

"Oh, yuck. I hate Nebraska."

"When you're right, you're right," I said after a beat. She smiled at my repetition of Paulie's phrase. After a few moments of silence, I pointed to the crossword. "Ten down, five letters: Retired Major League catcher Ivan Rodriguez's nickname. The answer is 'Pudge.'"

"Pudge. Huh. That's odd."

"He was my idol growing up. I wanted to be just like him."

I'd realized I wasn't going to be good enough for pro or even minor ball when I was in high school, but I had loved playing. Loved being on Diego's team.

Paulie and Daria came out of his bedroom then, and he grazed a kiss across my temple. Daria gave me a watery smile before slipping over to the refrigerator to get a can of pop. A loaded glance passed between Paulie and Aunt Ruth, and he smiled, as if he wanted to reassure her. When Daria returned, everyone settled around the kitchen table and helped with the crossword while the tater tot casserole heated in the oven, spreading fast-food smells through the house.

Hours later, Paulie and I lay side by side in his bed staring up at the ceiling, lost in our individual thoughts. The room was tinted blue from a desk lamp with a filmy sapphire shade, and the gossamer fabric over the window glinted silver from the moon. Paulie's hand was wrapped in mine, and he ran his thumb in a circle on my palm.

"They're changing her antidepressants right now," he said out of the blue.

I studied his profile. His plush lips and thick eyelashes didn't negate the masculine cut of his jaw, but I still couldn't get over how pretty he was.

"It's a good thing, I hope. Her last ones made her sick to her stomach. It's hard watching her distort everything sometimes. She has this tendency for all-or-nothing thinking, for minimizing positive accomplishments and blowing bad things out of proportion. I worry about her so much. Daria and Aunt Ruth are all I've got, you know?"

He slid his gaze to mine until our eyes were locked. Our faces were only about a foot apart, and his breath ghosted across my cheek. I wanted to tell him that he had me, but chickened out.

"I'm so glad you're here, Joel."

His voice cracked, a small hiccup that most people might not notice. I touched his cheek, running the tips of my fingers along his five-o'clock shadow. He took a shuddery breath, and his eyelashes fluttered closed helplessly, casting spiky-tipped shadows on his cheekbones. In moments like this—moments of openness and vulnerability—I was always stunned by his reactions to me, like I held the key to everything and he'd happily give himself to me completely.

"I love it here. Not just this area, but *here*, with your aunt and your sister and you." I didn't handle vulnerability or intimacy as well as him—didn't let myself sink into it like him—and that bald statement tore at me until I was practically shivering under the blanket.

He rubbed a thumb over my bottom lip to the corner of my mouth, and his eyes tracked over my face until I couldn't bear the attention any longer.

"Daria's taller than you," I blurted. "And blonde. I didn't expect that."

"My dad's family is tall and fair and my mom's family is a mixed bag. Daria told me that most of the older kids are taller than me now. Or, rather, when she left."

"I look like my dad." I wrinkled my nose at the thought, but it was undeniably the truth. We both had golden-brown hair, blue eyes, and tall, leanly muscled bodies.

"What's it going to be like seeing your dad again?"

"My mom says we all need to forgive each other, but I'm not sure we can."

"Wait!" Paulie frowned. "What does either of them have to forgive *you* for? You didn't do anything to them."

My stomach jolted. *Of course.* Paulie still didn't know anything about Diego or the shit after his death. He thought my dad didn't want me because I liked dick.

"We all said really horrible things to each other," I lied. "I'm not exactly innocent."

Paulie's eyebrows thundered down. "Your dad abandoned you. *He* gave you up. As far as I'm concerned, he doesn't deserve your apology. Fuck, he doesn't deserve *your* forgiveness. And he doesn't deserve to have the man you are now in his life."

Paulie's eyes filled with tears, and he turned his head away from me. My thoughts screeched to a halt and realigned as he swiped his hand across his cheek. His sudden anger was as much about his father as it was mine. I gathered him in my arms and molded him to my body, hoping to calm the storm of his emotions with touch and comfort. It was exactly how we normally slept, all pressed together, and part of me wished we could drift off now, away from this painful conversation.

"Do you miss your family?" I asked in his ear.

He nodded. "Christmas is hard. I always wonder what they're doing."

"I don't think a day has gone by where I've missed my dad," I admitted.

"Good. He doesn't deserve that either."

Paulie's fierceness made me smile. He really could be rather terrifying. I liked that about him. I liked his fight.

I rubbed the back of his head, letting his short, prickly hair sensitize the tips of my fingers, and he melted into me like surrender was what he'd been craving all along. Within minutes, his body was relaxed and heavy against mine, and I could tell he was falling asleep.

His arms and legs always jerked a little, as if he needed momentum to launch into a deep sleep. I wanted to ask one more question though.

"Baby, Aunt Ruth and Daria just call you Paul. Where does the name Paulie come from?"

"Pauly Shore," he mumbled against my chest. I laughed, which was surely his intent.

"Seriously. Tell me."

Paulie huffed and lifted his head until his chin rested on the center of my chest. He looked up at me with soulful, sleepy eyes.

"I didn't start going by Paulie until college, and I pretty much pulled that off by introducing myself that way. I liked the idea of being *Paulie* because it sounds like a woman's name, and I got a kick out of my parents finding out about it . . . which is pretty sad, I know. I'm twenty-three and still acting out to garner my parents' attention. But I'd been *Paul* my whole life, and it wasn't good enough. It wasn't *me.*"

I knew how he felt. *Jared* wasn't me either. Not anymore.

Paulie liked it when I called him Paul in bed, even though Paulie fit him so perfectly. But it made sense to me now. If I called him Paul, maybe especially when we were having sex, it was like a big *fuck you* to everyone who had rejected him. I was telling him that the boy who loved pink and had been abandoned by his parents was fine and perfect and accepted.

"I like *Paulie,*" I said.

"That's good," Paulie said, his voice slurred with sleepiness. "He likes you, too."

chapter eleven

It snowed hard the next morning, but Daria and Paulie still insisted on venturing into town to finish Christmas shopping. Paulie drove us in his aunt's SUV, and Daria fiddled with the radio the entire time. It was fun watching them interact. He pulled her out of her shell with good-natured teasing and prodding, and she responded with dry, sneaky puns and innuendo. They had a comedic dynamic and a camaraderie that was comfortable but also exciting to me as an only child.

It was also telling. Paulie was a wonderful brother, and Daria clearly needed him. If only their parents could realize what they'd let go.

Eventually, we arrived at the first department store. I bought my mom a big purse with Western-style rhinestone embellishments. I considered buying my dad a Kansas City Royals ball cap, but eventually put it back on the shelf. Paulie and Daria filled their arms with presents for Aunt Ruth and, discreetly, for each other; though, they'd agreed to only exchange gift cards.

Once we were leaving the last store, and Paulie was in the checkout line buying stocking stuffers, Daria hooked her arm in mine and whispered in my ear, "What did you get him for Christmas?"

Sweat immediately slicked the back of my neck. I hadn't gotten him anything. I wasn't actually going to be with him on Christmas Day, so I hadn't thought about presents.

When Daria saw my face, she chirped, "Uh-oh!" with obvious delight.

"Has he gotten me something?" I whispered frantically, hoping to learn the details before Paulie made it through the line.

Daria shrugged. "I'm sure he has because that's how he is. Just like I know he's gotten me something besides a gift card. He makes us all look bad."

I nodded because that was the goddamned truth, but by then Paulie was through the line and walking toward us. He was wearing a long gray peacoat and a fuzzy, chunky blue scarf today, and he looked graceful and stylish and gorgeous.

"What are you guys talking about?" he asked as he ripped open a package of chocolates and popped a piece between his sweet pink lips. I had the absurd thought that I wanted to follow that chocolate into his mouth and over his tongue until I was completely inside him.

He was so fucking sexy and way too good for me, for all my lies and deceit and baggage. One of these days he would realize it and spit me back out.

I managed to choke, "Nothing."

Paulie must have seen the need on my face, because after Daria climbed into the front seat and he'd loaded his bags into the back of the SUV, he pinned me against the car. I kissed the sensitive hollow below his ear, hoping my breath would warm him, and soon he was squirming in my arms and tilting the beautiful slope of his neck so I had more room, more access. He moaned when I sucked the skin and tight flesh between my teeth, and when I released him, he had a tiny blushing red stain that hopefully his aunt and Daria would think was simply chapped skin from the punishing cold.

When we got home, we ate grilled cheese sandwiches and canned tomato soup and pretended we didn't want to fuck on the kitchen table. Or, well, I pretended. Paulie didn't really hide it. He regaled Aunt Ruth and Daria with stories from Farm College, including several about Travis and me, but in between stories or when no one was looking, Paulie raked me with his dark eyes. By the end of the evening, he'd been eye-fucking me so much, and I was so worked up, I worried I wouldn't be able to keep quiet when he took me to bed.

The minute Paulie's bedroom door closed behind us, he turned the overhead light off and stripped. The only light in the room now was cast from a small desk lamp. The shade painted his creamy white skin blue and green, like he was underwater. *Oh.* Oh, I had to touch him, had to trace the medley of colors on his skin.

As soon as my hands met the curve of his neck and shoulder, Paulie moaned softly and melted against me. I whispered, "Shhh," against his lips, but then his cold hands digging underneath my clothes made me gasp louder than any noise he was making. He pulled my shirt over my head, and then we were chest to chest. The hair between my pecs scratched against his smooth skin, and I felt friction and fire. I licked into his mouth and swept my hands down the long bright line of his spine, making Paulie arch against my hands until they slid all the way to his ass.

When I gripped each cheek, Paulie shuddered and his head fell back. "Yes," he whispered. "Yes!" when I pulled them apart.

I rained down kisses on his neck until he made that sobbing noise that meant he was close. I wasn't even touching his cock, but when I looked, it was plum-colored and weeping at the tip. A growl rose up in my throat. He was gorgeous, and I was a lucky son of a bitch.

Surging forward, I used my weight and strength to bend him over backward until my mouth could wrap around his nipple piercing. I normally wasn't this aggressive, but Paulie didn't seem to mind. When I sucked on his nipple, he gasped. "Touch me!"

I reached for that beautiful prick and pulled gently on his nipple piercing with my teeth. His skin was salty-sweet, and he smelled like snow and sweat and oranges. He arched his back even more, and my other hand slid lower. My middle finger teased the soft skin over his tailbone.

He opened his eyes, and his gaze captured me so completely, I couldn't breathe. His pupils were blown and needy and dazed. I couldn't turn away from that desire. Couldn't walk away. I wanted it. I wanted him to look at me like that every fucking day.

I hadn't felt like this—possessive and stunned and free—since Diego. My stomach rolled, because no one could compare to Diego, and I couldn't imagine loving anyone like I loved him.

God, it was excruciating every time Paulie slipped inside the tight fist of my heart and made me want him with a power I had never experienced.

And I did want him. And it wasn't just sex. I wanted the afterglow when he tucked against my body. I wanted him to trust me with the gift of his painful past and his home. I wanted to hold his fierceness inside me when he thought I was selling myself short.

Paulie cupped my cheek. "Hey, you okay?" he asked, and I shook my head to empty it. Then I kissed him.

He pushed his butt hard into my hand, and I knew. I knew exactly what he needed, but I wasn't sure I could do it. Wasn't sure I could touch him how I had once touched Diego.

"*There*," he said softly. "I want you to touch me there." When I started to pull away, he gasped, "Just touch. Nothing else." He rolled those fluid hips again until there was absolutely no way to pretend he wasn't talking about his ass. We'd never tried ass play with him, and that was my fault because I hadn't thought to ask if he'd wanted it. Paulie had liked to bottom before me, so it would make sense that he would like to be fingered too. *Oh fuck.* I wanted to slip my fingers inside his heat and let it melt me, turn me to liquid, and spill me out all over the bedroom floor. I suddenly needed to be inside his body as much as I needed oxygen.

He hummed and purred against my mouth as I kneaded his strong butt muscles and whispered touches over him. Each lingering pass brought me closer to his entrance, but I wanted to draw him out until he couldn't see straight, until he couldn't feel or see or want anyone but me.

His lips opened on a gasp when I caressed the insides of his thighs, and I dove at his mouth, sucking on his tongue and plump lips until they looked so juicy and ripe I thought they might burst. He sobbed—"Please, please, please!"—and when I pulled him closer to me, his cock brushed my stomach. His eyes rolled back in his head, and his knees went so weak it was like someone had cut the cord of his spine. I couldn't resist any longer.

I licked my fingers and swept them along the furrow of his ass, and he sucked in a breath and held it. Then I finally brushed my fingertips over his entrance. His body clenched in my hold, his neck muscles sprung tight and his head tilted back. His hole flexed for a second against my finger—I'd barely slipped inside—and I started thinking about lube and slick and the warm honey orgasm I would coax out of him with my fingers planted in his perfect ass.

But then Paulie coated me in his spunk. He came from nothing more than my finger touching his asshole, and made a sound like he was being tortured—a desperate, keening cry. It blurred my vision—it was so fucking hot—and I could only make out the kaleidoscope of night shadows on his skin.

Before my mind could catch up with my body, I had Paulie on his knees, my jeans and briefs partway down my legs, and his spend running in rivulets down my abs and catching in my body hair. The picture of him kneeling in front of me, his face flushed and eyes still bleary from orgasm, made come rush to my nuts and jacked me so high I could barely breathe. I pumped my shaft once, twice, *fuck*, and Paulie leaned forward to wrap that wicked tongue around my cap, but his mouth didn't make it. I lost it too soon.

I cupped his chin with one hand and tilted his head back so he wouldn't get a facial. I painted his long, graceful neck, and I couldn't seem to stop, couldn't seem to stem the force that wanted him covered in me until every single person would know he was mine. A groan ripped from my belly, and the world tunneled until all I could see were Paulie's eyes and my jizz dripping from the barbell in his nipple.

After a long, dizzy moment, I listed forward, and Paulie steadied me. He guided me to the bed and used a towel to dispose of the mess. We'd both shot like teenagers, and I would have been embarrassed if it hadn't felt so fucking good.

Still, wariness soured my stomach, that black swirling cloud of my past growing large and scary in my chest. The last ten minutes felt like déjà vu, from the rushed groping to the white noise in my head when I put Paulie on his knees. Every time Paulie undid me with his sweetness and intensity, I felt bare, like he could peer into me and see my guilt. Guilt for killing the best thing that had ever happened to me. Guilt for wanting Paulie even more than Diego. Guilt for comparing them.

Paulie must have sensed my head spinning because he pulled out of my arms and looked up at me. The silver sheets against his pale skin made his brown eyes luminous, so I could see the exact moment insecurity flooded him.

"Was that okay?" he asked.

It should have been. It had been hot as hell. I had come so hard I could hardly move. But now, in the aftermath, I wasn't sure.

So I didn't try to answer. Instead, I said, "You're really sensitive."

Color rushed up his cheeks, and I was disgusted with myself. Why couldn't I just ease him for half a second and freak out in the privacy of my own head?

He nodded. "I always have been, but normally I don't shoot so fast."

I tried to think of something to say, something that would make him feel better without giving too much away. But my silence went on too long.

"Do you think it's gross? Like, do you think I'm gross?" he asked and broke my heart. I would never forgive myself for putting the insecurity and self-consciousness back in his voice.

I grasped his face between my hands and kissed him gently. "Paulie, I don't think you're gross. I don't think what we did was gross."

Suspicion crept into his eyes. "Then what's wrong?"

"Nothing," I lied. "You just melted my brain waves. I'm not thinking straight." He still seemed skeptical, so I said, "I liked it," and it was the truth. I had loved feeling him fall apart like that.

"Really?" His voice was still so small. He tilted that angel face of his down and picked at a loose string on his comforter.

I tipped his chin up with two fingers. His eyes were wide and vulnerable, and holy hell, I felt so much emotion, so much desire and faith and affection in that moment, I was sure it would burst from my chest and kill me.

I kissed him again—his soft lips, his chin, nose, eyebrows—but he kept his eyes closed.

"Paulie, look at me," I whispered against his lips. He opened his eyes slowly, and like always, they were deep and dark and full of feeling. "That was the hottest thing I've ever done."

It was exactly what he'd said the first time we fucked. He knew how to give his emotions voice, and I didn't.

He laughed. "You're such a plagiarizer. You always steal my lines."

"Yeah, well, you're better at words."

The smile slid from his face. "I know."

My stomach clenched, and I cupped the back of his neck, hoping to reassure him. "Hey, I've got you, baby. I'm so sorry if I made you feel uncertain. I loved it. My mind was just racing too fast afterward. But I want to do it again. I want to do whatever will make you feel good. So never, ever feel self-conscious when you're with me."

I said it and hoped that I could make it the truth.

chapter twelve

Paulie wobbled on his tiptoes and kissed me long and hard in his aunt's front yard: a good-bye kiss. I didn't want to leave him, even if it was only for a couple of days. I wanted his happiness and warmth to wrap around me until the thought of facing my father didn't make me want to puke and cry.

"I'll see you soon. Tell your parents your flaming boyfriend says hello," he said, playfully nipping my neck. Then he froze, his mouth open and suddenly slack.

"What's wrong?" I asked, a breath away from begging him to never stop.

"I said 'boyfriend.'"

"Oh." I hadn't even noticed.

"Does that freak you out?"

"No. You *are* my boyfriend." I cupped his pretty face in my hands and kissed his chin, his stubble prickly and abrasive against my lips.

When I moved down to his Adam's apple, he said breathlessly, "Well that's a relief. I was worried this was just the longest one-night stand in history."

The hollow in his throat looked so sweet I had to lick it. I trailed my lips up to the perfect shell of his ear and nibbled. "I can't get enough of you," I whispered hotly against his neck. "I wish I didn't have to leave."

He wrapped his arms more tightly around my neck, and then we were just hugging. I buried my face against his neck, and he dug his chin into my shoulder.

"We're probably giving the neighbors a show," I said finally, even though there wasn't another house in sight.

"Or Daria and Aunt Ruth. I'm sure they're watching from the living room window. Perverts."

I stepped out of his arms reluctantly, but he grabbed my face and yanked me down, a move so reminiscent of the kiss at the Yard all those months ago, it made me instantly hard.

Once Paulie had licked inside every part of my mouth, and I was contemplating places to get off before I left—the garage, my truck, the bushes on the side of the house—he pulled back into a gentle and tender kiss. Just clinging lips and hands smoothing through my hair.

"Bye, baby," I whispered. "I lo— I'll miss you." Heat rushed to my cheeks because I had almost said it without thinking. Said *I love you* because I was leaving and it felt natural. There was no way he hadn't noticed.

"You too, buttercup. You too." His smile was magic, big and playful, gap fully on display.

I ran a thumb down his nose, pressed chaste kisses all over his face, and then got in my truck and drove away. He stood on the front porch, melted snow dripping from the eaves, and waved until I was out of sight. A perfect good-bye, and it sustained me through my drive, making the hills sweeter and the flatlands less dull.

My mom's rental house was sad, and I always forgot that for some reason. I pictured our old house in Townsend when I imagined her, and even though it had been a shithole, at least it'd had some personality. But now she was a Hobby Lobby enthusiast, so everything looked kitschy and fake. No heirlooms, no character, only poorly constructed resin decorations with a Western bent.

She hadn't decorated for Christmas either. I wasn't going to mention it, but she brought it up almost immediately. "What's the point of decorating if it's only me here by myself?"

I guessed it didn't matter to her that I was here too. And I couldn't really blame her. I was only staying a couple of days. "We could decorate now, Mom."

"I don't have a tree," she said.

I almost asked her where our old artificial tree was, but I knew the answer. We'd left it in Townsend. The year before, she had decorated a small, waist-high tree, but evidently she wasn't up for that this year.

"When is Dad going to be here?" I couldn't stand not knowing, worrying he might be at the door at any moment.

"Tomorrow morning. We can do presents when he gets here, and then I'm making bierocks for lunch."

I refrained from rolling my eyes. Barely. Bierocks were my dad's favorite food, but I only tolerated it. In fact, it was probably the one meal we'd eaten regularly while I was growing up that I hadn't liked. Suddenly, I wanted to do a whole lot more than roll my eyes. I wanted to fling one of her gaudy resin sconces through a window.

"I have some Christmas shopping to finish. I'll see you later," I said, suddenly desperate to get out of the house.

She nodded and wouldn't meet my eyes. The anger seeped out of me like steam. I hated seeing her like that—scared or unhappy, the way she'd been with my dad. "Want me to pick anything up while I'm out?" I added to soften the blow of my tantrum.

"If you see any stockings on sale, maybe pick up three. It wouldn't be Christmas without stockings. I have stuff to put in them, even. I just never bought the stockings."

Three hours later, I found myself amid frantic Christmas shoppers in the middle of the mall. *What a mistake.* I could drive several miles out of Salina and I would hit hills, smaller but similar to the ones in Emporia. But I was stuck here. Trapped for three days and two nights, and I had already wasted most of one hiding at the mall.

A rush of teenagers rounded the corner and almost barreled into me. They were all laughing and wrestling, and I couldn't remember ever looking so free. Even as a teenager, I had been locked so securely in the closet with Diego I'd never let my guard down.

I slipped into the closest store to avoid the teen stampede and was affronted by white-and-silver figurines. Precious Moments figurines. I choked on my own spit and tried to hightail it before a saleslady sucked me in. But then something caught my eye on the edge of the window display. It was a nativity set, thankfully not of the Precious Moments variety. The figures were vibrant and realistic, and I couldn't stop staring. It was marked fifty percent off. All of the Christmas stock was priced down. I grabbed a little handbasket and ventured back inside. At fifty percent off, I could easily give my mom Christmas.

With shopping bags proudly declaring I had just spent a fair penny at a store mostly filled with cherub knickknacks, I wandered into a specialty bookstore that was going out of business. I browsed the Westerns for a long time, searching for any titles I hadn't already read. Eventually I made it to the back corner of the store, which housed antique books and odds and ends. I bought Paulie a set of timeworn dime novels—most of them Westerns but some romances. The covers were all still intact and colorful, even if the books were a little worse for wear. The copyright on the oldest was 1902. The owner threw in an old Bantam Books magazine shelf. It wasn't much, but it felt like a small piece of me that I could give Paulie. A few cheap words and stories to make up for the stuff I couldn't, *wouldn't*, tell him.

On the way out of the mall, I stopped at a hat cart and bought the cheapest Royals hat I could find for my father. It was a youth size.

My mom cried when I showed her the Christmas stuff. The tears seemed to be more out of guilt than happiness, so when she shoved money at me to pay for it, I accepted it.

For dinner, we ate frozen pizza, and she asked me not-so-veiled questions about school. They started the same way they always did.

"So, you're still getting the history degree, and don't want to be a teacher?"

I gritted my teeth. "No. If I ever teach, it will be in college. Mom, we've talked about this. I'm going to graduate school because I like to *research* history."

"So you'll get a PhD, or something?"

"Or a master's degree, yes," I ground out.

"Aren't those for really smart people though? You've just never seemed all that academic."

I looked down to hide my frustration. In high school, I'd made decent but not spectacular grades. And I certainly wasn't like Paulie, who made *A*s in every class and was every professor's favorite student. But history was different. It was important to me, and I excelled at it. And I was different now too.

"What did you think I would do, Mom?"

"Well, I always figured you'd play baseball in college, like you planned, and then get a business degree or become a coach."

Spending time with my mom made me want to throw things. And I had a pretty damn good arm. I was an ungrateful little shit, but for God's sake, she knew why I wasn't playing baseball in college. She knew I quit my senior year because I hadn't been able to handle it after Diego died. No one on the team had even talked to me. She knew Diego and I had planned to walk on to the team at the University of Nebraska together, and that without him the dream didn't feel so special. She *knew*.

When I didn't respond, Mom moved to my second-favorite topic.

"Meet any nice girls out there in the middle of nowhere?"

"Yep. Met plenty. There's this girl—Angie. She's an accounting major. Short black hair, dark eyes. Loves to dance." Mom's eyes lit up, and it hurt. So I twisted the knife. "Too bad I'm not heterosexual." Her face fell so fast it was almost laughable.

"How do you know, Jared?" She winced when she said the name, so I let it slide.

"How do I know I'm gay? Do you really need details? Most of them were in the paper before I turned eighteen."

"Well, have you ever been with a girl? You certainly started in on the gay thing young. How do you know you wouldn't like dating a girl?" she huffed. It was the same defensive tone she used when she fought with my dad, and it made me sick that I wanted to fight back. Lash out. Show her exactly how wrong and dumb she was being. But . . . I couldn't. Couldn't reiterate that cycle.

"Mom, I don't have to be with a woman to know I like guys. It's who I am, and I wish you'd accept it."

She stared at me for a long second, and I was tempted to fill the silence by telling her about Paulie. How he also had black hair and dark eyes and loved to dance. How when he laughed, I felt like I'd chugged champagne, and how the gap between his front teeth was the cutest shit I'd ever seen. I wanted to tell her about how confused I was, and how sometimes the Diego baggage fucked up my head so much I wanted to throw in the towel, even if it meant losing Paulie in the process.

But I didn't say any of that.

Mom nodded slowly, and it felt like a win.

"The new dentist at the clinic has a kid who's your age. I think you'd hit it off. I should introduce you."

"For God's sake, Mom! What did I just—"

"His name's Cory. He's gay."

I gaped at her, and she laughed like my surprise delighted her.

"Oh. Well, thanks . . . I think. I don't really need you to help me find dudes, though."

She wrinkled her nose and smiled. "Yeah, he's probably not your type anyway. Cory is—I don't know the PC phrase—uh, flamboyant? Let me put it this way—there is no mistaking him for straight."

"How do you know that's not exactly my type?" I asked, mostly teasing. I wouldn't call Paulie flamboyant, necessarily, but he was soft and pretty and swishy. And he most certainly was my type now.

"Well, *Diego*," she answered.

The pit of my stomach dropped. Diego definitely hadn't been flamboyant. He'd been reserved and withdrawn. Sometimes he'd been cold. He'd pushed away the prospect of joy and often refused to show any emotion at all, good or bad. It was only in secret, hidden flashes that he'd let me see his sensitivity, his happiness, his desire. And in those moments, he'd enthralled me.

Finally, I said, "I'm a different person than I was in high school."

She nodded, but I wasn't sure she got it. She didn't seem to understand that mentioning Diego like that, in such an offhand way, wrenched me apart. We'd rarely spoken about Diego after he died, unless Dad had been on a rant. When we had talked about him, Mom had used veiled phrases like *the incident* or *your problems in Townsend*, as if a dead boyfriend was *my* problem. And fuck! It *was* my problem. It *was* my fault.

But maybe Paulie's voice was in my head, because I wished, violently, that my mom had stood up for me like Paulie. That she would say it wasn't my fault, even if it was.

Mom surprised me then by kissing me on the cheek. "I'm proud of you. I don't always understand you, but I'm proud of you." Her simple words made heat burn in my throat, and I had to blink a couple of times. It wasn't exactly what I wanted, but it was close.

We spent the rest of the evening watching old Christmas movies. Eventually, she fell asleep in her chair, and I shook her awake and convinced her to go to bed.

At midnight, Paulie texted me. We didn't normally text, mostly because I didn't like it.

Merry Christmas, buttercup, his text read.

Back at ya, baby, I wrote.

When does your dad get there?

In the a.m.

Call if you need anything. We'll just be hanging out all day, so I can talk.

I clutched the phone in my palm until the plastic creaked. The need to hear his voice swept over me, so I called.

"Hi, sweetie," he breathed. "Hold on." When he finally spoke again, his voice was stronger. "Sorry, I was watching a movie with Daria."

"I can let you go if you're busy."

"No, it's cool. I can talk for a couple minutes."

"What're you watching?" I asked.

"Some Christmas movie on TV. We weren't allowed to watch much TV growing up, so I've never seen it. It's the one about the kid who wants a gun."

"*A Christmas Story.* That's what I'm watching too."

"Aw! How cute. We're the same!"

I laughed. God, I missed him. "I just wanted to say good night."

Paulie didn't respond for a couple of seconds, and I looked at my phone, worried the call had dropped.

"Don't let your dad make you feel bad tomorrow, Joel. It's Christmas."

"I miss you already," I admitted, even though it was pathetic. "I'll talk to you soon."

Paulie's voice softened. It was almost a whisper again. "Good night, buttercup. Sweet dreams."

I hung up and watched movies late into the night, Paulie's words echoing in my ear.

I jerked awake to knocking. I frantically scanned the slightly familiar living room, but couldn't really place it. My heart slammed hard in my throat, and sweat broke out along my hairline. After ten tense, heavy-breathing seconds, my eyes landed on the nativity set and everything clicked into place. I had fallen asleep on the couch at my mom's, rather than the futon in the spare bedroom. As I grabbed my phone to check the time, another round of knocking boomed through the house.

Oh, 9 a.m.! It must be Dad at the door. Anxiety bloomed fresh in my chest.

"Honey, would you answer the door?" Mom called from the kitchen. I wanted to yell at her for not waking me up before he got here.

When I swung the door open, Dad and I stared at each other for several long seconds. He gave me the slow once-over of disgust I had become familiar with in those months following Diego's death.

"Thanks for getting out of bed to greet me, Jared," he sniped. Or teased—I never could tell with him. He had always hidden his spitefulness behind good-natured joshing.

I turned around without a word and walked straight to the shower.

As I was closing the bathroom door, I heard him say, voice full of honey, "It's so good to see you, Pam. I've missed you."

With the water turned up as hot as I could stand, I tried to scrub the feelings of inadequacy and resentment from my skin. I tried to forget the sting of his hand on my face, or the smell of stale liquor. I tried to remember that he was my father, and I was doing this for my mother. But the heat of the water as it seeped into my blood branded my skin, lifted all of my anger to the surface, and made me want to hit something. Made me want to make him as miserable as I felt.

Mom and Dad were side-by-side at the kitchen table when I got out of the shower. They looked happy. I sat down with a cinnamon roll, and Dad reached across the table and patted my shoulder.

"It's good to see you, Joel." I almost laughed. He was trying hard. I had to give him that. He'd even called me Joel. "Tell me about school, son."

"Okay," I said, venom filling my veins. "I'm a history major. I have decent grades. I plan on going to graduate school. I work a tutoring job to supplement my student loans. I live with my best friend, Travis, who is gay. And black." Finally, the dismay began to leak through my father's carefully blank expression. I nearly whooped in triumph.

"I like to go to the gay bar with my friends. I still like dick, Dad. So let's just cut to the chase. Why are you here?"

He slammed his hand down on the kitchen table. I didn't even flinch.

"I'm here because I miss you and your mother. And I was informed that the only way back into your lives was to make nice with you. I'm trying here. You should too." He banged away from the table and strode out of the room. My mom narrowed her eyes at me as soon as he was out of sight.

"Was that necessary?" she hissed, and then she followed him into the living room, probably to soothe his easily wounded feelings.

The rest of the morning and afternoon was spent in painful politeness. We decided to open presents that afternoon because Mom was so excited about cooking Dad's favorite meal for lunch. She likely knew everything might fall all to hell at any second, and the meal was her big opportunity to impress him.

After the divorce, my mom had seemed to miss her toxic relationship with my father. It had always been messy, but they both craved it, thrived off of it even. When Mom chose me over him, I was secretly proud that I had pulled her away from his sarcasm, teasing put-downs, and criticism. But all feelings of happiness had quickly slipped away as my mom spent most of the summer before I started college barely speaking to me and heartsick over him. The day the finalized divorce papers came in the mail, she'd told me to get out. Said she needed me to leave, needed time alone. Later, she'd cried and apologized, but I'd known any semblance of a family I had before would never heal completely, not even Mom and me. I'd fucked it up too bad.

During lunch, my parents drank spiked cider, and another impending implosion lurked under the surface, like one of those sinkholes that pops open like a sign from Jesus and swallows people whole. The bierocks tasted exactly as I remembered, and I choked two down purely out of deference to my mother. She looked happy for the first time in years. I tried to tell myself that it was just me that brought out the gloom, that she was happy when I wasn't around, but I had no idea if that was true.

Eventually, we settled in the living room. My parents talked and even flirted. I fingered the phone in my pocket. It was my one link to Paulie, and I wanted to remind myself it was there.

"The Christmas decorations look really nice, Pam. You did a wonderful job."

"Oh, it was Jared," she said, clearly surprised by his compliment. He never had been one for praise, and it probably hurt her to give me credit.

"Joel," I corrected.

Dad's cheeks flushed, and I could feel the anger coming off him in waves. *Jared* was his middle name, and each time I reminded them of my name, I was rejecting him.

"Well, I had no idea you had such hidden talents, *Joel*," he drawled. "How very domestic of you."

I gritted my teeth to keep my mouth shut. The accusation was clear. Decorating Mom's house for Christmas was feminine, and that had always been one of his biggest issues with me. I couldn't be a man's man if I was gay.

He took a long swig of cider, but his eyes never left mine.

"Did you pick out the nativity set too? Even with how all the Bible thumpers hate you?"

Mom gave an aborted little gasp, and I had to swallow down the taste of bile gathering in the back of my mouth. That dig was getting close to Diego territory, and we all knew it.

"It's pretty, and I bought it for Mom," I replied.

Not to be outdone, he convinced Mom to open his present to her. It was a turquoise necklace, vibrant and expensive and exactly her taste. It made her cry. He wiped a tear from her cheek, and my stomach clenched. I suddenly felt claustrophobic—the walls too close and the air too thick.

My parents were murmuring to each other, but I couldn't watch them. I whipped my phone out of my pocket, and Paulie's texts from the night before appeared on the screen. I read through them a couple of times and began to calm down. I started to thumb a message, but erased it. Everything I wanted to say seemed pathetic. Finally, I wrote, *Merry Christmas. Again.*

"Jared!" my father barked. It startled me so much I looked up at him. He smirked, and the hair on my neck stood on end. Mom stared down at the new necklace, her fingers shaking as they fiddled with the chain.

I raised an eyebrow at him, trying to channel Travis. Hell, trying to channel anyone who was not me.

"Who are you texting?" he asked, his voice cold and teasing. "Or should I say sexting?"

"My boyfriend," I spat.

Mom gasped, "Jared!" as if I had said the most offensive thing in the entire freaking world. I probably should have told her about Paulie yesterday, when everything was nice between us. But yesterday I hadn't wanted her to know anything about me, thinking that could keep me safe from this.

"Well, sure didn't take you long to move on, did it?" my dad said, all innocent and wide-eyed, pulling out his down-home, aw-shucks bullshit.

My head spun for half a second, my breath catching in my throat. I clutched my phone so hard the skin around my knuckles pulled.

Before I even realized I had moved, I was in the spare bedroom. I grabbed my bag, and thank God, I'd never unpacked. I didn't want to ask my mom for a box of dental supplies. Travis and I could just *buy* some extra fucking toothbrushes.

When I walked back into the living room, bag in hand, Mom was crying and Dad was whispering at her furiously. At least they weren't yelling. I kissed Mom on the cheek and said, "I love you, Momma."

My dad stood up. Fuck, he was big. Tall and lean. I hated that I looked like him. "This is just like you, *Joel.*" Goose bumps bloomed under my clothes at his mocking tone. "You run away from all of your problems. You haven't changed at all."

I tried to keep my face blank, to hide my anger and hurt, because it was true. I *did* always run. This time would be no different. The doorknob was icy under my hand, and my palm still felt the cold burn when I was miles down the road and heading to Emporia.

When I was forty-five minutes away, I called Paulie.

"Hey! Buttercup, you're not going to believe what my aunt bought me! Wait—are you driving?"

"How can you tell?"

"Your truck sounds like an airplane. Where are you?"

I hesitated. "Marion." It was a quaint little town west of Emporia.

Paulie huffed out a breath. "Want to talk about it?"

"Not now. I'll tell you when I see you. Is it okay that I'm a day early?"

"Of course. See you soon. Watch for deer," he said, and we hung up.

When I pulled into Aunt Ruth's driveway, Paulie was already waiting on the porch, bundled up in a blanket and drinking tea. Before I was all the way out of my truck, my arms were full of him, surrounded by his warmth and strength and the smell of oranges. His mouth tasted like cinnamon, and his fingers were strong and nimble as they held my face. He looked almost rugged with several days' worth of stubble and wearing two layers of flannel, like a hot little lumberjack.

"I hope you like chili. We have enough to feed the whole town," Paulie said against my lips.

"As long as it's not bierocks, I'll be happy."

"I don't even know what that is."

I kissed him again. I had never been so happy to see anyone in my entire life.

chapter thirteen

Neither Aunt Ruth nor Daria asked me about my family. Paulie had probably filled them in enough with the lies I'd fed him to keep the interrogation at bay. We ate chili, played gin rummy, and snacked on pretzels and chips, until the knot of tension inside me loosened and broke apart.

At about 9 p.m., Aunt Ruth said, "I don't want to pry, darling, but did you tell your mom you made it here? She might be worried."

It was true. She had called about five times and sent me a handful of text messages, but I turned my phone off without responding as soon as I reached Paulie. Paulie rubbed a hand down my leg under the table. I caught his hand and entwined our fingers.

"I'll send her a text."

Aunt Ruth stood up and planted a kiss on the top of my head, making my face hot. "You're a good boy, Joel," she said, and then disappeared into the kitchen to grab more snacks. That one sentence almost undid me with its maternal kindness. Why couldn't my mom say I was a good boy and mean it?

It wasn't fair, though—my bias against my mother. She'd done so much for me. Changed so much. Given up everything, and how did I repay her? *I ran.*

"Joel, you should see your face. You're a radish," Daria said. Paulie's laugh cracked out of him like a gunshot. I threw a pretzel at her, and she tried to catch it in her mouth, unsuccessfully.

"I like it," Paulie whispered into my ear, and a shiver straightened my spine.

"Oh, get a room!" Daria groaned. She threw a pretzel back, which Paulie managed to catch between his teeth. He flashed me a grin, and heat curled in my belly.

Before Paulie could distract me too much, I dashed a text off to Mom. I didn't read any of the ones she had sent me, just wrote, *I made it to Emporia. Staying with my boyfriend.* Then I turned my phone off again.

Aunt Ruth returned with four beers and a bag of pork rinds. "I wouldn't sit that close to Paulie, Joel. He'll peek at your cards."

Paulie chuckled and moved a couple of feet away, but I grabbed the side of his chair and yanked him back toward me.

"Don't care," I said, and pressed a kiss to his cheek.

As soon as the bedroom door closed behind us that night, I tried to come up with a lie for leaving Mom's a day early. I could tell him my dad had called me a faggot. It'd happened once, so it wasn't technically lying, right? I could say that my parents got in a huge fight, and I couldn't stand to be there. That had been the cold, honest truth so many times in my youth it wouldn't be hard to dredge up the emotions. I could say anything as long as it didn't hint at Diego. But, instead, I said that my dad freaked when I mentioned having a boyfriend, and I didn't really want to talk about it. True, but not the full story.

"Your dad sucks," he said when I finished. "Your mom too, a bit. I'm glad you left."

"Me too." I ran my hands along his scruff. In a few days, it would be a beard. "Mostly, I'm just happy to see you."

Paulie crawled up my body then. The fleece of our pajama bottoms crackled with static electricity when our legs rubbed together.

He cupped my cheeks and slanted my head back, and I expected his kiss to devour me or light me on fire, but it was sweet and soft. The tip of his tongue caressed the seam of my lips, I opened them, and he slipped inside. While the burn of arousal was there, that wasn't what this kiss was about. His tenderness made my breath catch and tears prickle my eyes.

God, I hated the effect he had on me, the feelings he pushed into me, but I loved them too. Loved to come undone. I craved his intensity, and how it made me forget everything but him. I had to touch him, the sharp cheekbones and delicate nose, the hard pulse in his neck, the rippling muscles of his shoulders and chest. When my hands slipped over the sensitive skin of his waist, he pulled back and stared at me, his eyes wild like his heart was on fire as well.

I couldn't handle the emotion in his eyes, so I shoved my face into the crook of his neck and turned us onto our sides. He tipped my chin up and kissed me again, this time running his fingers through my hair and letting his lips cling to mine with every breath. When I scooted closer, my feet brushed his, and he jumped.

"Your feet are freezing," he said, pressing his warm feet against mine, and I smiled. He did that in his sleep too. "Tomorrow, I want to show you some of the little towns around here. We could go to the gay bar too, if you want."

"There's a gay bar?" Now that he wasn't kissing me and the warmth from his body was seeping into mine, I felt groggy.

"Yeah, it's a trip. It feels like Ropers, except they play eighties hair metal."

"Sounds great." I kissed him again, just sharing breath and sucking on his bottom lip. He pushed my hair out of my eyes, his touch lingering. It felt so good, so comfortable, his hands petting me and our legs tangled together. I was safe, here, with him. My hands found the warm, hard muscles of his back under his T-shirt, and we fell asleep.

I liked this town Paulie had brought me to—whatever it was called: Cottonport Creek or Cotton Creek Falls or something equally hokey and idyllic. Cold wind punched at us as we sat on the top of a stone wall on a bridge overlooking a river dam, but I didn't want to move. Snowmelt made the water rush loud and fast below us. It was exhilarating. I stole a look at Paulie. His ears and cheeks were ruddy from the cold. I moved behind him and wrapped my arms around his chest, my lips pressed to his neck.

"You're going to get us shot," Paulie said. "We are in *Kansas*."

I sucked a small bite on his neck, waited for his groan, then released him.

I had a view of the small town's downtown area, which had bricked roads and storefronts from the nineteenth century. A limestone, French Renaissance–style courthouse was framed on a hill at the end of the street. Paulie told me it was built in the 1870s and was the oldest operating courthouse in Kansas.

"Well, aren't you a little history buff!"

"I looked it up on Wikipedia so I could tell you," he said with a smile. I wanted to grab him and pull him into a kiss, but heeded his warning instead.

After walking through Cottonwood Falls—*that was the name*—which took all of five minutes, Paulie directed me to drive back into the country, where he pointed out a trickling stream that he called Middle Creek, but pronounced it *crick*, which was adorable. We drove through a couple of ghost towns and passed more crumbling ranches and farms. Finally, we hit a scenic overlook, and I pulled over.

After we got out, Paulie released my tailgate and jumped up. His feet dangled down and he swung them like a child. I joined him with a blanket I kept stashed in the truck during winter. The wind was still crisp up here, but it wasn't hitting us in the face. Without the snow, I could see the trails cattle had worn into the earth, and short limestone fences cutting across the landscape. The hills rolled into the horizon, and they never seemed to level off. For some odd, inexplicable reason, it filled me with hope.

Paulie took my hand and played with the webbing between my fingers. "This is my favorite place."

I kissed his ear. "I can see why. I bet you could hear coyotes here in the spring." I loved that he was showing it to me—this perfectly preserved stretch of prairie. Loved that he was sharing something important.

"We'll have to drive up sometime in the spring to see."

Such a simple sentence. But it made my heart soar because Paulie saw us together in the spring, and I'd never had commitment like that before. Never had a future that yawned out before me with someone by my side. With Diego, I had felt like a consolation prize, like he was looking for someone or something he wanted more and would cut me loose when he found it.

Paulie tipped his head to my shoulder, and I pulled him closer. I took a deep breath and was overcome with the musky scent of wet dirt, rotting vegetation, and the trace of citrus. It was like breathing in life, and I couldn't get enough. I pressed kisses into his short, shaved hair until he smiled up at me, and crinkly laugh lines framed the corners of his eyes. The sunlight illuminated the streaks of color in his irises. His expression was so open and playful, and I couldn't resist running a thumb over his lips, which parted on a small breath.

"Joel," he whispered, the word misting in the cold, clean air between us. The sun shifted behind a cloud, and his irises shadowed from brown to black. Unease filled me. Tightened me up.

"Joel," he said again and touched my hand resting on the side of his neck. "You know that—you know I love you, right?"

Shock snapped through me, and he clutched my hand hard, holding me in place, when I instinctually jerked away from him.

"Don't say it back," he said. My mouth dropped open, and my gaze shot around frantically, searching for something to ground me. "Not until you're ready."

His words froze me.

He didn't think I was ready, and if I were honest, I agreed with him. I was pretty sure I loved Paulie, but that scared the shit out of me. Felt wrong somehow to love him.

Maybe he didn't want to hear it back until I could react to the words with something other than dismayed clumsiness. And I definitely couldn't say the words with Diego between us. With my lies and omissions between us. So instead of speaking, I leaned my forehead against his. As soon as his eyelashes fluttered down, I kissed him in a way I'd never kissed anyone. I poured all of the tumultuous feelings that wanted to burst out of my chest into the kiss and enveloped him in it until we were clinging to each other and breathless.

When I released him, his eyes shuttered immediately, and a tight, brittle expression that seemed more grimace than smile flashed across his face. A cold weight settled in my stomach. I had majorly fucked that up. He jiggled his knee up and down, like it was on a spring, but stopped with a shuddering sigh when I began drawing shapes over his leg with my fingertips.

We sat on my tailgate until our asses were frozen, and dusk had settled over the hills. Darkness descended quickly. Blink and the beauty was gone, covered in a blanket of black.

Paulie suggested moving to the gay bar. It only took minutes to get there, and I wouldn't have known it was a gay bar if Paulie hadn't told me. The sign outside simply read *BAR*. Inside, Christmas carols pounded hard from the radio, and someone had hung dollar-store tinsel and a handful of stockings along the walls. Besides that, the bar was dark and the floor sticky. Most of the patrons were middle-aged and blue collar. There was an older couple at the bar, and when Paulie dragged me to a barstool near them, they bought us a round. The man closest to us said it was for daring to be seen with so many old fogies. Paulie shot them a smile that was practically obscene, all batting eyelashes and pouty lips. Both men laughed, and then returned to their conversation.

"Don't bite off more than you can chew there, babe," I said in his ear.

"I'm just teasing, and they know it. Mr. Barnes owns the pharmacy next door, and his husband is a retired girls' basketball coach."

I felt sad that they were spending the day after Christmas in the gloomiest gay bar in the Great Plains. If it weren't for the Christmas music, the place would be lifeless.

Paulie chugged his drink. He'd been jittery since his confession, and now he was fiddling with his watch and the sleeves of his sweater. His eyes darted around, never settling on one thing for long, and he certainly wasn't turning them in my direction. I stilled his hand and brought the knuckles up to my mouth. He finally looked at me, and that was what I wanted. I wanted his eyes and his attention and his intensity turned on me so everything else could melt away. I pretended I was going in for a sweet and chivalrous kiss on the hand before sucking his middle finger into my mouth.

Paulie gasped, and the shadow cleared from his eyes. "You're dirty."

I winked and let his finger slip from my mouth.

A Christmas cover from some sugary boy band—NSYNC, maybe?—floated through the speakers, and Paulie whooped, throwing his fists in the air. He slipped off his stool and flung his arms around my neck. I pulled him between my legs, and he bebopped to the beat, singing the stupid lyrics to me like a serenade. By the end of the song, he was pressing the dumb words into my mouth, and we were giving all of the Joe Schmoe gays of the Flint Hills a show. I glanced around and was surprised to discover no one was paying us any mind. How could anyone keep his eyes off of Paulie?

"This place is a little glum, isn't it?" he whispered into my ear. His hot, beery breath sent a shiver down my spine. I attempted an affirming grunt, but Paulie chose that moment to lick my earlobe, and the noise died on my lips. "I like it. These people are the nicest you'll ever meet. And it's pretty amazing there's a place like this at all here. It's amazing that we have a place to go and be ourselves."

Leave it to Paulie to see the extraordinary beauty in a shitty little bar. I captured his face between my palms, and he flipped me a cheeky grin and bit his bottom lip.

"Finish your beer, Joel. I wanna take you home."

I tipped my drink back like a shot, and Paulie primly sipped the dregs at the bottom of his glass. As soon as I finished, he wiggled his butt over to the old bears, kissed one on the cheek, and slapped some cash down for their next round.

My truck was parallel parked on the main drag, which was mostly empty, and Paulie pinned me to the driver's-side door. He kissed me until his body heat melted away the winter chill. Until my blood sang to the beat of his breaths and the Christmas carols still wafting through the bar door. Until the warmth from my beer had worn off and the only thing making me high was Paulie's tongue stealing my oxygen, and my urgent need to get in his pants.

When he drew back, the sparkle of Christmas lights reflected in his dark eyes.

"Have I helped you forget your shitty Christmas?"

I was too dazed to reply.

"Home?" he asked. I just nodded.

By the time we pulled into Aunt Ruth's driveway, the desperation had burned off into anticipation. We both knew what was going to happen, and that it would be good. Paulie brushed a kiss across my mouth and then hopped out of my truck. He waited for me by the hood, the smell of petrol sharp in the cold air, and the light from the front porch haloing his head. When I reached him, he pulled me along behind him, and I realized that I had been trailing Paulie from the beginning. With the exception of our first real kiss, I had been content to grasp his hand and follow in his footsteps like the track of an arpeggio.

But I needed to take some control. Show him with lips and fingertips that he mattered to me. Even if I didn't have the balls to say it, I could press my love into his skin like a tattoo, burn it into his memory so he would never forget it.

We stripped slowly, and I touched my mouth to every sliver of skin he revealed. When he was naked, I nudged him toward the bed until he toppled onto it. He looked so damn sexy, spread out and ready to go, that all I could do for several beats was stare. My brain finally kicked back online when he whined, "Come on!" and I grabbed the lube out of the bedside table and dropped to my knees. Paulie's hungry eyes met mine, and I filed that look away, determined to never forget what he was giving me.

This meant something. And maybe it was because I had slept with so many faceless men, or maybe it was because I had locked down my emotions for so long when it came to sex, but until Paulie, I had forgotten that sex could *mean* something. That making yourself vulnerable for another person was a gift, not a perfunctory stepping-stone to orgasm. It meant something when I did it for Paulie, when I spread my legs, just like it had meant something when Diego had done it for me. And being strong and careful, like Paulie always was with my body—that was a gift too.

I whispered my mouth across the inside of Paulie's thigh, and his legs trembled. The dark hair on his thighs tickled my lips, and I inhaled his amazing scent. Tangy, like a tangerine, undercut with the sweat and the musk of a man. He propped up on his elbows and watched me with wide eyes as I slicked my fingers with lube.

"Joel?" Nerves colored his voice. After last time, I didn't blame him. I needed to show him that he could trust me to make him feel spectacular. I was good for it. I could give this gift too.

"I've got you, baby," I said against his skin. "I'm going to give you the sweetest blowjob you've ever had. Then you're going to make love to me, aren't you?"

He swallowed thickly, and I licked the ridge of his mushroom cap. God, his cock was perfect, like a Greek sculpture or something. Like art.

Paulie's elbows collapsed out from under him. I lifted one of his legs over my shoulder and pinned the other out to the side. His thigh muscles jumped against my neck.

Taking his cock slowly between my lips, I teased my fingers close to his ass. He buried his mouth in the crook of his elbow.

When I finally slipped a slick finger over his hole, he jerked like he'd been electrocuted, and a splash of pre-come sizzled on my tongue. I whispered, "Don't come yet. Gotta fuck me."

He groaned but nodded frantically.

I sucked lightly on that cord of nerves under his head and traced my finger around his entrance before pushing inside. His ring of muscle tensed and slammed down hard. *Holy shit, that probably shouldn't turn me on so much.* Anticipation covered me in sweat. I worked him, pumping my hand gently, until he shivered and his body yielded to me. The sensation—hot and smooth and so tight, even on my single digit—made me moan.

Paulie choked off whimpers with his own arm, and I thrust inside him harder, wanting to draw out all of his noises. I licked the head of his dick until it was spit-slick and shiny, and then curled my finger, found that little knot that would zing his nerves with pleasure, and sucked his cock down to his pubes.

"Joel!" he cried out, his voice not muffled at all. I swallowed, my throat milking him. "Fuck! Joel, oh fuck."

I stilled my hand and pulled off his cock, bringing him back from the edge. I couldn't help but leer at him. His ass pulsed on my finger, and a red blush had crept from his chest to color his face and ears.

"I was just really loud, wasn't I?" he panted.

"I think we're lucky if you didn't wake every animal in a mile radius, much less Daria and Aunt Ruth." I wiggled that finger a little, and he hissed.

"You're going to make me come if you don't stop," he gritted out, so I slipped my finger from that wonderful, enticing heat.

I climbed up the bed, and as soon as my face was in range, his fingers were deep in my hair and his mouth was sucking small bites on my lips. He held my head firmly in place and kissed me, lips tender and giving. It was a thank-you kiss, but it made my skin prickle with warmth. Then he flipped me onto my back.

His silky skin slid against mine, and he moaned softly when his cock skated across the groove of my hip. He rubbed against me until I was desperate to move away from the making-love part of fucking and get to the fucking part of fucking. But Paulie was in control. He licked kisses onto my shoulders and throat. He kneaded the tightness in my neck. He scrubbed our cheeks together until his beard growth abraded my skin. He made me accept his love physically until my body shook with the pain of desire.

Finally, with my head tipped back, neck exposed, and body aching, Paulie pushed two lubed fingers into me. "Look at me, sweetheart."

He was demanding too much, making me give him my eyes so he could see everything. He overwhelmed me with the love in his gaze and his expectation that I would let him in—into my body and eventually into my heart. That I could give him all of me. But I wasn't sure I was capable of being that open, even if I wanted to be.

I glanced up into his eyes, and they were desperate with want. I wished that we could seamlessly shift into sex. That he could slink his generous body up mine and sink into me like a stone through water. Instead, we fumbled for the condom and awkwardly pushed it on with too many hands. I swiped lube on him haphazardly. With a whoosh, Paulie pinned my lube-sticky hand to the bed.

God, but I loved it when he manhandled me. My blood sang, and I lifted my knees to my shoulders.

Paulie pushed his tip into me, and I struggled to stay loose and relaxed. I knew how to do this. I mean, I was pretty much a verified cock slut. But with Paulie it was always a struggle. A struggle to be vulnerable and to give back.

Because *this* meant something.

I wrapped my legs around his waist, and the movement forced him in farther. It was too much, too fast, and my body clenched so hard it hurt. We both gasped. Paulie moved both of his hands to my face and forced my eyes on him again. His dark eyes raked over my face just as they had before he told me he loved me, full of surprise and wonder. I took a deep breath, trying to get us past this limbo of pleasure and pain, but his expression scared me and thrilled me and tightened me up with nerves.

"Let me in, love," he whispered, and it was like he'd said a magic word. My body gave in, my brain shut off, and he slipped in to the root. It didn't hurt at all but was so intense that wetness blurred my vision. He moved gently, just a deep grind and dreamy hip swivel, until every muscle in my body melted around him. My mind grew fuzzy, and his weird blue room cast an otherworldly glow over our bodies. It felt so good, I was sure I would float away. And I loved this. Loved the struggle. Loved the surrender.

Paulie gripped my chin, and my eyes met his. He shifted slightly, and his cock rubbed directly over my prostate. A scream rose in my throat, and I just let it fly.

Paulie froze. "You're never that loud." His voice was completely shot.

"I know," I panted, but I could hardly find it in myself to care. My fingers and toes were tingling.

He thrust again, like he was testing me, and it completely lit me up. I tried to smother the next cry, but didn't quite succeed. It freaked me out—the loss of control and the sensations Paulie pushed into my body.

"Paul?" I whispered. My orgasm was building, slow and scary, but still far enough off that I couldn't just close my eyes and fall.

"I'm here, honey. I'm right there with you." And, Jesus Christ, that was a gift too. To be in this together. To both have skin and . . . and emotions on the line. Paulie continued that perfect glide into my body, his smooth stomach teasing the head of my cock. His hands delved into my hair, and I wrapped my arms around his neck and held on.

Paulie shivered and his mouth fell slack. His thrusts turned brutal, and nothing was sexier than Paulie taking what he wanted. Taking me. His next stroke tightened my body like a bowstring, and he groaned. *Christ*, he was gorgeous. I would have given anything, done anything, to see him like this—flushed and sweaty and playing my body like a violin.

I loved him so much. Loved Paulie. I wanted to scream it. I wanted to release it like the gasps he was driving out of my throat. I loved him. My body started to spiral. I loved him but couldn't say it now, not when the first spasm of my orgasm was a breath away.

"Look at me!" he choked out, and blood rushed in my ears, and my eyes found his.

"I'm coming," I said, almost silently, like a prayer.

His eyes were huge, and I fell into them. Into the black.

Paulie's rhythm broke apart on a sob, and his last thrust forced another cry from me. My body pulsed around him for an eternity before I shot. And my orgasm didn't taper, just built and built from somewhere deep in my gut until I couldn't see or hear anything, could only feel the rush of sensation pouring from me. My body shook from the violence of it, and my skin was a blanket of heat.

After a while, my vision returned, and Paulie had already slipped free of me. He was pressing hot kisses to my chest and neck and saying something. I couldn't hear it at first over the pounding of my heart and the burn of my breath. But then I made out the words—the "I love you, God, I love you" he kissed into my skin, his voice full of awe.

I skimmed my hands over his sweaty back and hitched him higher in my arms. When his face was even with mine, I buried my forehead in his neck, shutting my eyes against his hot skin. He pressed one more "I love you" into my ear, and I trembled.

Paulie had crossed a threshold, regardless of whether I was following behind him or not. And it wasn't like every other instance, where he could just clutch my hand and pull me along. He'd certainly made me forget everything—my mom and the fawning face she reserved just for my father; the anger in my dad's face and his stinging, catty words; and perhaps most of all, Diego. And because of that, I couldn't hold his face in my hands like my body was screaming at me to do. I couldn't say it back. Not yet. Not until I had my head on straight and my feelings for Paulie didn't at once fill me with bliss and guilt.

But, *fuck me*, was it fair for me to not give those words back to him, to not return that gift? Was it fair for me just to take his love and give nothing in return? I honestly didn't know.

The next morning, Paulie woke me up with a mug of hot apple cider and a Christmas present. I was still naked under his covers because, after the best sex of my existence the night before, Paulie and I had wiped off with some piece of dirty laundry and then slept like the dead. Now, with him fully showered, dressed, and bearing gifts, I felt uncomfortably naked and groggy.

I sat up and the blanket fell from my bare chest. Paulie hummed low in his throat, placed the cider on the bedside table and the present on the other side of the bed, then straddled me. I curled into him for warmth, and he laughed.

"So, we were maybe a little too loud last night. I figured I'd butter you up with a gift before making you face the peanut gallery."

"What'd they say?" I grumbled into his sparse chest hair.

"Not much. Just veiled innuendo and knowing looks. I think Aunt Ruth now knows more about my sex life than any mom should ever know about her son."

I groaned and buried my face deeper in his skin. For some reason, Paulie calling Aunt Ruth his mom always made me ache.

"You're kinda adorable when you first wake up. Have I ever told you that? You're all growly with bedhead and golden stubble." He lifted my chin and sifted his fingers through my tangled hair. "Here, open your present."

He sat back slightly so I could move the flat, square present between us, but he didn't get off my lap. It was wrapped in cowboy Santa wrapping paper, which I loved. His present was in a plastic grocery bag in my truck because I was the least romantic sad sack in the history of the West. Maybe I could find a bow to slap on it before handing it over.

"Your gift is in my truck," I said. "Do you want me to go get it?"

"Maybe in a minute. I'm enjoying your nakedness too much at the moment to let you get dressed. Open yours," he repeated.

I ripped the paper off my present, and saw hills and green grass and a pink sunset. It was a large photography print, and it looked like it had been shot from the overlook Paulie had taken me to yesterday where'd he told me he loved me. There was even a low limestone fence cutting across the foreground. But the photo had been taken in the spring when the grass was verdant and the wildflowers in bloom.

"A local artist sells his prints from a little shop in Cottonwood Falls. I thought you'd like it," Paulie said softly. My heart slammed an irregular tattoo in my throat for a couple of beats, and I tried to smile up at him. It was perfect. Did he have any idea how perfect it was?

How this place, this land, had burrowed into my soul and set up a pup tent? How did he know? I felt a connection here, like the history wasn't quite history, and I had the chance to witness the shift of time without losing it. Later in the afternoon, as we headed back to Elkville, I would hate watching the hills disappear behind us.

"Paulie, this is amazing. I love it," I said, even though the words weren't enough. They would never be enough. This was a gift like his love was a gift. One I wasn't worthy of but I'd grab with both hands and hold fast.

chapter fourteen

Paulie and I spent the days following Christmas pretending to live together at my dank old rent house, sans Travis, reading the silly dime novels I'd given him and banging in the living room every chance we got. New Year's Eve rolled around without much fanfare. I'd never had a boyfriend on New Year's Eve, except Diego, and for the first time, I kind of wanted the fanfare.

Diego and I had pretended to be straight best friends at the big high school parties. Our junior year, while at a New Year's Eve kegger at the river, I'd tried to talk Diego into sneaking into the trees to kiss at midnight. He'd wanted to—it appealed to his romantic side—but in the end, we'd been too scared. It should probably cut me to think of all the moments we'd missed out of fear, but part of me had loved the secrecy. Still craved it sometimes. Missed the thrill and excitement of pulling one over on the idiots around me. Missed the knowledge that no one in the entire world knew Diego the way I knew him. And it had made those moments when we could be together, those stolen breaths of time, even sweeter.

But now, for the first time ever, I had a boyfriend I could wrap my arms around in a crowd of people and kiss senseless when the clock tipped over into a new year. And that was just . . . *better*.

We ended up at Angie's house because she was throwing a raging, blowout, orgiastic party—her words. I recognized about every third person there from the Yard, and all the others were fratty. The queer guys smoked hookah, the frat guys played beer pong, the girls comingled, and we all existed in perfect harmony.

And Paulie was like this bright beacon among all of them. He was the funniest, shiniest, most irrepressible person there, and I was so awed that he was there with me. That he was holding my hand and sitting on my lap.

As the seconds ticked down to midnight, with people all around us screaming "ten, nine, eight . . ." I looked at Paulie, really looked at the play of emotions on his face and the miniscule flaws in his skin, and felt like I *knew* him in that moment. Like I could see the real him, just like I'd always seen the real Diego. The way I could see the inside of him—the tendons and grit and bone that made up all the things I loved about him.

And I wished, violently, that I could say, *I love you too.* That I could say the words with nothing but truth between us, like Paulie deserved.

But I couldn't, and I didn't, because I might know Paulie, but he didn't know me.

So instead, I held his precious face in my hands and kissed him like I loved him and wanted him and couldn't breathe without his breath. He smiled against my lips and deepened the kiss. It was clearly designed to turn me on, his tongue stroking into my mouth and lips sucking sweetly on mine. I groaned when he pulled away, and the noise around us slipped back into my consciousness—cheering and shouting and loud music. But no one seemed to notice us. No one seemed to realize this moment was monumental, even if only to me.

When we got back to my house, techno music from the Lumberyard's New Year's Eve rave was filtering in through my bedroom's old windows, the bass vibrating the floorboards. I had never noticed that the music carried this far before, probably because I was normally at rave night, rather than at home.

I needed to shower if we were going to fuck, and I definitely wanted to fuck. Paulie had that effect on me. So I took the fastest shower known to man, and when I got out, I slipped into boxer briefs, sweats, and a sweatshirt, because it was freezing, and set out to find him.

He was in front of my bookshelf, which was full to bursting with ratty paperbacks. It was also the only space with any personality in my whole room. I watched from the doorway as he pulled out several books and thumbed through them. The last one he drew out was an old sci-fi thriller I hadn't read in ages. Something fluttered to the floor.

Paulie bent over and picked up what looked like loose pages.

"What the hell?" he said, glancing at me. I moved to sit on my bed, my mind still tripping on lust and horniness. He gathered up the papers and cupped them in his palms like he was holding water. They weren't loose pages. Uneasiness prickled the hair on the back of my neck. Paulie frowned. "This is that guy from the article. The boy. It's the same picture from his obit."

Obit?

"Oh God, Joel. This is you."

Clarity tackled me. *My pictures.* Diego and I together during baseball season. His senior portrait. A couple of photos of us on a tractor in the Martinezes' back forty. All these memories I'd hoarded and hidden away and forgotten about. Snippets I'd shoved in a book I hadn't read since high school.

A scream drew up in my throat—a literal scream-in-fright scream—and I didn't think I'd ever screamed that way before. Not even when I heard about Diego's death and realized I had caused it. But I wanted to scream. Scream and hide. Scream so loud my body fragmented into a million pieces, and I wouldn't have to do this. Wouldn't have to face Paulie. I could just scream and float away. Scream and disappear. But nothing came out.

Fight or flight set in, and I gripped the edges of my mattress, ready to propel myself out of bed and away. Suddenly, Paulie was right there, straddling my legs and grabbing my face.

I was shaking, sweating, my whole body rejecting what was about to happen. Because Paulie was smart. He would figure it out.

"You knew that boy, didn't you? That's why you left class that day."

My breath burned as it worked its way out of my throat. I was going to hyperventilate. Or puke. I tried to rip my face out of his hands, but he held me fast and forced my eyes up by shaking me a little.

"Diego Martinez." My voice sounded wooden. It hurt saying his name out loud—I had hardly uttered it since he died—but I couldn't stand Paulie calling him *that boy*.

It was so clear the moment the puzzle pieces clicked into place in Paulie's mind. His eyes shadowed, like a cloud had blacked out the light in them. I was sure he could see the cracks in every conversation we'd had, every moment of intimacy—none of it was exempt from my lies.

"You're the boyfriend," he murmured. "You're Jared Smith."

I shook my head, but it turned into a convulsion. A tremor that hurt my entire body with its strength. "I changed it to Joel before I started college."

Anger passed over Paulie's face. He had every right to be mad at me. This was too big a secret. He hadn't known that I was raised in Nebraska, for fuck's sake. He'd thought I was from Salina. He knew me better than anyone, and he didn't know me at all.

But then Paulie's anger gave way to pity and understanding, which was just as bad.

He kissed the corner of my mouth, and I tried to jerk my face from his hands again. His sweetness would ruin me.

With one hand still cupping my cheek, Paulie rested his forehead on my shoulder, the move so tender it made my whole body tremble. That action burrowed down into my heart and cracked it wide open. His kindness and gentleness always exposed me, like a giant nerve with no protection.

A salty tear slipped into my mouth—I hadn't even realized I was crying. But suddenly a sob leaked out. I tried to stifle it, but it burst from my stiff-closed mouth in a weird lawn mower noise. That was somehow worse. So I let myself ugly cry until snot blocked my breath, and my head felt like a precariously balanced top.

Diego had once sat in my lap, exactly as Paulie was now, and cried into my shoulder. That memory didn't hurt as much as the present, which was pulling me into the undertow and dragging me across the reef. Too painful. And too much. And no air.

But that day, the day Diego had cried, we'd lost in the final game of Regionals our junior year, which seemed so trivial now. But Diego had played terribly—multiple errors and strikeouts for every at bat. He had been the last out in the last inning, and it had wrecked him. So I'd held him in the front seat of my truck, and told him I loved him. He'd cried and needed me, and as much as I hated to admit it now, I had needed *that*. I had needed him to need me because so often he had been ashamed of us. But not that day. That day I'd held him together, and he'd actually let me.

Big, hiccupping sobs wracked my body, and I was so embarrassed, because tonight Paulie was holding *me* together. I distantly accepted his consoling noises and his hands on my face and in my hair. I cried into his shirt and covered it in snot and tears. He felt strong and warm, and I just couldn't stop.

Eventually, the crying slowed into exhaustion, like my body didn't know what to do about all the upheaval except shut down. By finding those pictures, Paulie had pulled a stopper, and my tears had drained all the resistance and secrecy and grief out of me.

He probably had a million questions, but I could hardly keep my eyes open. Rather than demanding answers, though, Paulie, in all his infinite gentleness, laid me out on the bed and brushed his fingers through my hair. The edge of sleep crept up on me, but sad, sniveling little shudders kept pulling me awake. I couldn't make them stop.

In the morning, I would have to face the fact that Paulie might not want me anymore. How could he look at me, kiss me, fuck me, and not wonder if I was thinking about Diego? Hell, I normally *was* thinking about Diego. Sometimes I was so wrapped up in memories of him that it was a miracle I could function at all.

And why would Paulie want the man who had caused the death of his first boyfriend? Why should he have to deal with the baggage left from that? He could be free of all of this. Surely, he would see my fear and my damage and know there were so many men who were more worthy and less work. Men who wouldn't lie to him for months about who and what they were.

But at least I had tonight. Dredges of electro-pop floated around us, a ridiculous soundtrack to my meltdown. I curled into a ball, my hands over my face, and let Paulie comfort me until I fell into oblivion.

My eyes were a desert, so arid and swollen there was a dry *click* each time I tried to blink awake. Little crusties crumbled in my fingers when I rubbed my eyelids. I attempted to draw a deep breath, but my nose was too stopped up.

Paulie's hand closed over mine, and something so simple shouldn't have felt life altering, but it did. His lips brushed over my cheek, his breath warm and humid. I finally managed to crack one eye open, and he smiled at me, his grin so kind and uninhibited that my stomach turned over like an old engine.

"You look like you have the worst hangover in all of history," he said with a deep, singsong lilt.

I turned my face back into the pillow, and nausea rolled through me.

"Joel, sweetheart, don't hide. Please." The endearment was loving, not acerbic. It made me burrow deeper. Paulie ran his fingers through my hair and tried to coax me into facing him again, but I couldn't.

Finally he said, "Seriously, Joel. Please don't hide from me any more." This time he sounded so sad and hurt that it prompted me into action. I flung my arm over his waist, snatched him up just like a person might snatch a lightning bug out of the air, and held him to me like he was precious. Because he was.

We just lay there for minutes or hours, caressing and cuddling, but not saying a single word. I'd have to face him eventually, to fess up, but I'd take this while it lasted.

It didn't take long for Paulie to press me into talking, but he didn't ask a question. Only said my name, so timidly it almost made tears prickle in my eyes again.

"I'm sorry. Are you mad at me, Paulie? I'm so sorry."

"Of course I'm not mad at you! I could never be mad at you when you're hurting so badly."

I wanted to tell him that he could be mad at me. He was allowed. Practically everyone I knew was mad at me when I was hurting this bad. When I was hurting worse, even. My dad, who never forgave me for causing a sordid news story that had thrust us into the public eye. My mom, who'd reluctantly chosen her son over her home and husband, but had never been able to fully hide her disappointment. I wanted to tell Paulie that Diego's parents had told me they hated me for pushing their son into perversion, and then proceeded to drown their pain in a pointless campaign and pretend they loved him.

I *could* tell Paulie all of that now, but I had no idea where to start.

"The beginning," he said, as if he had read my mind. "Just tell me about Diego."

So I let the words tumble out like rocks down a hill, no regard to where they fell. "He'd been at work at a local diner, and we'd been sexting all day. He told me he was driving and would text me when he got home. But I sent him two more sexts anyway. He read the last text from me, swerved a little at a point in the road where there was no shoulder, just a sharp drop-off into the ditch, and rolled his car. He was expelled from the vehicle." *Expelled* was such a police word; I must have read it somewhere after his death because it was always the one I used in my head; *expelled*, like he'd been kicked out of school rather than launched through his own windshield. "He wasn't wearing a seat belt, and he was impaled on a metal fence post."

Paulie sucked in a pained breath and closed his eyes. *Breathing*—something so simple and automatic, until it wasn't.

I was going to tell him how Diego hadn't actually died right away and how, miraculously, his cell phone had been unscathed. How they'd been able to medi-flight him to the hospital in Omaha, but he'd died soon after arriving. All the words were there, raring to escape, like they had been waiting on the tip of my tongue all along. And, I guessed, they had.

"No," Paulie said before I could speak again. "Tell me about *him*. Not how he died."

"Oh." What was safe? What would hurt the least to talk about? Because talking about Diego's life was harder than talking about the mechanics of his death, the gears of a body slowly turning off. "He was sweet and sensitive. But he didn't show that to anyone but me." *And I exposed him to everyone.* That was almost as hard as his death, knowing that I let him down in the end.

"How long were you together?"

"Almost two years. I kissed him for the first time right after I turned sixteen. My parents had bought me my truck, and we were so excited to be free to drive without an adult in the car. So I headed down some back road and just pulled over and kissed him. I was worried he'd deck me." I was pretty sure he'd thought about it.

"And?"

"He kissed me back, and it was wonderful. He was my best friend, and I was crazy about him. But, on the way home, I had to stop twice for him to throw up." Paulie flinched, so I explained. "He hated being gay. His parents weren't going to accept him, didn't accept him when he was dead and they found out. Anyway, we pretended like the kiss never happened. Then a couple months later, when we were playing videogames at his house and his parents were gone, he jumped me—tongue in my mouth, hands down my pants, the whole nine yards. We never stopped after that, but he never got over the shame. Not sure he would have."

Paulie let out a sad, wounded sigh, and I looked away.

"Have I told you about starting public school?" he asked out of nowhere.

I shook my head, thankful for the reprieve. A moment for me to clear the rubble of Diego's shame, our shame, from my mind.

"I'd known I was gay forever and that my parents thought it was wrong, and once I talked to Aunt Ruth and found I had a way out, I started to build up public school as this type of utopian, open-minded, magical kingdom. My aunt lives in Kansas, mind you."

"Not exactly the friendliest place if you're queer."

"*Public school* isn't the friendliest place if you're queer. Pretty sure that's universal. My third day of school, I got called a slutty little faggot and was pushed into a locker by some meathead, and I felt shame, true shame, for the first time in my entire life. It was *awful.* I had given up my family for *this*? And then I met a bunch of boys just like me: small and effeminate and fey. And 'straight.' I remember thinking, 'Finally. My people.' But they all had girlfriends. And I realized that these gay boys knew what they had to do to stay safe. They'd been there longer than me. They weren't getting pushed into lockers. They knew the score. So I followed suit and stepped primly back into the closet.

"When I was a senior in high school, I even had a girlfriend. She was pretty and nice and we both liked theater and the same types of music. And, remember, I was so naïve I didn't watch gay porn until I had my own dorm room, but my girlfriend and I decided to have sex so we wouldn't go to college as virgins—à la Britney Spears in *Crossroads.* And I did it, not because she talked me into it, but because I wanted to feel *normal.* And that shame was worse." Paulie took a shuddering breath, and I closed his hand in mine. "All I'm saying is that it takes some time to figure that shit out. I left my family because I was gay and then caught a girlfriend. But I figured it out eventually. Diego would have worked it out eventually too."

Sometimes, Diego's fear and guilt hurt the worst, even more than his absence. Knowing he died filled with shame was almost too heartbreaking for me to fathom. He had never been able to say he loved me, and there were days he'd been so sad he wouldn't speak to me. We'd planned to go to the University of Nebraska together, and I'd asked once if we could be out when we got to college, and he'd told me no. I had to believe that would have changed. It was too painful not to.

"And your name?" Paulie asked after several minutes.

"I changed it as soon as I could. I didn't want to be connected to a tragic news story forever. Maybe it's stupid, but I was worried the Sweet Mouth Texter stuff would follow me everywhere and prevent me from getting jobs or being treated without pity. I didn't want people to be able to Google my name and find the news articles."

"I don't think that's stupid."

"Thanks." I shrugged. "It wasn't just that, though."

"What was it, then?" Paulie brushed hair off my forehead.

"I wasn't Jared Smith anymore. I wanted to be free of that boy." I was a little struck by how exposed that statement made me feel after all the other things I'd revealed. I tried to smile. "Plus, 'Jared' is my dad's middle name and he's an asshole, so there was some sweet revenge to changing it. I chose Joel because I liked it."

"I like Joel better than Jared. Jared's so pedestrian."

"You're just saying that."

"Of course. But I go by 'Paulie,' like I'm from Jersey or some shit. So I'm not the best judge." Paulie's eyes shadowed with suspicion and then hurt. Would I ever be able to make up for the hurt in his eyes? "What actually happened with your dad at Christmas? I know there has to be more to that story."

"After I told him about you, he made a comment about how it hadn't taken me long to move on from Diego."

Paulie tensed and pulled away from me slightly, withdrawing into himself. "What happened with your dad in high school?"

Talking about Dad, and my parents' divorce, wasn't as hard as talking about, *thinking about*, Diego. Wasn't as hard as thinking about moving on from Diego. Dad had always been mean, but because I was big and athletic, he let me into his club of machismo and bluster. I had not been that crushed when he took it all away.

"He hated that I was gay—he's not religious; he just thinks it's icky—but he hated that I pushed us into the spotlight in our backward town even more. Him and my mom had always fought, but it got worse after Diego died. He slapped me once, and my mom promised me that as soon as I graduated, we'd leave. It was my fault, though. I'd been back-talking him, taking everything out on him and my mom, and it wasn't like he hit me hard, you know? It was just a tap, but he called me a 'faggot,' and I'd never been called that before. It became a common occurrence at school soon after. I guess he was just preparing me."

"He hit you? After everything you'd been through?" Paulie's eyes burned with anger. It was almost frightening to see his kindness turn to hardness and fight. I couldn't take my eyes off of him.

The muscles in his sharp jaw ticked a couple of times, and when his eyes scanned my face, they softened. He followed his gaze with his fingers, running them lightly over my cheekbones and jaw. I closed my eyes, and he touched my nose and my lips, like he was learning them again. Like he was learning this new version, the one he hadn't been aware of until last night. It felt so good, and I shouldn't feel good after talking about Diego, but *my God*, I wanted to feel good. My breath hitched when he slipped the tip of his finger into my mouth. His skin tasted salty and familiar. My eyes flew to his.

"I think we've had enough of memory lane this morning, don't you?"

I nodded, Paulie's finger still in my mouth. He looked brilliant, like the sun shone through him. All alight and intense. He smiled, and his soft gaze turned predatory when I sucked his digit in even farther.

He wasn't leaving me, and I could hardly believe it. But Paulie was tougher than me. He had been through hell and still managed to be happy and kind. I should have realized he wouldn't balk at a sordid past. But, part of me—that part that was hidden down deep inside— wanted Paulie to balk. Because if he didn't freak out, then why had I been hiding? If he didn't leave me when he learned the truth, or at least part of the truth, then my lying was nothing but slim and selfish self-preservation. And how sick was that?

When Paulie tugged his finger out of my mouth, I almost begged for him to fuck me. I wanted to feel something other than pain and memories. I wanted to stop thinking about Diego, to be pounded until the only thing I could keep in my mind was the rush of losing it. But I hated that feeling suddenly, because it was what I had always done. It was how I had coped with losing Diego for years, and I hated reducing Paulie to that.

"It's okay, sweetheart. You can just let go. Let me make you feel good," Paulie said against my mouth before pressing his tongue inside. Morning breath melted away until all I could taste was heat and the sweetness of Paulie's lips.

After I'd stripped off last night's clothes and fallen back on the bed, I pushed impatiently at Paulie's sweatpants and briefs. He stripped them and then landed on top of me. His mouth sought mine, and I grasped his slender hips like a lifeline. Like the feeling of his silky skin could anchor me and keep me from falling apart.

"Let me make you feel good," he repeated, and I realized I was crying again. I didn't even know why. I started to scramble away, but then his hand was on my cheek and his dark eyes were so close I could fall into them and swim around. "Let me love you, Joel. Please. Let me give you this. I just want to make love to you."

His words should have sounded cheesy, but they didn't. They sounded like sex and love and safety. And I couldn't believe he still loved me, couldn't believe he was still here. I opened my legs, and he nestled between my thighs. He humped against me, and I groaned.

"Paulie?" I whispered.

"I've got you, sweetheart."

Paulie readied with spit and lube, skinned a condom on, and flipped me onto my stomach. He pushed into me gently, and I let it all happen with a hazy sense of desire and pain.

"I'm yours now. And you're mine, aren't you, Joel?" Paulie said in response to my delirious cry. After I'd adjusted, he hammered into me hard, again and again. It was too much and I was too close, so I gripped his hip to stop him.

"Are you okay?" he panted, voice full of concern. I laughed and clenched my muscles around him. He groaned, "Oh my God, Joel. Don't do that to me!"

"Let me ride you."

He was right. He was mine, and I was his, and we were *good*, and suddenly I needed to be able to face him and prove it.

We disentangled and awkwardly fitted ourselves back together, this time with me straddling his thin hips, his fists in my hair, my mouth on his chest, and his cock even deeper inside me. The hickey I sucked below his pierced nipple pushed him over the edge, and I treasured the sight of him coming apart below me. He was gorgeous and bold, allowing himself to fall into his pleasure completely and without reservation. Taking what he wanted and needed in order to let go, his cock still pumping hard into my body until he clenched and relaxed in blissful relief. After a breath, he pulled out and shoved three fingers into my ass. My body was open, lubed, and used from his cock, but the rough glide of his knuckles past my rim whited out my vision with pleasure. He spat into his other hand and jerked me unevenly. He owned me, and I needed that. I shot hot and thick across his chest and neck, some splatters landing on the pillow by his face. He thrust his fingers gently until my tremors stopped.

After a few seconds, he pulled his fingers out, and I collapsed next to him. He had a couple of love bites on his chest, but the most vivid one was below his collarbone. I ran a thumb over it, and he jerked.

"Hurt?" I asked.

Paulie shook his head, and when he lifted his eyes to mine, my heart bounced into my throat. Like . . . *oh God*, it was like Cupid had shot it from my chest into my mouth with the flick of a wrist. I could open my mouth and hand my heart to him.

"I really am yours. You know that, right?" I asked.

Paulie closed his eyes, and I kissed the thin, bluish skin of his eyelids. He almost imperceptibly shook his head. His breath caught like he was in pain, like he didn't believe me, and fresh tears threatened to form behind my eyes.

I helped him strip the condom and wiped him off with a T-shirt.

"It would be nice to skip that step," he said, suddenly alert. I glanced at the T-shirt in my hand.

"The T-shirt?"

"No. The other part."

Oh. The condom. As understanding barreled through me, he visibly shuttered his emotions, a move so unusual for him it startled me. I had never had sex without a condom. Paulie was the only guy besides Diego I had ever even blown without latex.

When I didn't respond, Paulie said, "That was a dumb thing to say. I wasn't thinking."

But it wasn't really that dumb. Paulie and I had been together for months now. I only wanted him—*I was his,* as I had literally just said—but the thought of having nothing between us made me feel raw and vulnerable. Everything in me wanted to rebel at the idea.

"I'm not sleeping with other guys, Paulie. And I don't want to. But I'm not sure I'm—"

"I know," he interrupted in a rush. "Me either. It slipped out. Please, let's not talk about it. God, I'm such a fucking idiot."

He climbed off the bed and turned his back to me while he dressed, another uncommon occurrence.

His words hurt my stomach, and this whole conversation felt wrong—the way it fell on the tail end of Paulie finding out about Diego, which I still hadn't wrapped my mind around.

Finally, I told him, "I'm not ready for that yet. But maybe someday. Is that okay? You're definitely not an idiot."

"Yeah. Fine. It's not like I wanted to jump right in. Please let's just go back to sleep. It's still early."

"Sure," I whispered, even though I felt a little sick.

But then he curled into me like always, his head against my chest and our legs tangled together.

As sleep started to creep in on me, he whispered, "I'm sorry, Joel. About everything."

"Me too, baby. You have nothing to apologize for."

His legs jerked a little, a telltale sign he was falling asleep, but he murmured, "Love you."

I pulled back to look at his face. His mouth was slack, and his limbs heavy against mine.

I didn't say it back. I didn't want to anymore.

I kissed his forehead and tried to follow him.

chapter fifteen

The next week flew by me in a haze, like I was emotionally hungover. Everything too vivid and my brain too sensitive to face the light. Paulie never forced me to talk about Diego, but I would catch him peering at me when he thought I wasn't paying attention, and his eyes would hold confusion or pity or pain. He never pushed me, but I could feel this gulf growing between the questions he wasn't asking and the past I was ignoring.

Travis was due to come back the Saturday before school started, but as the evening wore on, I began to think he wasn't going to show. Paulie had been on the phone with Daria for two hours fielding a meltdown—the second one this week—and I was working on an internship application that was a ridiculous long shot, when Travis rushed through the front door at half past eight in a flurry of sleet.

He dumped several big bags of presents and his suitcase on the living room floor. I hadn't gotten a present from anyone but Paulie, which I probably deserved for bailing on my parents. It actually bothered me—my lack of gifts—especially in the face of Travis's impressive load.

"Check this out, Joel. I asked my parents for spare toothbrushes for Christmas, and my haul was spectacular!" Travis dumped a plastic grocery bag over the kitchen table, where I was working. Toothbrushes, all in their original packaging, rained everywhere.

"Oh my God, Travis," Paulie said from the entry to the hallway. Travis and I both turned toward him. "Why did you want toothbrushes for Christmas?"

"Well, normally, Joel brings a box of them home from his mom, but since you guys are all cock docked for life or whatever, I figured he'd skip it. And our stash is getting low."

"Wait!" Paulie laughed. "Did you tell your parents you wanted toothbrushes because you have so many overnight guests that you need a bunch of extras?"

"*No.* I told them I needed them for an art project. My parents support my creativity."

We all laughed for a couple seconds, but Paulie's chuckles fizzled off the quickest. He seemed a little distracted, and I was sure his mind was still on the phone call with Daria. He gave Travis a quick hug and then slumped over to the couch. Last night, protected by a cocoon of blankets, but still so sad and vulnerable, he'd admitted he was scared about Daria. And I was a horrible person because I couldn't help but be relieved that her increasing number of breakdowns meant Paulie had been too distracted by her to ask about Diego.

I saved my work and sat down by him. He doubled over, his face against his knees so I could rub his back. If Travis weren't in the room, I would have taken Paulie's shirt off and really given him a massage. Rubbed out the stress in every way possible and kissed him until he was sweet and pliant and normal. Like he used to be.

"Paulie, think fast," Travis said. Paulie sat up, and Travis tossed him a small wrapped present. He pitched a similar one to me.

"Are these sex toys?" Paulie asked. I eyed the package, suddenly scared they were.

But it wasn't a butt plug or anal beads or any other number of playthings Travis would have loved buying us. It was a desk calendar with a different picture for each day. Mine had cats dressed up as historical figures. January first was Marie Antoinette. It was tacky, and I loved it. When I glanced over at Paulie though, he was staring too intensely at the gift in his lap for it to be funny. He flipped through the calendar in his hands, but I couldn't see what the pictures were. Travis's gaze was glued on him.

"Thank you," Paulie murmured. His smile was sweet—the one I always thought of as mine—and his eyes were shiny.

He handed me his calendar, and the picture on the front was of two men, obviously a couple, with a quote about love in the face of adversity. The next page of the calendar was a picture of a gorgeous drag queen with a quote about being true to oneself. Every page was about the blessing of being queer. It gutted me—simultaneously filling me with hope and guilt and pride. And maybe it was normal to feel that way about being gay: proud and sad and scared and full of guilt and shame and excitement. Maybe it was part of the cycle of being okay with who you were, who you were born to be. Part of being proud to be gay hinged on the flipside, which was dealing with the pain of the closet and the disparaging looks and the disappointed parents. And learning to overcome them all. All three of us had been there, were still there, probably. Still living in that limbo between simply accepting being gay and learning to love yourself for it.

"Well, fuck. All you gave me was pussy," I said, hoping to lighten the mood. Everyone laughed, and Travis moved on to tell us stories of suburba-hell, as he called it. Travis, much like Paulie, could tell a story that wrapped you up and held you hostage, but even as he regaled us with a tale about walking in on his little brother wanking it to pony-play porn, I couldn't tear my eyes away from Paulie. And Paulie was staring at the couple on the front of his calendar, obviously in love and happy.

He was huddled in on himself, like he'd been kicked in the ribs, and I, as was my habit, pretended not to notice, pretended that the pain in his eyes wasn't because of me.

The next morning, I woke up in Paulie's bed with my tackle twisted under me. I started to roll onto my back and elbowed Paulie by accident. He chuckled. I moaned a little, because it felt ridiculously early, and then cuddled into his side for warmth. He was already sitting up.

"Why are you awake?" I grumbled. He was reading one of the silly dime novels I'd bought him. He'd appeared to find my present cute when I'd given it to him right after Christmas, but it certainly hadn't affected him like Travis's gift.

"I rather like these ones about cowboys," he said. "I think I'm developing a cowboy kink. You have the boots, right?"

I laughed a little and pulled him down to kiss me. When his mouth was close, I smelled mint and oranges. He'd already showered and brushed his teeth, which totally wasn't fair. He hadn't gotten dressed though, opting for only sweats. I started to roll out of his arms because even though I was all for spending our last free day in bed, I was not up for doing it when he smelled so good and I was disgusting.

He pinched my butt when I walked by but didn't even glance up from the book. I showered quickly and slipped into a pair of gym shorts I'd left at Paulie's before Christmas. When I crawled back into bed, Paulie had a movie pulled up on his laptop. It was one of those old, horrible Westerns full of Native American stereotypes and bad acting. He waggled his eyebrows at me.

"I have a cowboy hat too," I said. He growled, a sound so obscene and hungry I choked on my laughter.

We watched some of the movie, which was bad, made out a little, and dozed off and on. Before the credits started rolling, he snapped the laptop shut and put it on the floor.

"When you think about your life, like the future, what do you picture?" he asked. It was an odd question, but then it was also odd that we had never talked about it. That was probably my fault.

"Like a career?"

"Sure."

"Umm . . . I want to get a master's degree or a PhD and then either teach, or work at a museum, or as a historian somewhere. I don't really know. I just want to study history."

"If you could choose, though. If you could pick the exact career you want, what would you pick?"

"I'd be somewhere here in the Great Plains or Midwest and doing a job that helps preserve the area's cultural heritage," I said easily, even though I had never put the plan to words before. It sounded academic. I was almost impressed with myself. "What about you?"

"Well, I get my bachelor's next spring, and Farm College has a one-year master's program for accounting. So I figure I'll do that. I'll get my CPA and then find a job as an accounting manager or something for a company. Small potatoes, though. No public accounting firms. No huge corporations. Just somewhere small and friendly."

"Why accounting? I've always wondered. Accounting just seems so bland, but you and all your friends are wild and funny, so I obviously have some misconceptions."

He wrinkled his nose. "I like math, I guess. And organization. And it's normal and steady. I've never felt *called* to be anything, like some people. So why not go into a profession that's stable and dependable?

My job will never be my whole life, and I don't want it to be. I want my life to be fulfilling because of the *people* in it."

"I like that philosophy." It made sense for him. All of his connections had been ripped away from him when he was fourteen. A situation like that probably pushed you in one of two directions—running from every connection possible or hoarding them as precious. And Paulie had chosen to treasure his relationships, to hold them close to his heart and protect them. I'd always been the opposite.

"So you'll go to graduate school. Do you know where you want to go yet?" he asked.

"Well, here, if possible. I've thought about the University of Oklahoma, but it's pretty close to the city, and I don't think I'd like it. Oklahoma State is a better option."

"What about Kansas? Schools in Kansas, I mean."

My insides melted into something gooey and soft because it was suddenly so obvious what this conversation was about. Paulie was digging about *our* future. And I actually didn't want to run from it.

I rested a hand on his cheek. "I like Kansas. My mom's up in Salina, and your family's in Emporia. So we have connections there." Why was it so easy for me to say *that*, but I couldn't say, *I love you,* or even, *Sure, let's ditch the rubbers*?

A slow smile stretched across Paulie's face, happy and shy at the same time.

"Come here." I pulled him close. "I want you in my life, Paulie. I'll be honest—I haven't thought much about the future. For such a long time, I've only thought about how to get through the next day without breaking down." I hated admitting that, yet it was undeniably true. "But I can't imagine a future without you, okay? So you wanna start planning? We can start planning."

He pressed his face against my neck.

"I was worried," he whispered, his voice muffled.

"About what?"

"That I was the only one who felt that way."

chapter sixteen

dr. Yamato called me while I was at the library, trying to get back into the groove of school after slacking for the first several weeks.

After the requisite greetings, she said, "Well, Joel, no easy way to say this, but you didn't get the research fellowship."

That sucked, but it wasn't like I was surprised. My classes were full of bright, ambitious students and the competition had been fierce.

"That's okay. I'll apply for some internships for the summer and maybe something will come out of that," I told her.

"I'm actually calling to offer you a job." *What!* I fumbled the phone and got it back to my ear in time to hear, "I've received a grant for a historical preservation project to preserve, digitize, and exhibit prairie newspapers. I get a student assistant as part of the grant, and this is in your wheelhouse, what with all of the work you've done with prairie diaries and journals. You wouldn't make much money, and it'll be mostly legwork, but I thought you might be interested. The job would start in May."

"I'm in." Maybe I'd make enough money to quit my tutoring gig. The summer was always the worst because that was when the athletes came out of the woodwork. I didn't hate tutoring student-athletes. We spoke the same general language, but I couldn't help but see a life there that I'd abandoned. Couldn't help but see Diego in every dark-headed, corn-fed ball player.

"Really?" she blurted, like she was surprised.

"Of course. It sounds awesome."

"Great! I'll send you over my grant proposal and everything else I've written up so far, so you can review it and familiarize yourself with the project."

We scheduled a couple of meetings over the course of the coming months. I was taking her Civil War seminar, so it would be easy to catch up after class.

I was so excited, I didn't even call Paulie. I just drove over to his apartment and waited for him to get home from class. He arrived about thirty minutes later, and when I told him the news, he jumped into my arms and made one of those faux-excited screams. I'd never realized how wonderful it would be to have someone to cheer my triumphs.

"Come on, buttercup! I'll make you and Travis dinner to celebrate. But it'll have to be in your kitchen, with your supplies, and with food that you bought. I need to grocery shop like *whoa*."

"Travis is eating meat again." I didn't want there to be any misconceptions about whether we could or could not eat meat.

"Good to know. Want to walk?" Paulie asked. The day was clear and sunny, chilly, but fairly mild for January. The walk from Paulie's apartment to my house was a little over a mile, and I loved making it with him. He always held my hand, or danced around me while we were walking.

We were a couple of minutes away when my phone rang. I pulled it out of my pocket and stopped walking. The screen was lit up with missed calls and text messages from Travis. He was probably all worked up over *Golden Girls*, which he'd recently discovered, or one of the gay freshmen in his biology class for non-majors.

"Hey, Trav. Paulie's making us dinner," I said, as way of greeting.

"Oh, that's fabulous, but I don't care. I've been trying to get ahold of you." He was whispering, and his voice was sharp.

"I saw. What's up?"

"Well, you see, Joel, my dear, an enormous white guy showed up about fifteen minutes ago and wanted to see someone named *Jared* Smith."

I stumbled, almost dropping my phone, and Paulie grabbed my shoulder.

"What's wrong?" Paulie said. I shook my head.

"Travis?" It had to be my father, and I had no idea what he might have spilled to Travis. Travis didn't know dick about Jared Smith!

"Your dad looks just like you, by the way. So just a heads-up, the dad you hate, whom you never talk about, is here. At our house. With me."

"What are you guys doing?" I asked.

"We're smoking cigars and drinking coffee on the back porch. Actually, he's drinking coffee. I'm drinking hot chocolate."

"Sweet Jesus, tell me you're joking."

"Nope! Sure ain't." Hysteria cracked Travis's voice, and he laughed, which was perhaps better than my reaction. I wanted to throw up.

"Why in the world are you doing *that*, Travis?"

Travis paused for a moment. When he spoke, he sounded thoughtful. "Well, he seems like a coffee-and-cigar kind of guy, and we're on the back porch because I wasn't sure you'd want me to let him in the house. But I'm getting cold, so I need you to hurry home. *Immediately.* This is your official warning. I'm going back out there now before he comes a-looking. You get your ass over here and save me." He hung up.

I turned to Paulie, and I must have been pale, because he looked pretty alarmed.

"My dad's at my house," I croaked.

"Uh-oh."

I stared at him, my mind reeling too fast to think of an adequate response to him. "Oh shit."

"Do you want me to go home? I don't have to come with you," Paulie said. And, fuck, he got right to the heart of it, didn't he?

Paulie's brown-black eyes were wide, and those long lashes curled like perfectly arranged feathers. He was wearing his peacoat with a handsome plaid scarf, tight khaki corduroys, and red canvas tennis shoes. I had no idea what he was wearing underneath his coat, but it was probably femme-y and tight. I almost groaned. My dad was going to eat him alive.

But I couldn't make it without him. If I had to walk on by myself, I would stall out on the way. Farm College was supposed to be safe. I could be myself here, and no one got to know about Townsend or Diego or my fucked-up parents unless I wanted to tell them. And I'd never wanted to tell anyone, so no one knew, except Paulie.

But now my dad was here, with Travis, smoking freaking cigars and talking about who knew what!

I gaped at Paulie, my head spinning like that girl in the *Exorcist*.

"Or . . . we could pretend to just be friends," he continued. "He doesn't have to know I'm your boyfriend. I know what I look like."

"No!" I snapped. Paulie's perception was excruciating, and I would never forgive myself if I asked him to lie. I wasn't ashamed of him. He was hot and kind, and I needed him. Dad didn't get to change our narrative because he showed up unannounced.

"It's going to be okay, Joel. Let's see how it goes. If it comes up that I'm your boyfriend, then that's great. If not, that's okay too. We don't even know what he wants. I might be completely inconsequential. What's Travis doing to keep him occupied?"

"Cigars and coffee."

Paulie laughed so hard he doubled over, and I had to admit it was just absurd enough to be funny. But I was pretty sure my dad hadn't carried many conversations with a black guy, much less a gay one, and I couldn't even think about all the ways that little chitchat could go wrong.

"Let's go meet your daddio, buttercup."

Paulie started off at a brisk pace, and there was nothing I could do but quit stalling and follow him.

Much too quickly, we made it home, and voices wafted toward us from the back porch. When Paulie and I cleared the corner of the house, we spotted Travis and my dad. Dad had his feet up on an empty lawn chair and ominous cigar smoke curled around his head. He stood when we got close, and made like he was going in for a hug, but I took a quick step back. The moment hung long and awkward between us.

"Thanks, Travis," I said to him. He nodded and fled into the house. "Paulie, this is my dad, Harlan. Dad, this is Paulie McPherson. He's my—"

"Nice to meet you, sir," Paulie said, cutting me off. He held out his hand, and Dad eyed it for a drawn-out second before grasping it hard in one of those my-dick-is-bigger-than-yours handshakes, which he was probably only giving because he expected Paulie to be limp-wristed.

Paulie's smile was ferocious and fearless. I wished I could follow suit.

"Please, why don't you boys sit?" Dad said as if we were in his nonexistent office and not on my shitty back porch. Paulie plopped down, but I leaned against the railing. It felt safer, like it would be easier to bolt from here.

"Only for a minute. I promised Joel I would make him dinner. He just got a job offer, so we're celebrating," Paulie said. "You can eat with us, if you want."

I glared at Paulie, trying to incinerate him, but he ignored me.

"Well, I would hate to intrude," Dad said. I couldn't tell if he was trying to sound humble and gracious, or dismissive and bitchy. Either way, I was on fucking edge.

"Oh, *honey*, it's not an intrusion at all! I like to cook," Paulie said, his voice lilting and more singsong than usual.

My dad and I were both so shocked Paulie had called him *honey* neither of us responded. Dad's mouth was even slightly agog. The smile Paulie shot in my direction was sly and predatory. I would have laughed if I could have unkinked my locked jaw for half a second.

"You got a job?" Dad asked, directing his blue-fire gaze back toward me. He sounded incredulous. I wanted to remind him I currently had a job tutoring, but he didn't respect that type of position. It wasn't what he considered *hard work*.

"Yes."

"A good one?"

"Yeah, sure."

"Oh! It's a really good job. Joel will be working for one of his history professors on a preservation project," Paulie chimed in. Part of me was touched he was trying to come to my rescue, but I also wanted to sink into the floor. My dad disliked intellectuals, almost as much as he hated homos. He'd told me once, before I graduated high school, that he no longer had to worry about one of those *liberal colleges* ruining me. I'd already done that all on my own.

"That's fantastic," my dad said flatly.

I was suddenly so done with him being here in my space, talking to my boyfriend, pretending to be harmless, and dropping petty shade all over the place.

"Why're you here, Dad?"

He pulled a wrapped present out of the inside of his jacket and tossed it across the patio table to me. I didn't catch it, so it *thunk*ed onto the tabletop.

"Open it."

"Is it from Mom?" I asked because I couldn't imagine it being from him.

"No, it's not from Mom!" he snapped. The present made my gut hurt. I wanted to hate it. I wanted to hate that he had driven all the way from Nebraska to give me a gift. But a small piece of me also wanted to rip into it like a kid at, well, Christmas.

Instead, I sat in the chair beside Paulie and fiddled with the wrapping paper. I could tell it was a book, but for some reason, I was scared to open it in front of Paulie.

"Here, sweet pea, I'll give you some time alone. I need to start cooking anyway," Paulie said, like he had read my mind. He ruffled my hair as he stood up, and I couldn't help but watch the sway of his hips as he walked into the house. He was working the walk a bit more than usual, and I wasn't sorry to see that either. He still melted my brain.

"So what's with the little woman?" Dad asked, and I slammed my hand down on the patio table. I was very happy to see him startle.

"Watch yourself," I warned.

"Open the fucking present, Jared."

Oh my God. I couldn't do this anymore. Two years without having to worry about my fucking father, and now *this*. I pressed my palms to my forehead so the top of my head didn't blow off.

"Shit! Joel. I meant 'Joel.' It's just hard to remember! I've called you Jared for your whole goddamn life."

He sounded upset, but I didn't trust him. His eyes were red-rimmed, the blue irises startling. It was how my eyes looked when I was hungover, but his had looked that way for as long as I could remember. I reached for the present and tore it open.

It was a Western, of course, because they were the one thing my dad and I shared that I hadn't completely rejected over two years ago.

Comstock Lode. One of the first Westerns I had ever read—an oldie by Louis L'Amour.

"I know it was always your favorite, but your copy is still at my house. This is an original edition," he said.

I didn't tell him that I had purchased a new copy at a library book sale my freshman year. This was actually a sweet gift.

I flipped the paperback over in my hands. It smelled old and perfect. The cover was a little worn around the edges, but still firmly attached to the spine. The pages were yellowing, but there were no visible stains or markings. I thumbed it open. Dad had written, *For Joel*, on the inside cover. My heart clenched with a weird mix of want and fear. I wanted to trust this olive branch, but I couldn't. My dad wasn't a safe bet.

"I was an asshole, Joel. I still am most days, and I'm going to work real hard at that. I'll admit I don't understand the gay thing. I don't get guys like your friend in there. But I want to be in your life, so I'm working on it."

"You want to be in Mom's life, and she's making you, you mean."

"No," he said, the word catching in his throat. He leaned toward me. "I miss you both. I'm even going to counseling."

I laughed a little because this situation was so bizarre I could hardly stand it, but my laugh sounded wet, and I hated that he was seeing me vulnerable. I knew from experience that he was a pro at using it against me.

"Joel, the stuff with that kid in high school—"

"Diego."

"Right. Diego. It was a surprise. You're my only child. I thought you would have kids and a wife one day. I wanted you to have a perfect life. I wanted it to be better than the life I gave you . . . And I got a lot of lip from the guys at the plant when the shit hit the fan. I handled it poorly."

I suspected the real reason for his disdain lay more in the contempt he received from his coworkers than in his sadness over his expectations for me.

"Dad, you think I don't know how hard it was for you afterward? People treated us like pariahs. I'm aware that didn't only extend to me. You and Mom didn't deserve it."

I paused because some of Paulie's words from weeks before thundered in my head. Paulie had said it wasn't *my* fault, either.

That my parents had nothing to blame me for. I took a deep breath. I wasn't sure I believed it, but I wanted to say it.

"But I was only a kid. I had just lost my best friend. I didn't deserve your hatred. I didn't do anything to you, and you should have been there for me."

"I know."

I gawped at him in shock.

"You know?"

"Yes. I'm sorry, and I want to be better from here on out."

"You didn't act better at Christmas." It came out as a whine, and I winced.

"I know that too. I was an asshole. Your mother has already told me that in a million different ways."

I traced the characters on the cover of the book for several seconds. "Okay," I whispered.

"Okay? We're okay?"

"No! We are definitely not okay, but I'm thirsty and I can't stand talking about it anymore." I pressed the heels of my hands into my eye sockets and then stood. He watched me warily. "What now?" I asked.

"I'd like to try talking more often. But it's all up to you."

I nodded, and he stood so we were face-to-face.

He stretched his neck and then said, "Well, I'll get out of your hair, I guess."

"Where are you staying tonight?" I felt drained, like I could sleep for a week. My dad's revelations and apology jumbled my brain. It was such unfamiliar footing.

"I was going to get a motel room and head back tomorrow."

"You can have the couch," I told him, and regretted it immediately. There were so many ways Dad could spill my secrets to Travis.

"That's right gracious of you." He sounded so formal I almost rolled my eyes.

"What did you tell Travis about my name?"

His gaze cut toward me sharply. "Does he not know why you changed your name?"

Huh? Dad had clearly misunderstood my question. Until today, Travis hadn't even known I'd changed my name, much less why.

I shook my head.

"Well, I didn't tell your roommate anything," he said. "He took it in stride when I slipped and called you Jared, so I figured he knew. You probably shouldn't close yourself off from your friends like that, son."

I didn't know how to respond. "You probably shouldn't have written in a first edition Louis L'Amour."

Twenty minutes later, we were all eating dinner, and Paulie was acting odd and distant. I was at once grateful and incredibly pained. I wanted to reach over and drag him closer to me on the couch, but he was radiating *Don't Touch* signals so strong even my dad could probably see them.

"This is really good, Paulie," I told him. We were eating pasta salad and breakfast sandwiches. I was pretty impressed by what he'd managed to scrounge together from our fridge.

"Thanks, buttercup," he said absently. He lifted his gaze from his plate, which he was balancing on his lap, and winked at me. Relief welled in me for no reason I could really pinpoint.

My dad grimaced anytime Paulie spoke, but we were all ignoring it.

"Travis," Dad barked abruptly. A mouthful of shell pasta dropped from Travis's fork when he glanced up. Travis watched it wobble on his plate before focusing back on my dad. "Tell me where you're from again."

"Katy, Texas, sir. It's a suburb of Houston."

"Big city," Dad replied, but I felt like he wanted to say, *Inner city*.

"Katy is pretty much just suburbia."

"What do your parents do, Travis?" Dad asked. He kept saying Travis's name, like a car salesman, over and over.

"My mom's a divorce lawyer and my dad's a nurse."

Dad blinked like a confused puppy. Travis's parents' occupations clearly did not align with his normal view of the world at all. But instead of making some crackpot comment like I expected, he said, "That's nice." It was forced, but I supposed it was progress.

He turned toward Paulie, and I flinched. Sweat broke out along my spine. But Paulie shot him a calm little smile.

"And Paulie," my dad started, "what about you? Where are you from?"

"I was raised outside of Springfield, Missouri, but moved to Emporia, Kansas when I was a teenager. It was *dreadfully* dull."

"And your parents? What do they do?" The assessment was clear in Dad's eyes, like he was testing for cracks.

"Oh, hon! I don't rightly know anymore. Last I saw them, my mom was having babies and teaching homeschool, and my dad was an engineer. It's been about nine years since I've spoken to either of them."

Dad looked at me funny then. Paulie stood up with his plate and began to gather up the other dirty dishes around the living room. When he caught my eye, he twitched his head toward the kitchen, so I grabbed my plate and followed him.

As soon as we were clear of company and our hands were free, I clutched Paulie's shoulder. He barreled into my arms and hugged me hard. We remained silent, but Paulie pressed himself against me so forcefully I could hear his pounding heart.

"Your truck is at my apartment," Paulie breathed into my neck. "Travis said he would drive me home."

"Why? Just stay here."

He huffed in exasperation. "If I stay here, there is no way your dad won't realize I'm sleeping in your bed." He bit his lip and scowled. "I guess I could sleep with Travis."

"You are not sleeping in Travis's bed!" I hissed.

"Ooh, sheath those claws," he teased but sobered quickly. "I don't want to cause any trouble. Your dad's a dick. I'll just make it worse."

"I don't care what my dad thinks," I whispered, even though it would probably never be one hundred percent true. "I care what you think, Paulie, and what Travis thinks, and what *I* think. And *I* think I want to wake up and see your face in the morning. Can you live with that?"

Paulie stared up at me, and his gaze wasn't full of its normal, happy sparkle. Instead, he radiated resignation and uneasiness. I cradled his face in my hands and kissed him softly, trying to reassure him and convince him to stay. His lips were so sweet. I couldn't resist going in for another taste. Paulie opened for me, and I held back the moan that wanted to rise in my throat. It was heaven every time Paulie let me in this way. I kept expecting the effects to wear off, to get used to kissing him, holding him, having him, but these feelings didn't show signs of stopping.

Paulie slipped his hands under my shirt and trailed them up my back. I tipped his chin up and bit his bottom lip. He shivered and whispered, "Fuck."

Then Dad walked into the kitchen.

Dad sucked in a startled gasp, and I reflexively jumped back. Paulie closed his eyes for half a second, pain flitting across his face. I immediately reached for him again, willing to do anything to stop the hurt that was gathering there, but he stepped back.

Without looking at my dad, Paulie said to me, "I'm going to go to your room to do some homework, and then I think I'll turn in early. You sure you don't want to have Travis drive me back to my apartment?"

"I'm sure. I want you here," I said, even though the words felt like peanut butter stuck to the roof of my mouth. He nodded and left the small, dirty kitchen without a backward glance.

I expected to see disgust on my dad's face, but instead he seemed sad.

"You really do have a boyfriend," he said. "I thought you were just saying that to get a rise out of me."

I stifled the tide of anger surging in my chest and shook my head. Dad would obviously always be an insensitive dickhead. I didn't want to fight with him, but I also hated letting his shitty comments slide.

Dad walked back into the living room, and I followed him. Travis had retreated to his bedroom, so we were alone. The wind battered the outside of the house, and all of the walls creaked in protest.

Finally, Dad asked, "Paulie's parents are religious like Diego's?"

I didn't want to talk about Diego anymore. I wanted him safely locked in my memories where no one could touch him. Where no one could know that my mind was still full of him.

"Yes and no. Paulie's parents are probably more extreme. He's from one of those families with a million kids, like you see on TV. The end result is the same, though. Both families rejected their son."

Dad jerked back. "I never rejected you, Joel. That wasn't what I did."

"That's exactly what you did. Maybe you never said the words or told me to *get out*, but you made sure I didn't feel welcome. You made sure our home couldn't be my home anymore. Or Mom's."

He took in a shuddering breath and scrubbed a hand across his mouth. "Paulie isn't what I expected for you."

"Well, last I checked, you expected a girl," I snapped.

"No, I mean, he's nothing like Diego. I assumed if you were going to be with a man, it would be a *man*, you know?" I just stared at him. I couldn't believe I had offered him my couch. The irritation must have been plain on my face because he rushed on. "Shit, I'm screwing this up. I just don't get it. If you're going to be with some guy who's girly, why not be with a girl?"

"I'm not talking about this with you."

It didn't matter what I said about Paulie. I could try to bolster him up as the most masculine man in the world, and it wouldn't matter. It could be true, and it wouldn't matter. My dad would only ever see a swishy priss.

"Fine," he barked, anger rising visibly on his face in a red rash. "I finally got used to picturing you with Diego, so it's hard for me to imagine you being with another man. That's all I'm saying."

My heart flopped over sickly, and fear congealed in my stomach like day-old macaroni. Dad had no idea how much those words hurt. I locked down my expression and donned apathy like a Halloween mask. He'd used signs of weakness against me in high school, and I had no intention of letting it happen again.

But Dad had given words to one of my darkest truths. I loved Paulie, I did, but I had trouble envisioning a life with anyone except Diego, because it felt unfaithful to him somehow. I still felt that loss—the loss of a future, a life together, the potential—like it was taken from my flesh. When Paulie was in my arms, it was so easy to forget. But, in moments like this, I resented how effortlessly Paulie encroached on a space that wasn't his to take.

It would pass. I knew it would. I would go to bed and take one look at the curve of Paulie's naked spine, and the longing I felt for him and *him alone* would knock back my reservations. He would whisper my name or call me *buttercup*, and I wouldn't hear the echo of Diego so acutely.

But now, sitting here with my father, the past choked me.

So I changed the subject. Asked Dad about his work at the plant and listened to him talk about missed promotions and suck-ass bosses for an hour, just like old times. And then I went to bed.

Paulie was already asleep when I slipped inside my bedroom, and part of me was thankful. I needed to wallow in the pain a little longer. Maybe I deserved the pain.

The next morning Paulie was running late for class, so he didn't do more than shower, press a fast kiss to my mouth, and wave at my father before scurrying out the door. Dad had to leave soon after, and he gave me an awkward hug with a big swat on the back before getting in his truck. I wasn't sure what this weird visit meant for us, but I suspected he would soon move to Salina with my mom, or she would move back to Nebraska.

I felt torn up, like his visit had stirred all of the scum and detritus hidden away in my life to the surface, and now everyone would be able to see it. Maybe that was why my relationship was so strained with my parents. Maybe it wasn't just because I had wrecked the thinly veiled disaster they'd called marriage.

Maybe they reminded me too much of the misery I'd buried inside.

chapter seventeen

Paulie and I trudged hand in hand out from the warmth of the library and into the snow. We'd been studying for a couple of hours, but Paulie's bubbly, take-charge attitude had melted away until he'd seemed completely beat. He'd practically been falling asleep at our table. He needed some fresh air, and I was done anyway.

The flat, sparse landscape of the college stretched before us. There were hardly any trees on campus because it had been established on an open field. About twenty years ago, someone had decided the campus was too bare and planted a scattering of Bradford Pear trees in strategic locations. Not all of the trees had made it. The wind and the winter were too harsh here, and the trees too weak.

Paulie paused to tie his shoe after we stepped onto the lawn in front of the library. Seconds later, a snowball exploded against my neck. The snow was wet and sticky, more slush than powder. I spun around to see the culprit, but the only person in sight was Paulie. The minute my eyes met his, he dropped his bag and took off running.

"You little shit!" I yelled, but he only snickered. I ran after him and laughed when his surprised squeak reached me. He hadn't expected my speed. No one ever did.

I caught him easily and trapped him in a bear hug, then effortlessly wrestled him to the ground. He grinned up at me. His nose was running a little, and he kept wiping it with his sleeve. I just wanted to kiss and fuck and hold him. I glanced around quickly; we were completely exposed but totally alone. Weathermen had predicted an ice storm would hit the Elkville area that afternoon, and we'd received a campus alert to "be prepared for bad weather." Everyone with a brain had probably already hunkered down.

I pulled my gloves off with my teeth so I could touch his skin. I traced my fingers over his cheeks, which were warm to the touch, and his smile grew. He turned his head and pressed a breathless kiss on my palm.

"I feel hot, but my nose is cold," he said.

I kissed it. Then I kissed the bottom of his earlobe, which was peeking out of his beanie. The sharp angle of his jaw called to me, so I bit it gently, just enough for him to need a sweet kiss to settle the sting. Paulie drew his arms up around me, but we were both wearing so many layers, it was like two marshmallows trying to hug. The slick nylon of our coats whistled together.

I captured his lips between mine, and his breath was hot and quick. He smiled at me when I pulled back, and the sight of his slight gap made me dive in for another. Then I sat up onto my knees and pushed a wet snowball into the side of his head. I sprinted off before he could even sputter.

By the time we made it back to my house, I was desperate for him and he seemed practically feverish for me. Travis was curled up on the living room sofa when we stumbled in, reading an obnoxiously long novel for one of his classes. *Show off.*

I'd been avoiding Travis since Dad's visit. I'd given him some half-baked excuse about changing my name. *"Jared is my dad's middle name, and I don't want it connected to me,"* I'd told him. But it had sounded muddy at best, and I could tell he hadn't quite bought it.

Travis started to greet us, but I shuffled Paulie through the living room so fast we didn't even hear his full sentence.

If we hadn't been wearing a million layers of clothes, I would have had Paulie horizontal and calling my name in ten seconds flat. But he couldn't get his arm out of his hoodie, and I had some issues with my boots. Finally, we were both down to jeans, but the intense, gotta-have-you-right-fucking-now passion had receded. I still wanted him, but didn't feel like my dick was about to explode anymore.

And *Je-sus*, I could have just stared at him all day. His creamy skin and pebbly nipples. The mind-boggling, erotic flash of his piercing. The warm blush on his chest and face. The dark shadow on his jaw. His wide, black-as-licorice eyes. The pouty, plush lips. Under his denim, I would find strong, wiry legs with a light dusting of black hair; curly pubic hair that always held that smell that was distinctly him and distinctly male; and his perfect, long cock with its dark-pink head. I could tongue that baby all fucking day.

But his body, and the way he so expertly used it, was not even half of my desire for him. When I woke up in the morning, the first thing I wanted to hear was his musical voice. And being near him—it felt right . . . in my heart, I guessed. Like a coal settling in my chest to keep me warm forever.

And then there were these moments when shyness and vulnerability filled the deep pools of his eyes. And, in those moments, he slayed me.

If only I could stop letting him down. But I couldn't. Or maybe I hadn't. Since the visit from my dad— No, really since he found out about Diego, I had been chasing the distrust and pain from his eyes. It was exhausting. And maybe it was all in my head, but I didn't think so. The only time he looked at me with open joy anymore was when we were naked.

We finally fell tangled on the bed and strained together until Paulie's body tightened with tension. I held his perfect, elfin face in my hands and kissed him through the wrenching of climax. It took him longer than usual to stop trembling and come down, but once I was sure he was aware of his surroundings, I gave him some space. He smiled at me sleepily and climbed out of bed.

As soon as he was upright, he gasped.

A sudden wind rattled the frame of our house, and the atmosphere changed like it did when a storm rolled in, the air turning thin and empty and choking. Paulie turned back toward the bed and thrust his hands out, like he was trying to grab the mattress, but then his eyes rolled back and he fell to the floor.

I shrieked and vaulted out of the bed. His eyes fluttered open as I knelt by his head and lightly touched his cheeks. I was so alarmed I almost yelled for Travis. But we were both naked. Like really naked. Sex naked, which was a different and stickier kind of naked than shower naked or changing-clothes naked. And as much as I didn't care about my nudity at the moment, Paulie seemed so fragile and small and exposed. I couldn't let anyone see him like that. Not even Travis.

"I'm dizzy," he murmured.

I pressed my palm against his forehead, like my mom always had when I was feverish, and he was burning up. But was he sick hot or sex hot? I had no idea.

He started shaking. *Sick hot*, obviously.

"Baby, I think you're sick."

He nodded solemnly, his eyes wide and his skin ashen.

"Let's get you dressed and then—"

"I want to go home," he said. "I want to be sick in my own space, please, Joel."

"Okay, baby. I'll take you home." The wind gusted against the house again, and I closed my eyes. It sounded bad out there, and if it wasn't yet, it would be soon.

"You get your flu shot?" I asked as I helped him wipe off our come and get dressed.

"No! Did you?"

"Yeah. Trav and I got them at the clinic on campus the first week they had them."

"Why didn't you take me with you?" he asked, so forlorn and precious I wanted to lock him against my chest and rock him to sleep.

"Well, it was before you and I started hanging out. We got our flu shots and STD tests." Both were free at the student clinic, and it was sort of a back-to-school ritual for Travis and me. I'd been with several guys between my test and when I hooked up with Paulie. I was probably due for another one.

"Fuck me, are you for real? That's adorable," he said. But by then he was shivering pretty badly, so I dressed quickly and then shuffled us out the door.

Travis took one look at Paulie and said, "Oh shit. You're taking him home, right?"

Paulie gave a weird little giggle and a wave, and we hiked into the brand-new blizzard.

On the drive to his apartment, I stopped at the drug store to buy a case of Gatorade, Ibuprofen, flu medicine, soup, and a thermometer. The Doomsday crowd had cleaned out the water, milk, and bread.

When I got back in my truck, Paulie frowned at me, all bleary-eyed and miserable.

"My body hurts."

"I'll take care of you."

"You know how?"

Nope. "I'll figure it out. I can call your aunt."

"Don't! She'll drive down here. It'll be so embarrassing."

I kissed his temple. His skin was hot and slick with clammy sweat.

A couple of hours later, Paulie was running a 102.3-degree temperature and sleeping fitfully under three layers of blankets. His eyes and nose were swollen, and he was even coughing weakly in his sleep. When he woke up, I crawled into bed and cuddled him against my chest. He burrowed into my neck and breathed heavily against my skin until he fell back to sleep. Every couple of hours, he would wake up, re-medicate, hydrate, and then doze off.

At about four in the morning, Paulie woke me up with a cold hand on my side. He was nauseous, so I got him some Gatorade, a trash can, and took his temperature.

It was still high, and I wondered if I should take him to the ER, since the student clinic was closed due to the weather. What could they do for him, though? It was obvious he had the flu. And I'd always heard you could treat symptoms with over-the-counter meds, which I had already bought him, but you just had to wait for the flu to run its course.

I researched Paulie's symptoms on my phone while he slept, and entirely freaked myself out by falling down the rabbit hole of WedMD. People died from the flu, I learned. Every year. It was uncommon, but it actually happened in this twenty-first century full of medical advancements and emergency rooms.

Paulie could die. Yeah, sure, he wasn't elderly or an infant and he didn't have an autoimmune disease, so the flu was probably *not* going to be the thing that made him kick it. But something would, one day. And, surprisingly, that God-awful truth had never occurred to me.

I watched Paulie's face like a laser, scared I would overlook a warning sign, and he would be sicker than I thought. I felt sick, not with the flu, but with the realization that I controlled *nothing*. We were all just puppets to fate and pain and the crunch of car metal and the placement of barbed wire fences and unwashed hands and viral contagions.

Every few minutes, I touched his forehead, because it made me feel proactive. But it changed nothing. Eventually, I contented myself with curling him back into my arms and measuring the minutes and hours with his breath.

I must have fallen asleep at some point, because I woke up to an empty bed. The shower was running. I pressed my ear to the door and heard only rushing water, not even movement. A jittery fear filled me, so I jiggled the doorknob until it gave way.

Paulie was huddled in a ball on the floor of the tub, his forehead resting on his upturned knees, and water from the shower pattering against his back. My stomach dropped in sympathy.

"Baby, you okay? You should have woken me up."

"I know," he said, his voice laced with misery. "I felt sticky, though. And I wasn't dizzy until I was under the water." He tipped his face up, water catching in his eyelashes and running in rivers like tears down his cheeks. But he smiled, even with the flu.

"School was canceled," he continued. That was a relief; though, I would have happily missed class to watch Paulie obsessively while he slept. "I saw on my phone that we're expected to get more ice on top of the inch we got last night. We might be out for a couple days."

I almost laughed. In Nebraska, we handled winter weather much better than they did here. In Oklahoma, several inches of ice was an apocalypse. An *ice-pocalypse*.

"Sounds like you picked a good week to be sick."

"I know. I haven't asked anyone to take notes for me in my Cost Accounting class yet."

I turned the water off, because I couldn't stand to watch it slap against his poor, sick body anymore, and stepped into the tub. Paulie uncurled a little, but I still had to squat down and help him up. He swayed when he was upright, so I swooped him into my arms and carried him back to his bedroom.

"This is embarrassing," he said against my neck.

"No, it's not. It's just me and you here."

When I sat him down, his body glittered with water droplets, and normally the sight would have made me hot, but his face was pallid and his eyelids kept rolling shut like he was drunk. I toweled him off, dressed him, fed him medicine and chicken broth, and eventually he fell back asleep.

His temperature was higher when he woke up, upward of 103, so I put some cool washcloths on his skin. His body shook—tremors that vibrated the whole bed—and his muscles were so achy he couldn't sleep. He wasn't particularly lucid either, though. Every so often, he would mumble little fragments of phrases that I couldn't seem to make out. I called Aunt Ruth and filled her in. She told me I was doing everything I could do, but to take him to the ER if he started vomiting a lot or if his temperature spiked. Her instructions calmed me. Sometimes you just needed a mother to tell you what to do.

"The roads are too bad, or I would drive over." She dropped her voice. "And Daria isn't doing well. Don't tell Paulie—I don't want to freak him out—but I think she's stopped taking her meds. It's probably not a good time to leave."

Later, I cleared the ice off my truck, stocked it with blankets, and refilled my emergency kit in case I needed to take Paulie to the hospital. When I came back inside, Paulie said my name, so I crawled into bed with him. His eyes were closed, but he was awake.

"Tell me more about Diego."

We had hardly talked about my past. There had been times when Paulie had obviously wanted to ask me about Diego or my parents, times when I could see the questions forming in his eyes or almost hear the words on the tip of his tongue. I'd always sidestepped. But since he was sick and I was pretty sure he wouldn't remember any of this conversation, I didn't see the harm in appeasing him. And maybe it would feel good to unload a little for once.

So I told him about how Diego had had an innocent sense of humor and how he liked poetry. I told him that Diego had been a good kisser, but hadn't liked making out. I told Paulie about how Diego had written in his journal every night, but *didn't* tell him how Diego's parents had found those journals after he died. I talked about playing baseball with him and how he'd been one of the best first basemen in Nebraska. I told Paulie about our plan to go to the University of Nebraska and walk on to the baseball team there. I got stuck, though, when I tried to describe the feelings I'd had when I'd been with Diego—the excitement and fear and wonder that I had found someone in that scary, small town. The sense of belonging. It wasn't coming out right—the words too weak and thin to truly capture what he meant to me.

"You loved him," Paulie said, his voice a sigh of exhaustion.

"Yeah."

Love. Such a feeble word for something that had consumed me so much. I loved Paulie too, but not like I had Diego. Like I still loved Diego. With Diego, it was just . . . different, and I didn't want to look too closely at it.

"Tell me about the things you didn't like."

"About Diego?"

"Sure. Everybody has something he doesn't like about his boyfriend."

"Is there, now? What don't you like about me?"

"You snore," he replied without missing a beat. His lips curled up into a sad imitation of his normal smile.

I wasn't sure I could talk about Diego like that. I worried it would make me feel disloyal. But I couldn't deny Paulie either. Especially not now.

"He never told me he loved me back." The words came out so easily, like they'd been waiting there on the roof of my mouth, just gearing up to break free. "I said it all the time, and I think he liked hearing it, but it also made him sad. I wasn't the life he wanted. Sometimes I worry that he would have dumped me and married some girl and had the kids and the perfect nuclear family because that's what he actually wanted out of life."

Paulie lifted a hand and placed it on my chest right over my heart. It was beating fast. His touch loosened my tongue.

"He didn't want to come out once we got to college. God, I used to ask him that all the time. It was probably one of the only things we fought about. But I wanted to get out of Townsend and stop hiding. Diego made me so happy, but I don't think I ever made him feel that way. He was gay and hated it, and part of me thinks he hated it about me too, like it was my fault he wasn't going to be the man he had planned to be."

"He wasn't ever going to keep you," Paulie said. His voice was soft and slightly slurred, but it vibrated through my body like he had rung a giant gong. Because he was right. It was a truth I tried to avoid. I always told myself that there was no way to know for sure that Diego wouldn't have come around eventually, but I *knew* that Paulie was right.

He gazed at me with misty eyes. "Just like you and me," he said. "I love you, but you ain't ever gonna keep me."

A tear spilled out of one of his eyes and slipped into his hair. He closed his eyes, and it pushed another set of tears out onto the pillow under his head.

"Oh, Paulie. That's not true," I told him, but his tears were falling fast now. I pulled him against me and held him loosely in my arms. He was an oven, the heat radiating off of him, but I wasn't letting him go.

I could tell him I *did* love him and I absolutely intended to keep him, but it would feel weak and placating. Still . . . if it would make him feel better, I'd do it in a hot minute. I opened my mouth to say the words, but, as usual, they choked me.

He cried for about five minutes. He didn't make a sound, but hiccups juddered his small frame and his tears seeped into my shirt. I told him over and over that I wasn't giving him up, not for anything. I knew he was just sick and in pain and his body was exhausted from fighting so hard, so I held him until he fell asleep.

The next morning Paulie threw up. He managed to make it to the bathroom to do it, for which I was very thankful. He was still feverish and achy, but after vomiting, some color returned to his face. He was scared to leave the bathroom in case he had to puke again, though, so I made him a little pallet on the tile floor. He slept with his head resting on the lip of the tub, and I sat with my back to the door and watched him.

"I hate throwing up in front of people," he told me after about an hour. His eyes were clearer and his voice strong.

"I've seen it before. You ralphed right in front of me a couple months ago, remember? Want to move back to bed?"

"I want a baked potato."

"Okay, weirdo."

Paulie made his way back to his bedroom, but not before tossing me a cheeky smile over his shoulder.

After eating and sleeping for the rest of the day, his fever dropped to around one hundred degrees. We watched a couple of bad movies on Netflix, and Paulie kept down the baked potato and some soup. He slept through the night, and the next morning he wanted to take a shower. I was nervous for a repeat of his last shower, so I climbed in with him. His movements were measured and sluggish, but he smiled the whole time and insisted on shampooing my hair.

The next day, I worked on an assignment for Dr. Yamato's Civil War seminar while Paulie dozed. He no longer had a fever, but he couldn't seem to stay awake for more than a couple of hours at a time. School had been canceled for another day, and it didn't seem like they would open campus up until the temperature rose over the weekend. I was focused on my homework, so when he spoke, it startled me.

"I got tested about two weeks after we got together." His eyes were alert, like he'd been awake for a while, probably watching me work.

It felt like I had been dropped into the middle of a conversation without a map.

He sat up and scooted to the edge of his bed. "You said something about getting tested with Travis when you asked me about the flu shot."

I laughed. Paulie was picking up a conversation from about four days ago. "I wasn't sure you would remember that."

"I think I remember most of what we talked about." The intensity in his voice made me cringe. He obviously recalled our conversation about Diego, which I'd been hoping would be lost in his flu fog. "I haven't been with anyone but you since I was tested."

"I have. My last test was in August, way before we got together."

"You could get another."

Heat rushed under my skin, and a prickly, uncomfortable sensation tickled my palms.

"I could," I hedged.

I didn't know what to say. I needed another test. But I wasn't sure I wanted to get one just so we could stop using condoms, and that was clearly where Paulie was heading with this conversation.

"We don't have to go bare, buttercup," he said gently. His use of the nickname was probably intended to lighten the mood, but it didn't. In fact, the mood was so thick and ugly it was practically visible in the air like an unpleasant sludge. "I don't want to do that until you're ready, Joel. But could you tell me *why* you don't want to? Do you not trust me? Or do you not want to be—"

"Of course I trust you, Paulie! And there's no one else. I don't want anyone else." I didn't know how to put my reticence into words. I didn't really understand it. I only knew that the thought made me itchy. "I'm just not ready. Not yet."

He nodded and smiled, but the smile was forced, like he was trying to put on a mask to keep me at ease. He eventually closed his eyes, and if he hadn't fallen asleep, he was doing a good job faking it.

Evidently, I was capable of telling him no after all. But we'd be fine. I had to believe that.

chapter eighteen

It took Paulie a couple of weeks to recover from the flu. He lost seven pounds, which was not really weight he could afford to lose. He slept more than usual, and dark circles shadowed his eyes. The flu wasn't entirely to blame, though.

On our first day back at school after the ice storm, Daria called Paulie and completely freaked him out. She was sobbing uncontrollably and wouldn't tell him where she was. He was ready to pack a bag and take off for Kansas, even though his body was still wrecked, but I talked him into calling Aunt Ruth, who had driven to Wichita to buy a part for her sewing machine and wasn't home at the time. Aunt Ruth eventually discovered Daria in her closet surrounded by tissues and family photos she had stolen when she ran away. Neither Paulie nor Aunt Ruth had known Daria had pictures of her and Paulie's parents and siblings, and the news broke him. When he found out, he threw one of his secondhand mugs at the wall. I shuffled him into his living room, where he sat with his head in his hands while I cleaned up the chunky pieces of enamel.

After that, he called Daria every night, and more often than not, when he crawled into bed, his beautiful face was pinched and his eyes full of pain. I would hold him and tease him until the light returned to his eyes, and then he would either fall asleep or come with a smile on his lips. But cracks were beginning to show—moments of sadness or anxiety that reminded me of Diego.

Travis talked us into going to the first rave night of the semester at the Lumberyard. I hoped it would pull Paulie out of his funk. We shivered in the cold on the walk to the club, but the moment we made it through the door, air warmed by writhing bodies enveloped us.

Bouncers were passing out glow-in-the-dark snowflake necklaces at the door, and Paulie attached one to his jeans like a belt.

"Are you trying to draw attention to your package?" Travis asked him, and Paulie just grinned.

Travis was more dressed up than usual. He had on tight jeans, which made his legs seem a mile long, and a toffee-colored sweater, the sleeves rolled up and showing off his forearms. He was also wearing his glasses, which hardly ever happened. It was very coffee-shop-hipster chic, which was a good look for him. Like a *really* good look.

"Are you trying to impress someone?" I asked him.

My comment drew Paulie's attention, and he said, "Oooh, Daddy. Who's the guy?"

Then Travis did the most surprising thing. He glanced down self-consciously and mumbled that he needed a drink. I gaped at him. I'd never seen him insecure before. He pulled Paulie along with him, and I watched them whisper to each other at the bar. It should probably have bothered me that Travis would choose to divulge his secrets to Paulie rather than me, but it didn't. Paulie was better at relationships and, well, people in general.

"Joel?" someone said in my ear. It startled me. When I turned, I was assaulted with the sight of a neon-orange sweatshirt belonging to none other than David McDavid. I hadn't seen him at the Yard since the night we hooked up, but he had been wearing neon that night too. Maybe it was all he owned.

"Hi, David."

In the space of a breath, Paulie crowded against my back and slipped under my arm. I wrapped my arms over Paulie's shoulders and pulled him in front of me. David's eyes scanned us, panic growing on his face.

"David, this is my boyfriend, Paulie. You might remember him from last time."

David's face paled. "I didn't know you were together."

"Oh shit, sweetie, we weren't! We didn't hook up until after that," Paulie explained, and David visibly relaxed.

"I just wanted to say hi and see how you were doing," he said finally, eyes boring into mine. He was clearly just checking up on me out of some misguided chivalry. He had been so kind, and I had acted like a basket case. If we were somewhere without strobe lights, techno, and the smell of man and sex, I might have tried to explain myself.

Oh, who was I kidding? Of course I wouldn't have tried to explain myself.

I wanted this encounter to end so much I simply nodded and smiled.

A cute twink strolled by at that point, and he gave David a solid once-over and grin before sauntering off.

"You better go catch him before someone else does," Paulie teased, and David scurried after the guy without another word to us.

"That was a little awkward," I said. "I'm sorry."

"He was worried about you?" Paulie asked, and I nodded. "I worry about you too, buttercup. Pretty much all the time." I glanced at him in alarm, but he just smiled kindly, and I flushed. "Let's dance, Joel. I want to show you off. I want you to kiss me out there so everyone knows you're mine. I don't want the David McDavids of the world to get any ideas."

That wasn't a hardship at all. Paulie undulated against me, all loose and sexy, and I was completely mesmerized by the impossible arch of his spine. I couldn't stop running my hand down it, feeling the hot skin under his shirt. His ass was perfect in my hands, and Paulie rode my thigh hard until we were practically pawing each other's clothes off, our shirts were soaked with sweat, and I had sucked love marks all over his throat.

"Let's go home," Paulie breathed into my mouth after about an hour. The colorful lights illuminated his face, and his eyes sparkled with desperate hunger. "I'll tell Travis. He's at the bar trying to get some cowboy's attention."

"A cowboy? Is that who he dressed up for?" I asked.

"Yep. Maybe the hipster thing turns the cowboy's key?"

I followed Paulie to the edge of the dance floor, which was where we found Travis. He was chatting with a couple of girls about an assignment in their Southern Literature class.

"We're going home. You gonna be okay?" I asked Travis.

"Yeah, yeah. I'll be fine. I'm going home with that guy. He just doesn't know it yet."

I followed his finger, and sure enough, there was a cowboy sitting with a group of men and women in one of the booths. He was clean-cut and redheaded. He wasn't wearing a cowboy hat and I couldn't see if he had boots on, but I could tell he was a cowboy anyway.

"Good luck," I told Travis, and Paulie gave him a big, sweaty hug.

We headed for the shower when we got back to my house. I could smell the drying sweat on me, and my skin felt clammy and tight. In the bathroom, Paulie peeled his T-shirt off like a stripper, and I wrapped my lips around his nipple piercing, tasting salt and metal. I licked up his midline, from his navel to the notch in his throat, savoring the tang of his skin. He was sweaty too, but I liked it.

"Let's hurry," he said. "I want you in a bed."

He pushed me under the hot spray, and then soaped us both efficiently and effectively. I dried us off afterward and wrapped him in the biggest towel I owned.

It took us five minutes to make it from the bathroom to my bed. I couldn't help but press him into the wall every few feet, devour his cherry-red mouth, and relish his smooth, creamy skin against me. By the time we made it into my bedroom, my head was spinning. I felt drunk off the sweetness of his lips and the scent of soap and *him* flooding my senses. Drunk on him. Hungry for him.

I ripped his towel off, and he tumbled onto his back in the middle of my bed. I started the kisses at his calf and nipped and licked and sucked gently all the way from his calf to the back of his knee, from his knee to his fleshy thigh and the tendon in his groin. He twisted in the sheets, moaning. I liked him desperate. Needed him that way.

He smelled amazing: oranges and earth. I planted kisses around his balls, spread his butt cheeks, and ran a thumb from his taint to the enticing little bud of his ass. He whined in the back of his throat and lifted his legs so I had more access. Without thinking, I licked that perfect pink hole, and it was like a bomb detonated in my head.

Boom. Fuck. *Perfect.*

Paulie gasped my name, and I had to lick him again. Like, right now. I dipped my head again, but he seized my hair and pulled until I had no choice but to lift my head away from him.

"Joel, I've never . . . I haven't done . . . I don't know how I—"

"I haven't done this either," I said and tried to get my head back down there, but Paulie's fingers gripped my hair too fiercely for me to move.

"I'm not sure," he whispered, and I tried to slow down. To take a breath and understand what was freaking him out so much.

But it was obvious. Rimming left you vulnerable and open to your lover. It exposed you completely. And Paulie had been burned before. His eyes held that distrust, that insecurity I had seen so much of lately. I wanted it fucking gone.

"We just showered. You taste amazing. I want you like this, Paulie. Please let me keep going," I begged. After a long moment of wide eyes and harsh breaths, Paulie flipped over onto his stomach, and I groaned in relief.

Paulie's inhuman cry when I spread his cheeks and ran my tongue over his tightly puckered hole made all of my blood rush south. My whole body thrummed an unsteady tattoo, and I tasted him again. Sharp and sweet and amazing.

Fucking hell, he was sexy. His spine flexed and arched, and he made the hottest, choked-off little whimpers. I kissed and sucked on his hole until it softened, and when I pushed in slightly with the tip of my tongue, Paulie pulled the fitted sheet off the corners of my bed and writhed against my face. I needed to make him scream, make him forget everything in the face of his desire for me.

I licked him loose, savoring the feel of him against my mouth and the way his body responded. His inner muscles were tight and hot on my tongue. I wanted them wrapped around my cock, but, *God*, we'd never done that, and I was too out of control to ask for it now.

I added a finger into the mix, and Paulie's back bowed, pushing his butt up off the bed. When I found that hot spot inside of him, he screamed into the pillow. He seemed shameless now, totally wanton, not caring at all that neither of us had done this before or exactly how vulnerable of a position he was in. He pushed his body against my face, his noises needy, insistent, and incoherent.

"Fuck me. Joel, please fuck me!" he begged, desperation pitching his voice until it was deep and ravaged—no longer incoherent but, suddenly, perfectly clear. "You licked me open. Now I want you inside me."

"No!" I gasped. I couldn't. The need pounding through me was too scary.

His whimper washed my vision white. "Lick me again," he cried. So I did, and it was torture.

"Please, please, please," he pleaded at each pass of my tongue. The room spun around me. "Please, Joel. Please, it feels so good. Please fuck me. I need you. Please. Oh fuck, I need you."

And I needed it too. I wanted to be inside him so badly, so tremendously. My mind turned off with a *snap* and instinct took over. I sat up and reached for the lube. He pushed the bottle into my hands, and shit. Oh God. I was slick and balanced right at that perfect precipice of his body.

I pushed in hard and entirely too fast, but Paulie's body swallowed me like he was made to take my cock. He sobbed his relief into the pillow, real tears on his cheeks. Holy hell, he was tight. His muscles quivered and squeezed me in an extraordinary vise; slick and so hot I felt like I was going up in flames. My second stroke inside, slow and hard, forced another wild wail out of Paulie, and I couldn't believe that this was happening. It really shouldn't be happening *bare*.

Oh fuck, I was bare. But, God, it *was* happening now, and it felt so good, and I couldn't stop. Didn't *want* to stop. Paulie turned his face, and I could see his profile—the shadow of his eyelashes on his red cheeks, the stubbly jaw, his wet mouth. He bit his lip on a groan on my next stroke, and I needed him on his back so I could kiss that sinful mouth.

I licked a path up his spine, feeling each vertebra under my tongue, and then I couldn't help but suck a hickey onto his shoulder blade. He shook underneath me, his body strung taut.

"Need you on your back," I gasped against his neck, and he nodded.

He released a cry when I pulled out and flipped him over. This was when logic should return. This was when I should slow down and suit up. Or stop completely. Yeah, I should stop completely. This was too crazy. Too out of control. But I didn't want to stop. Paulie's eyes rolled back when I pushed inside him again.

"Yes. There. Right there," he sobbed, so I hit that spot again and again. Paulie's fingernails scrabbled on my shoulders, and I'd have scratches there in the morning. I loved that. I wanted his marks all over my skin. I kissed him and tried to make it gentle and loving, even though my whole body was feverish and slick with sweat, screaming at me to take him hard and fast. Paulie threw one leg over my shoulder, flexible bastard, and the other up around my waist and carded his fingers through my hair. He clung to me.

"I've never felt like this before," he gasped into my mouth.

Me neither. Nothing had ever felt as good as Paulie's ass pulsing and milking me. The way his muscles pulled me in and tried to keep me there. His soft lips clinging to my mouth. I was flayed open, and so close to him, closer than I'd ever been to anyone. Everything was sharper. Brighter. Better. I loved when he fucked me. But this . . . God, this was unprecedented.

Paulie surrendered, his body bared to me and his eyes wide and glazed. He arched and tipped his head back, the vein beating in his neck, his very lifeblood, offered up to me. I licked it and imagined the taste of copper.

He grabbed for his cock with both hands, clearly trying to push himself over the edge. And . . . *nope.* I wanted control. I pulled his hands off his prick, and pinned them above his head. His leg slipped off my shoulder, and I completely covered him, our bodies in contact everywhere. He stared up at me, frantic and desperate, so I kissed him lightly.

"You can come like this, right?"

He whimpered, a little noise of abandon and affirmation.

"Fight for it, then," I whispered against his lips. The cry that ripped from his throat was part frustration, part arousal, and my whole body throbbed. He struggled against my hold, hips snapping against me and arms straining to find a weakness.

"Yes! Joel, fuck!" he groaned, long and drawn out like he was dying.

"Reach for it, love. Come on."

His eyes snapped to mine, and he looked so fierce and happy, my heart ached. All of me ached. I thrust inside him hard, trapping his drooling cock between us, giving him just enough pressure, and with that familiar, wonderful sob, his body tensed. His eyes rolled back in his head again, and *oh*, I had never realized how sexy that could be.

Paulie's ass gripped my cock so tightly I could barely move. Sweet and perfect. His hot come splattered between us, painting my chest and making my glide against him wetter, smoother. My skin washed cold and hot, pleasure radiating out from the base of my spine and shooting to the tips of my toes and fingers. My whole body clenched.

I'd never felt this good before. This close to someone. This in love. Never been so consumed, so lost. My heart beat his name. Paulie. *Paulie.* I loved him, and he was beautiful and perfect and better. His ass still pulsed around me, harder than Diego's ever had. And it was better. *Better.* With that final thought flying through my brain, my vision slipped to black, the joy of release rushed over me, and I came so violently I collapsed.

chapter nineteen

I was never able to predict when regret would pummel me. I had been the type of child who had been surprised to get sick after gorging on too much candy. I had been the teenager who hadn't considered the repercussions of sending a dirty text message to my high school sweetheart when he was driving until it was entirely too late. I was the man who'd finally fucked my boyfriend, and I hadn't expected the regret until it swallowed me whole. Like a black, torrential downpour, when you only anticipate a sprinkle. Like the obliterating pain when someone dies without warning.

Like the anger that filled me when I saw Paulie's sated smile as my carefully constructed world collapsed around me.

Moments before, I had been so full of hope and desire and love, but now I felt empty. I felt regret. I felt Diego slipping through my fingers with a frightening finality. All it had taken for me to betray him, to betray the memory of Diego, had been a sweet smile and some begging from a guy I had known for a couple of months. A guy who was not the sort of man I'd ever pictured myself with. Fuck, even my dad had seen that.

Come leaked out around my cock, hot and sticky, and my stomach roiled. I ripped myself from Paulie's body, and he yelped in surprise, then froze, still and wary, like a cornered animal. I was going to vomit. Or cry. Probably cry. I paced to the other end of the room.

"Don't make me do that again," I panted. I couldn't look at him, naked and covered in sweat and spunk. His and mine.

"*Make* you do that?" The incredulity in his voice was unmistakable. *Good!* I wanted to fight. He sat up and started getting dressed.

"Yes!" I snapped, jerking on my boxers and sweatpants. I couldn't be naked in front of him. Didn't ever want to be naked again.

"I didn't make you do anything, Joel. What's wrong?" He inched his way toward me, slowly, like maybe I was the cornered animal. The room was spinning.

"Well you certainly begged for it like a . . . like a—"

"Like a slutty little faggot?" he asked, voice quiet and deadly.

"Exactly!" I faced him head-on then, ready to rend apart the patchwork of our relationship even more, but his expression stopped me. His eyes were wide, and rather than bright and lively and full of fight, they were dull.

He sucked in a gasp, like he couldn't breathe.

Ah, shit. He'd been called that before. And my world cleaved in two. How could I hurt him so badly? I loved him. Despite my haze of confusion and anger and disgust, I knew I loved him. But I also wanted to rip us apart, to wash him from my skin, to punish us both for crossing a line I hadn't even known was there until we'd barreled through it. It was a relief, almost, to ruin everything, and a sour rush of euphoria crashed through me.

"Paulie," I started, ready to end things completely. I couldn't stand to look at his wounded expression any longer.

"Don't," he snapped. "I know this is about Diego. I'm not fucking blind."

I shook my head in laughable denial.

"Answer this, Joel," he said, voice low and slippery in its anger. "Why did you hide your past from me? From everyone? I never asked you that. Why didn't you tell me about Diego from the beginning? I've done nothing but be there for you. Why is it such a big fucking secret? Why! Why! Why are you such a scared little boy?"

I reeled back like he'd smacked me. And I didn't know how to answer. I only knew I'd feared exposing my grief. I'd dreaded facing pity.

"I'm not him, Joel. And I'll never be him, so just . . . don't say anything else. And stay away from me."

He bent down for his backpack on his way out the door, and a fat teardrop dripped from his nose to the carpet. He didn't look at me as he left. He just . . . left.

It wasn't until hours later when the sky was icy pink with dawn—hours after Travis came home alone and I'd stared up at my popcorn ceiling for ages, holding off the emotions broiling beneath the surface—that I remembered Paulie's car hadn't been at my house. We'd left it at his apartment. He'd had no means to get home without calling someone else or walking in the frigid cold wearing nothing but a long-sleeved T-shirt and jeans with a glow-in-the-dark belt.

I stood, rushed to the bathroom, and threw up. It was violent and painful and much less than I deserved.

It took me no time at all, once I was done retching, to grasp the enormity of my screw-up. Paulie was like vanilla ice cream, and clean sheets, and the smell of mint toothpaste. He was all the good things. He'd pulled me out of this darkness I'd let fester inside of me, that I was still letting fester inside of me. Every day more sun seeped in, and I didn't want to live without the light.

Yeah, maybe the intimacy was getting to me. Maybe we were moving too fast, but that seemed like such a miniscule issue now. Something I should have talked to him about rather than blamed him for.

I waited until 9 a.m. to go over to his apartment. I didn't sleep at all, and part of me didn't want to shower. I could still smell him on my skin—oranges and spunk and lube—and I hated to wash that away. It might be the last time.

When I pulled into Paulie's apartment complex, I knew in my gut that he wouldn't be home. He would have risen early and set out to distract himself from his fuckup of a boyfriend. I parked my truck right in front of his apartment and sat on his stoop to wait.

The wind was cutting and cold, but I didn't feel it. I rested my head in my hands and tried to stave off the headache building from my lack of sleep and holding back tears. An hour later, I glanced up.

It was like the particles in the atmosphere vibrated to alert me to his presence. He hadn't made a noise, but I knew he was there as surely as if he'd shouted my name. He was leaning against the side of my truck, and it looked like he had been there a couple of minutes at least. While I had been drowning in my own personal misery, he'd been standing there waiting for me to notice him. There was a lesson in there somewhere, and it probably had to do with me being a selfish asshole.

Paulie didn't seem happy or angry to see me. It felt like he hardly saw me at all.

"Hi," I said with a brittle smile. His expression didn't change. "Paulie, I'm so sorry. I feel so horrible about last night."

"*You* feel horrible. Is that why you're sorry? Because *you* feel bad?" The derision jolted me. This was not going to be pretty.

He walked past me and through his front door. It was left open, so I followed him into his colorful kitchen, where he'd braced himself against the counter. I was surprised . . . I couldn't believe that the kitchen of all places was where this was going to go down. He spun to face me.

"Do you have any idea what it feels like—" His calm broke and anguish washed through his eyes. "Do you have any idea what it feels like to be treated s

o callously by the man you love? To insinuate I pushed you into something you didn't want? That I'm a slut? Can you imagine that? I was still naked, for fuck's sake!"

And I couldn't imagine. While Diego and I had had our share of problems, he'd never treated me so cruelly, and if he had, it would have crushed me. More than that, if *Paulie* had acted that way toward me, I would have been wrecked. Because I did love Paulie. I had for so long. I'd just never had the stones to say it.

Maybe I could tilt us back to an even keel.

"Paulie, I'm sorry. And I love you. I love you so—"

"Fuck you!" he shouted. I jumped and he took a step toward me. "You don't get to say that now. For one, it is totally unfair. And two, I don't believe for a second that it's true."

I started to object because it was really, truly, absolutely true, but Paulie talked over me.

"You're a liar, Joel. You lie. That's what you do. All the time as far as I can tell, and you have from the beginning. And you don't lie to spare others' feelings or to simplify things or to make others feel better. *Oh, hell no*! You lie to avoid personal pain. You lie to save yourself from discomfort and hurt. It's selfish and cowardly. So yes, you know that losing me will hurt, at least a little. If nothing else, you're going to lose a steady fuck. So lie some more, Joel. Go ahead. Lie to postpone the pain."

He had my number—that was for fucking sure. I *was* a liar, but losing him would hurt more than "a little." The heat of tears pushed behind my eyelids, and I tried to blink it away.

"I'm sorry, Paulie. And not because it hurts that you're mad at me. I'm sorry because I've caused you pain when you didn't deserve it. And I'm sorry for every time I've lied or kept something from you. I promise, I never did it with the intent to hurt you. You *have* to believe me."

The space between us, the distance from one counter to the other in Paulie's narrow galley kitchen, felt vast and wrong. I wanted to reach out and grab him, but didn't have the nerve.

"No. I really *don't* have to believe you. What is it you want, Joel? You've apologized, and, guess what? I'll even accept your apology. I won't be getting over last night anytime soon, though."

I knew he wouldn't. Paulie was insecure about sex. He'd been through too many one-offs where he'd felt used afterward, and I could hardly imagine the pain I had inflicted on him the night before. The thought made my gorge rise again.

"I don't want to break up. I don't want to lose you."

He looked at me fiercely. "Then stop hiding, and tell me the truth!"

I nodded. This would end poorly.

"What the hell was last night about? You were like a crazy person. You just snapped."

"What we did felt good," I said weakly.

"No shit it felt good, Joel. *Jesus Christ*!"

"I love him, Paulie!" I bit out. "I love him and I don't want to lose him, okay? And I am losing him. I can feel it. Each time I kiss you or love you, he's slipping through my fingers and I'm not ready. I can't lose him yet. I don't know how to keep going if I lose him again!"

That had all spilled out way too easily, like it had been building there for ages, and Paulie's jaw-dropped, gobsmacked reaction to my words would have almost been funny but for the tears in his eyes.

He scrubbed a shaking hand down his face, and something inside me cracked.

I reached for him, but he turned toward the sink full of dirty coffee cups. He ran his fingers over the rim of a bright-green one with a weenie dog on the side. It was *my* mug—the one I always used.

"I love you," I said. "And it's scaring the shit out of me. Last night, how much I needed you, how close I felt to you—I've never felt that before. Not even with Diego. I don't know how to cope. I'm not ready to feel that yet."

"You love me?" he asked, facing me again.

"More than anything," I said, and realized it was the truth. He closed his eyes, and a tear slid a track down his cheek. I stepped up to him and rested my forehead on his shoulder.

"You never said it back. Guess now I know why."

"You told me not to. Not until I was ready." This next bit was going to hurt him, but now that I'd started telling the truth, it was a relief. "I'm not sure I'll ever be ready."

Paulie pulled out of my arms.

"Is that why you didn't want to go bare? Because you did that with Diego, and you weren't ready to do it with me?"

Oh God. Paulie had wanted to ditch the rubbers for ages, had wanted to be that close to me. And then I'd taken what should have been a positive emotional experience for us and made it horrible and traumatic for him.

"Diego and I always used condoms. I've never had sex without a condom until last night. I swear, Paulie."

"So was the issue that you never got to experience it with him, so you didn't want it with me?"

I'd never been able to really articulate my reticence about going bare, but his suggestion nudged at me, like it was closing in on the truth.

"Maybe a little. I don't honestly know. I was just scared," I admitted.

His tears stopped, and anger lit his eyes again. He squeezed the bridge of his nose. "One day, you were on the phone with your mom. She asked you who you were talking to, and you told her *no one*. You said I was no one."

I racked my brain, trying to remember the conversation he was talking about, but everything was happening too fast. I hadn't told either of my parents about Paulie, not until I screamed it in their faces. But, even then, I hadn't really told them *about* him. That he was sweet and kind. That he was a good dresser and a better dancer and could make anyone smile. That he looked at me like I was something special.

"I'm sorry," I whispered.

"You were also embarrassed to have your dad meet me," he snapped.

"No, I was nervous he would be an asshole to you. He's not a very nice person."

"I heard what he said that night, about me not being what he expected for you. I'm too swishy. He made a big deal about how I wasn't like Diego."

"My dad's opinion means very little to me." But, shit, Dad's words had hurt. They had made me second-guess Paulie, if only for a moment.

"How can that be true, Joel?" he asked, and tears flooded his eyes again. He wiped his cheeks angrily. "My dad threw me away like a gum wrapper, but if he showed up tomorrow, it would matter to me what he thought of my life. It's not right or fair, but it's true."

"Paulie," I said raggedly, gutted. I reached for him again, but he backed away, his eyes huge and scared.

"Don't touch me." His words ripped a hole through me.

Paulie took a deep breath and let it out slowly. "This is how I see it, Joel. I wanted it too bad. Wanted everything. That's where I failed here, and that's on me. I wanted you from the moment I saw you in class that first day. Then I l-loved you, even though it was too soon." His voice hitched and faltered. "And then I wanted you to fuck me so badly I begged for it like a little—a little b-bitch. And that's unattractive. It's so embarrassing, I hate that I have to face you at all."

Shame pushed a sob into my throat, and I choked it down. "You're twisting the truth, Paulie! That's not how it happened! I fucked this up, not you. And I wanted you too. From the beginning. I wanted to be inside you so badly, with you so badly, sometimes it was all I could think about. And I loved you from the beginning. I just didn't realize it right away." My voice cracked at the end, and I pressed trembling fingers against my lips, trying to stem the tumult that wanted to burst forth.

"I don't believe you," he whispered, and my tears started to fall. "I know that you . . . that you still love Diego, and I would never in a million years want you to stop loving him. But you have filled up your heart so full of memories, and lies, and rules that you haven't left room for anything else. Or *anyone* else. And I can't be Diego, Joel. You know, maybe I'm selfish, but I don't want to be s-second. I want to be with someone who loves me first, not as a consolation prize or because the person they really want is d-dead." Paulie wiped the tears off my face but let his own fall freely. "One day, sweetheart, you're going to learn that there is room for both. There is room for Diego and your memories of him and your love for him. But there is also room for a healthy new relationship. Your love for Diego and your memories will always be there, but they won't rule you. One day, when enough time has passed, you'll fall in love with s-someone else and it won't hurt so much. The new love won't compete with your love for him." He took a shuddery breath and let it out slowly through his nose. "But I don't want to wait, and I deserve better than second fiddle."

The room tilted, and I grabbed the counter. My chest hurt, like a spike had been shoved into my ribs. And my heart was beating too fast. My breath coming too quick.

I was losing him.

No. I'd *lost* him.

I ate him up with my eyes, trying to imprint every bit of him into my mind as fast as I could before he kicked me from his life completely.

Stubbled jaw, chapped lips, sharp shoulders, smooth skin, dark eyes.

But, *God*, his eyes. They weren't right at all.

No, they were red and swollen and full of tears. I touched his bottom lip with my thumb and the slight movement caused one of his tears to slip into the corner of his mouth. I probably wouldn't see his smile again.

My tears fell faster, and a sob caught in my throat. He closed his eyes, perhaps trying to shield me from his pain or protect himself from mine.

I crossed my arms over my chest. "If it hurts us both this much to break up, maybe it's not the right thing."

He opened his eyes and smiled then, but his smile was sad and watery. I caught a tiny peek of that gap I loved so much. And then he kissed me—a light touch of lips and a soft hand on my cheek—and said, "People break up, Joel. That's just part of life. You need to learn to live yours." He stepped back, his hand falling away from me. "Bye, buttercup."

I never knew how I got home. I didn't remember leaving Paulie's apartment or getting in my truck, but eventually I ended up back in front of my crappy house. I stumbled inside and found Travis's stash of beer. It was juvenile and stupid, but I got drunk and passed out in bed so I didn't have to think about the huge hole that would be there when I woke up.

chapter twenty

travis ambushed me in the kitchen Monday morning before class. I had woken up, showered, and dressed, but our expired carton of milk had been one obstacle too many, and I had just decided I was too sick to go to class when he found me.

"What the hell is going on? Did you and Paulie break up? You've been hiding in your room for two days. I texted Paulie yesterday about this cowboy from Grindr and he said, and I quote, 'Please don't text me for a while. You're his friend first, and I need some time.' Then he said that if I didn't know what he was talking about, I needed to make 'that idiot' talk to me. So here I am, idiot, and we're talking."

Travis pulled me toward the living room, and I set the sour milk on the kitchen counter as we passed it.

"Milk's bad," I told him numbly. He pushed me down on the couch and cupped my face between his hands. The touch was gentle and tender, which was not like us at all.

"What happened, Joel?"

The tears didn't come like I expected. I'd pretty much cried constantly since I left Paulie's and was tapped out. I started to shake, though.

"We broke up," I said, but Travis had obviously already figured that out. "I did something horrible, and I can't fix it."

I saw Travis wanting to ask me more details, to force me to tell him everything. And I saw the moment he decided it was a lost cause.

Absurdly, that made my eyes fill with tears again.

Travis hugged me. "It hurts, doesn't it?"

I nodded, and he made shushing and consoling noises in my ear. Eventually, though, he had to get up and go to class, and I went back to bed.

A week later, the days still passed in a fog. I hadn't seen or spoken to Paulie, but Travis had. After about two days of finding sweatshirts, colorful socks, a scarf, and a notebook full of class notes, Travis and I had purged the whole house, and he'd kindly taken the box to Paulie.

When Travis had returned from Paulie's apartment, he'd looked the way I'd normally felt after spending time with Paulie—invigorated and joyful. I'd almost asked how Paulie was doing, but Travis's good mood had been proof. Paulie was fine.

I was evidently petty enough to wish he were suffering as much as me.

Every morning it hurt to wake up without him in my bed. Every afternoon, mental muscle memory made me want to call him or drive over to his apartment. I craved my connection to him.

Eventually, Travis tired of my moping, and begged me to figure out a way to fix my mess, but I didn't know how. Besides, Paulie deserved better than someone as fucked up as me. If nothing else, I believed that.

Another week went by, and I managed to catch up on my homework without having to explain myself to any of my professors. Most nights I had to convince myself not to get drunk, but even in my funk, I could see that was a poor idea. It mirrored how I'd handled losing Diego a little too closely. When Diego died, I had drowned out my grief with casual sex. I refused to do the same thing with Paulie and alcohol. I wasn't going to hide from pain this time. I wasn't going to be a coward.

As the semester wore on, Dr. Yamato and I started meeting after her seminar class, supposedly to discuss the preservation project. More often than not, though, we just chatted about history and life.

One day, without any forethought, I told her that my high school boyfriend had died reading a text message from me while driving.

I'd never told anyone about what happened with Diego without being pushed or bullied into it, and my world didn't even crash down around me. When I said the words, over *tea* of all fucking things, she didn't look at me with pity but with understanding. She reached across the expanse of her modern desk and patted my hand.

"Is that where your interest in history comes from?"

"No, I've always liked history."

"I was just wondering. I've found through the years that some people who have traumatic pasts or have experienced acute loss feel powerful connections to history. It's like the past holds more weight to them because they understand that it stays with the people living in the present."

"I'm not sure that's exactly served me well," I admitted. "I've allowed my past to screw up every relationship in my life. Family, friends, boyfriend. Well, ex-boyfriend."

"It'll make you a good historian, even if it makes you a lousy partner," she teased, and I actually smiled.

A small framed picture on a bookshelf beside her desk caught my eye. I stood up abruptly and walked over to it. It was a picture of Dr. Yamato and a man, but I hardly noticed the people. Rolling, grassy hills with scattered cattle and twisting creeks stretched out behind the smiling couple. It looked like the Flint Hills, and my heart lodged hard in my throat.

I'd taken the photography print Paulie had gotten me for Christmas off the wall because I wasn't getting any sleep with it hanging above my dresser. At night, I had found myself staring at it, eyes glazed, and longing to drive to the middle of nowhere. I hadn't thrown it away or returned it to Paulie, but now it lived out of sight between the back of my desk and the wall. Seeing this picture was like ice water in a drought.

"Where was this taken?"

"Scotland," Dr. Yamato said. "Our honeymoon. That's my ex-husband."

"Oh!" I yelped, and placed the picture back on the bookshelf and turned toward her. "I'm sorry. I shouldn't have touched it."

"It's fine. We're still close. What drew you to the picture? Really into kilts?" she teased. I glanced at the photo and noticed for the first time that the man was in fact wearing a kilt. I'd been so sure it was the Flint Hills I hadn't even noticed the sexy highlander garb. Heat crept up my cheeks.

"No, it looks like the Flint Hills in Kansas. I really like that part of the country," I said.

The next day I got an email from Dr. Yamato saying she had arranged for us to meet with the mayor's office in a small town south of Emporia about digitizing their old newspapers. *It'll be a treat for you*, she wrote. We wouldn't go until late in the summer, so maybe I would have enough time to prepare for the flood of pain I'd surely feel being back there without Paulie.

After I read the email, I locked my bedroom door and cried. Just a little bit.

Then I hung the photography print back on the wall. Best to start preparing now.

"I'll think about it," I told my mom. She wanted me to visit her for spring break in three weeks. I didn't want to go but couldn't think of an easy excuse off the top of my head.

"Okay. I guess that's all we can ask for."

Wariness prickled in the back of my mind.

"'We'?"

She sighed, and silence stretched between us. Finally she said, "I was going to tell you but didn't know how: your dad will be here. He got a job at a plant outside of town. He has his own apartment."

I closed my eyes, but the sick panic didn't hit me like it would have in the past. Maybe I was numb now.

"I'm glad you guys are working it out, Mom." I even kind of meant it.

"Thank you, baby boy. Think about coming. I miss you."

"Miss you too."

I hung up, and not for the first time—more like the *ten millionth time*—I wished I could talk to Paulie.

A couple of days later, Dad called, which was a college first.

"I just want to make sure it's okay with you that I'll be around if you come up at spring break," he told me.

"Mom said you would be," I hedged.

"Right. I know. But I could be scarce if you would rather not see me."

"It's fine, Dad. I don't really care."

I was tired of caring about my parents' fucked-up relationship. Maybe if I stopped caring, it would finally work itself out.

"What's wrong? You sound out of sorts."

"It's nothing," I told him. Then Paulie's words floated back to me through the piles of dross drumming through my mind. I hadn't claimed him to my parents all those months ago, when it counted. And Paulie was so much more than *no one* and *nothing*. Even as my now-ex-boyfriend, he was everything. "Paulie and I broke up."

My dad made a little choking noise, and I laughed. This was certainly more than he bargained for. "I'm sorry, son."

"Oh, no, you're not! You didn't even like him."

"Now wait just a damn minute. I did not dislike that little fruitcake. He made me dinner, which automatically makes me like him. I was just surprised that he was the man you chose." I didn't have the energy to touch the fruitcake comment. I rested my head on my desk. "Joel," he continued, using my name for once. "He's not like Diego, and I was worried you were dating him because he's the opposite."

And all the thoughts, all the realizations I'd had in the weeks since I'd lost Paulie came barreling out. "I was dating him because I love him. And you're right. He isn't like Diego at all. He treated me better, for one. He was proud of being my boyfriend, even though I gave him all kinds of reasons to distrust me. He's open and funny and warm, and those were things that Diego simply wasn't. Diego was dark and serious and so sad to be gay, and I felt unsure of myself every day I was with him. But Paulie made me feel normal and happy. And I screwed it up."

"Sounds like you need to figure out a way to get him back, then, son. It's not easy, though. Let me tell you."

"It's too late. He doesn't want me anymore." Dad didn't respond, and embarrassment at unloading on him crept through me. "Shit, I'm sorry for—" *dumping my heartache on you.* I couldn't finish the sentence. I should have been able to talk to my parents about my problems. "I just wanted to tell you what's going on in my life."

Dad paused, and blood pounded in my ears, making the silence heavy.

"I'm glad you told me," he said finally.

I sighed and laid my head back down. "I am too, Dad."

chapter twenty-one

travis was up to something, but I didn't have the energy to figure him out. He grilled us real-life sirloins on his George Foreman *and* let me pick the movie. I picked a Western, *Unforgiven*, and Travis actually didn't complain. He also didn't bring up Paulie or ask me for the one zillionth time how I was doing. The house smelled like steak and kettle popcorn. And I felt okay.

"Will you go to the Lumberyard with me tomorrow?" he asked. I must have looked alarmed, because he made a soothing sound. "It'll be fun. I promise. You need to get out of the house, Joel. Tomorrow's a Wednesday, so it won't be super busy and neither of us have class Thursday morning. We can get a couple drinks, dance a little, and be home before midnight. Just two dudes blowing off some steam."

"I'll go with you to Ropers." There was no chance of running into Paulie at Ropers.

"Paulie won't be there," Travis said, because I was transparent as all fuck. "He only goes on the weekends."

I shut my eyes against the small shock of pain that raced through me. I would love to see Paulie. I would love to see his smile and drink up his warmth. But it would gut me to see him dancing and flirting with other people.

"Why can't we go somewhere else?" I whined.

"Okay, cards on the table, dude. I want to know your opinion on this guy I like. He's there fairly often on Wednesdays. And I would know—I'm practically stalking him. But I can't get a good read. His Grindr profile says he's bi, and he's always with a group of people, and there's this girl that hangs all over him. I need my extra-special wingman—that's you—to tell me if I have a chance. He acts like he doesn't even fucking see me."

Travis looked down at his lap. I couldn't remember him ever being this worked up over a guy. Normally, he didn't have to try that hard. It kind of delighted me.

"What does he look like?"

"He has reddish hair and this farmer-cowboy vibe."

"Whoa!" I gasped. "Is this the same guy you were trying to get with before Paulie and I broke up?"

He nodded, and his expression was so forlorn I sighed. "I guess it won't kill me to go to the Yard."

Travis grinned and pointed at me. "You're not going to regret this, Joel. You need a fun night out. You need to let loose a little."

"You might be right."

But the next night, the Lumberyard felt off. *Everyone* on the dance floor seemed to be grinding hot and heavy, and a sense of hunger blanketed the room. The place, even though it was less crowded than a weekend night, screamed, *Young and down-to-fuck.*

We beelined for the bar, and Travis ordered us both Crown and Coke. My head spun. This was wrong. Being *here* wasn't right at all.

"Do you see your cowboy?" I asked Travis, and he shook his head.

"Maybe he'll get here in a bit," he said.

We drank in silence until a hot tank of a man walked past us, and Travis reached out and grasped his huge biceps. The guy wasn't tall, maybe five foot nine or so, but he was barrel-chested and beefy.

"Leighton! Nice to see you," purred Travis.

The guy—Leighton, evidently—smiled, slow and sexy.

"Dance with my friend here." Travis snatched the drink out of my hand and pushed me into the dude. Leighton laughed and helped me balance myself before pulling me toward the dance floor. I shot Travis a dirty glare, but he just grinned at me.

"I'm a horrible dancer," Leighton said. His voice was a high, feminine tenor and completely at odds with his bulk. "But I like to have fun. Name's Leighton." He gave my hand, which he was already using to drag me onto the dance floor, a rigorous shake.

"I'm Joel. I'm not looking to hook up, but I could be down for some dancing." Paulie had taught me that dancing could be fun. Maybe I could learn to have fun with someone besides him.

"Oh, you heartbreaker! I can be your dance partner, but like I said, I suck at it."

By now, we were in the writhing throng of bodies, and an old Britney Spears remix flowed through the speakers. Leighton let loose, and he wasn't actually a horrible dancer. He was just silly. He vogued and performed amateur break-dance moves and sashayed around like the dance floor was a runway.

It was *perfect*. I wanted to go back and smack a kiss on Travis's conniving mug because he must have known what he was getting me into when he pulled Leighton out of the crowd.

Leighton's dancing was infectious, and soon a whole mob of people was dancing with him in a small circle. I swayed and jumped and sang along. During the next song, Travis joined us, and he flung an arm over my shoulder.

"No cowboy yet," he breathed into my ear.

"Yee haw."

We danced for about an hour, but eventually Travis and I ducked out to get another drink. While I was leaning against the bar, waiting for the bartender to make her way down toward Travis and me, someone tapped on my arm. I almost clipped Angie's chin with my shoulder when I turned, and she took a quick step back.

"Oh! Are you okay, Angie? I'm so sorry!" The hair on my arms and the back of my neck stood on end. Travis froze beside me.

"I'm fine, Joel. I just wanted to say hi and tell you that I'm really sorry things didn't work out with you and Paulie." She gave me an awkward but sweet hug. "He told me what happened. I know that maybe sucks a little because I'm sure you didn't want your history spread all over the universe, but he needed to talk about it. I think I'm the only one that he told."

A shiver of anxiety worked its way up my spine. I hadn't considered the fact that Paulie would tell people my story. I didn't like it, but I couldn't blame him.

"That's fine. It's good he has someone he can talk to." I forced a small, fake smile.

Angie rolled her eyes. Per usual. "Paulie's such an idiot. He has no idea what he gave up. You're too sweet. I've told him that a million times."

"He's not an idiot. I was an asshole, and he deserves better. Don't give him a hard time about it."

"See, you're sweet. I'm glad to see you back out in the scene. You shouldn't hide away." She smiled, squeezed my arm, and sauntered off to a table of her friends. I recognized all of them.

I turned to Travis, who was still frozen in place, anger etched on his face.

"He wasn't supposed to be here," he gritted out.

Panic and excitement both closed in on me at once. The desire to see Paulie mixed with the fear of actually facing him again. The lights of the bar suddenly seemed too bright, and my drink soured in my stomach.

"Bathroom," I croaked at Travis before turning out of the grip he tried to get on my shoulder.

I strode toward the bathroom, which was through a seedy hallway. Couples sometimes snuck into the hallway to get their rocks off without the bouncers seeing. It was very *Queer as Folk*. Management let it happen. Thankfully, the hallway was clear. I slipped into the empty bathroom and tried not to have a panic attack. Or dry heave. After a couple of minutes and a face full of cold water, I felt composed enough to make it back through the bar. *Puking not imminent.*

I turned the corner out of the bathroom and almost smacked into a couple pressing each other into the cement wall.

I could tell immediately one of the men was Paulie, even in the dark with another guy all over him. The shape of him, the graceful way he moved, his noises—he would be burned into my mind forever. Paulie's head was tipped back, his eyes closed, and the other guy was kissing his neck. My skin prickled, and I imagined the smell of oranges. A familiar low moan reached me, and I rushed past. They didn't seem to have noticed me standing there.

As I made it back to the main area of the bar, Travis tried to slow me down, but I needed fresh air. I needed to breathe. Like right fucking now.

"I'm sorry, Joel. *Oh fuck.* I didn't know he was going to be here. And I didn't see them all arrive because we were dancing. I'm so sorry. God, I'm sorry. Joel, slow down!"

I had to get out of here, and if I opened my mouth to respond, I wouldn't make it.

I stumbled outside, and a cold wind knocked the air out of my lungs. Travis kept talking, but I couldn't hear him over the thunderous throb of blood in my ears. I hurried away from the entrance of the bar, hoping I could make it to the back alley before it was too late. Travis and I rounded the corner, and with a hand on the wall, I ralphed up the Crown and Coke. Travis rubbed a rough circle on my back.

My head pounded like the worst hangover ever, and I was pretty sure I was going to puke again. I needed a couple of minutes before I could move. Travis leaned his back against the building and apologized over and over. Eventually, footsteps pattered toward us from around the corner, but I was too miserable to straighten up.

"Joel! Oh my God, are you all right?"

I whipped upright at Paulie's voice. His whole face flushed crimson, and his eyes were wild.

And, holy hell, did this really have to happen right by my puddle of sick?

Paulie was slightly unsteady on his feet, and redness rimmed his eyes. Embarrassment and anger soaked me with sweat.

"You're drunk," I said, because I was super smooth. Paulie hardly ever got drunk.

The crunch of another set of footsteps rounded the corner, but I couldn't peel my eyes off of him.

"Shit, Paulie! There you are! I thought I'd lost you," said the new addition to our happy little group. And yep, we were still standing next to my vomit. Just wonderful.

It was Alex, the guy I'd hooked up with in sophomore year and who Paulie had fooled around with before we got together. It had to have been Alex making out with Paulie in the hallway by the bathroom. I turned on him.

"What do you think you're doing?" I yelled. "He's drunk! You can't take advantage of a drunk guy like that. What's wrong with you?"

Travis tried to grab me, but Paulie got there first and gave me a tiny shove in the chest. "Back off, Joel!" he barked.

"They're together," Travis breathed in my ear, and my head snapped toward Travis so fast my neck popped.

"What?" I gasped.

"I'm sorry I didn't tell you. Paulie and Alex are together."

My knees threatened to buckle, and I clenched my gaping mouth shut to try to prevent the bile rising in my throat from making an escape.

"Yeah, asshole," Paulie snarled. "You don't get to care what happens to me anymore. You don't get to tell me what to do. You're not my boyfriend. I wasn't just going to wait around for you to get over your dead high school lover. I wasn't going to just be here whenever you decided you might want me! He's my boyfriend now." Paulie jabbed an angry finger in Alex's direction. "And guess what? He'll actually fuck me like a man!" He spun around, albeit unsteadily, and marched to the end of the alley.

Travis followed him, and I could hear heated words being exchanged. Paulie wiped at his cheeks with sharp, stilted movements, and I sucked in an unsteady breath.

Alex took a step toward me, and I fell back a little.

"Whoa! Hey, it's okay," Alex said, his hands up in a calming gesture. "Joel, Paulie's really drunk, and he's going to regret saying that to you tomorrow. I promise. His sister hasn't been doing well, and he's stressed. And I'm not taking advantage. I'm taking him home. I'm sorry."

I nodded stiffly. Alex was nice. He always had been, but when we'd fooled around, he hadn't been interested in relationships. That must have changed.

Travis's raised voice floated toward us. "I fucking asked you if you were going to be here, and you told me *no*, Paulie! What the fuck were you thinking?"

"Hey!" I shouted toward the end of the alley. "Don't yell at him, Trav."

Travis threw his hands up in the air and strode back to me, leaving Paulie alone and dejected. My eyes met Paulie's, and his obvious misery was so gut-wrenching that I wanted to scream. Tears were slipping down his face unchecked now. He turned on his heel without another word and walked away.

After seeing Paulie at the Yard, the pain was as acute as it had been right after we broke up. Maybe more so now that I knew the extent of his anger and hurt. And I had been doing better. Opening up to people, like my dad and Dr. Yamato. But none of that mattered if Paulie hated me.

I went to class, ate with Travis, and retreated to my room every night. Sometimes, I called one of my parents, just to chat and think about anything other than how sad I was. I felt entirely too pathetic.

My main regret was that Travis was so mad at Paulie they had stopped talking. Travis also quit chasing his cowboy, but he wouldn't give me the details. I suspected something ugly had gone down, but he acted like the guy had never existed at all.

With just a week until spring break, Travis talked me into camping out at Black Kettle National Grassland over the weekend. We brought the bare minimum: tent, sleeping bags, flashlights, camp chairs, beer.

The campground was just a flat, grassy field with a couple of trees, and there was only one other campsite occupied by a family with small kids. When we arrived, the dad was playing folk songs on the guitar, his wife was listening, and the children were tossing a Frisbee around. I sat on the picnic table at our campsite and watched them while Travis unloaded our stuff from the back of my truck.

"Hey, asshole! You gonna help me set this tent up, or what?" Travis teased as he skipped over to me. He followed my gaze, and then sat beside me.

"My family never seemed that normal. Did yours?"

"We were normal in a different way. We do the dinner parties and the over-expressions of wealth. We're upper-middle-class normal. Not tent-camping normal."

I smiled. Travis complained, but he knew how lucky he was.

"Paulie's family probably looked like that when he was a child. Happy, like an AARP commercial. But, really, they were so fucked up."

"He hasn't had an easy life," Travis said.

"Nope. He deserves an easy life. A good one, you know?"

Travis scrunched his nose up and frowned, but then nodded.

"When I think about my future, that's what I want," I said with a gesture to our neighbors.

"You want a wife and kids and a guitar?"

"Well, not the wife bit. And I'm not sure about the kids. I want camping with my family; whoever that is. I want normal."

"Isn't *normal* one of those ideals that gay kids hear about but never experience? Like uninhibited acceptance and Hogwarts."

I stood and started to set up the tent. I didn't want to believe that normal was out of my reach. Didn't want to believe it had been ripped from me the day Diego died.

When the sun went down, Travis and I roasted hotdogs and marshmallows over the gleaming coals of our fire and killed a six-pack of beer. The family across the campground was playing cards by the light of a lantern. The sky was completely clear, and the path of the Milky Way visibly meandered across the dark-navy sky.

I leaned back in my camp chair and licked marshmallow off my fingers. Everything felt *just right*, like all the stars had aligned, like the metallic *crack* of a ball off an aluminum bat. Like the perfect dance partner and your favorite song.

Like every cliché ever.

Everything felt right, but it wasn't. Paulie wasn't here with me, and he would have loved this. I could imagine him in my lap with his head tucked against my neck. I could hear the banter between him and Travis and his teasing voice whispering "buttercup" in my ear. I could see his dark eyes and huge smile.

"When I think about the future, I imagine Paulie," I admitted pathetically. "Do you think that will go away with time?"

"Yeah, probably. Maybe one day you'll meet another nice boy and fall in love, and then you'll be able to picture a future with him instead."

That sounded horrible.

"I don't want that."

"What happened between you guys, Joel?" Travis asked.

"I rejected him, like, right when he was the most vulnerable. I tore down all of his defenses, and then treated him like shit. Threw all of his kindness and love back in his face like he meant nothing to me," I said, voice brittle.

"Yeah, I know," he said, and I glanced at him. He shrugged. "He told me that. *Why* did you do that, though?"

I started to shake my head, to shore up the walls that I'd always used to protect myself, and it was such a deep-seated reaction, one I'd been fighting against since Paulie had called me out on it. But it was much harder to open myself up to Travis, who I lived with and cared deeply for, than someone like Dr. Yamato.

But Travis deserved my trust, and maybe I deserved a life where I wasn't held captive by my own lies and omissions.

So I let the floodgates open, and it was such a relief. I told Travis about Diego and his death and my name and my parents. Travis reached a long, spidery arm over and held my hand when I talked about Diego's parents hating me, and the way the newspapers had had a field day with the story. I shuddered through the teenage events until they were all out, and then I started on the next story, the one that hurt worse now.

"I'd never felt so close to someone, Travis. Paulie looked so happy, and it felt so good, but right before I came, this thought of Diego popped into my head. It felt like infidelity, you know? It felt like I was losing Diego."

"Man, you can't cheat on a memory."

I nodded. I realized that now.

"Paulie loves you. He has from the beginning. You guys can figure this out."

"We can't. You saw him at the Yard. He hates me."

"You can work through that. It was one fight. One episode."

"No. The main thing, according to him, is that he wants to be loved first. He doesn't think I can do that with Diego taking up so much of my headspace. And I don't think I can convince him that I've changed or, at least, that I'm *changing*. Because I *do* love him, so much, but I'm also screwed up. He deserves better."

Travis held my hands between his own. "Joel, here's some unsolicited advice. Get your head on straight with the Diego stuff. I can't imagine going through what you've been through. It has to hurt not knowing what could have been with Diego, and I know that what you've done so far, you've done in an attempt to protect yourself. But won't it be just as bad to *not* know what could have been with Paulie?"

"I'd do anything, give anything to go back and be honest with Paulie from the beginning," I admitted.

"Alex ain't gonna last, honey. There's no way. Paulie's on the rebound."

"And?"

"And . . . you'd be an idiot not to try to win him back. You love him. It's almost sickening how much you love him. And you've stayed away out of some belief that he's too good for you and that he deserves better. But you're *wrong*, Joel. He deserves someone who feels things strongly. He deserves someone who learns from his mistakes. Paulie deserves someone who will put him first because that boy has never been put first in his entire fucking life. That person is you. Maybe it wasn't back when you broke up, but it is you now."

I looked up at the stars. "I could be that person," I said softly, as if I were only talking to myself.

"That's all I'm saying."

We eventually wrapped ourselves up in our sleeping bags and crashed out for the night. A barn owl hooted in the distance, and after a while, I was sure that I could hear coyotes singing from far, far away.

My Friday morning class was over and spring break was officially here. Travis was blasting alternative rock through the house while we both packed to go home. He had a flight out of Oklahoma City to Houston that he needed to catch that evening, and I was driving to Salina as soon as I could get my shit in a suitcase.

I had just packed every pair of clean underwear I owned and was working on gathering up an enormous basket of dirty laundry to wash at Mom's house, when the doorbell rang.

"I got it!" yelled Travis. He belted the chorus of the song, off-key, before opening the front door. After a couple of seconds, Travis shouted for me. I picked up the last errant socks scattered around my floor before jogging to the living room.

Angie was at the front door. Her hair was shorter than it had been when I last saw her, and now she had a red streak racing through her bangs.

"Nice hair," I said.

She rolled her eyes. She really was the queen of the eye roll. "Can I come in?"

Travis turned down the music and retreated back to his room while I led Angie to the couch.

"Is everything okay?" I could tell it wasn't. Her very presence was a sign that something was off, and it could only be because of one person. "Is Paulie all right?"

"Daria tried to kill herself," she breathed.

My stomach plummeted. I remembered the dark circles under Paulie's eyes after fielding calls from her after Christmas. He had to be wrecked. They were all probably terrified.

"What happened? She's okay, though?" I asked. "She didn't die?"

"No. She had to stay in the hospital for a couple days, but she's back home now."

"Is Paulie there?"

"He left last weekend," she said. "I've been taking notes for him."

"Have you talked to him? Is he okay? Is she? Fuck! I wish I could do something."

I jumped up, no longer able to stay seated, and Angie jolted.

Then she said, "She's doing better. And Paulie is putting on a brave face, but I can tell he's freaking out. I think he needs help, some support. I thought you should know."

I paced away from her and gripped my hair in hard fistfuls. I wanted to help, but I couldn't do anything. I wasn't Paulie's boyfriend anymore. I wasn't even his friend, and he had made it abundantly clear I was not who he wanted to spend time with.

"Alex and Paulie broke up," she said, like she'd read my mind. "They broke up almost immediately after he saw you at the Lumberyard."

I sat down heavily on the couch again and rested my forehead in my hands.

"Daria and Paulie—they're at Aunt Ruth's house?"

"Yeah."

I straightened up and pulled my cell phone out of my pocket. Angie watched me dial with a disconcerted look on her face. My call connected.

"Hi, Mom. I'm sorry, but something came up, and I have to go see a friend over spring break. It's an emergency."

Angie's smile spread slowly, like syrup, and I felt the answering call in the heat on my cheeks and the dizzying relief that came from finally taking action. I told Mom I would give her more details later, then hung up without listening to her answer.

"One more thing, Joel," Angie said. "Paulie's parents are there too."

chapter twenty-two

Smoke whispered in front of my truck as I raced through the Flint Hills. A heavy ash hung thick in the air, and it smelled like barbeque: acrid, yet woodsy, like the tang of sweat on a man who'd been working outdoors in the spring sun.

When I first slipped over a rough hill and was confronted with flames on both sides of the road, I thought I had driven straight into a grass fire. Or the apocalypse. But then a man on an ATV waved a ball cap at me from the barbed wire fence running next to the road, and I realized the fires were controlled burns. Every spring, farmers and ranchers patch-burned grazing land, and weeks later the black terrain would be as green as a golf course.

Hot flames were licking over the prairie, obliterating it so it could be new and well again. Men and women worked the fire, spreading it exactly where they desired. It was beautiful to see. The sight almost distracted me from the fact that I was probably making a horrendous error. Probably, *definitely* making a huge mistake.

What if I hurt Paulie even more? What if he hated me for showing up unannounced? I pulled onto a gravel road and stopped on the grassy shoulder. My fingers were trembling, and blood throbbed in my ears.

I banged my hand on the dash. "Fuck, fuck, fuck! What am I doing?" No one could answer; I was utterly alone. The sticky-sweet smell of burning indiangrass slipped through my cracked window, and I rested my head on the steering wheel for a couple of minutes before calling Travis, who would be close to Oklahoma City by now.

He answered by asking, "Where are you?"

"Almost to Paulie's. I'm doing the wrong thing, aren't I? Holy crap, I'm going to make everything worse. What if he doesn't want to see me?"

"I think you need to prepare yourself for that scenario," Travis said after a long pause.

"Fuck you, dude! Couldn't you have lied?"

He chuckled, and I closed my eyes.

"It's worth trying though, isn't it, Joel? Even if it ends poorly."

"What if I add stress to everything? I don't want to be another cause for worry. I mean, I'm about to barge in on a very personal family situation." I moaned. "What was I thinking?"

"Okay, calm down, princess! You were thinking that Paulie might need someone, and you can be that person. You're right. He might turn you away. It might upset him that you're there. *Or* he might be relieved to have a friend nearby. Paulie knows that you care about him. He'll know that you're there for him and Daria, not to stir up drama. If it's really uncomfortable and Paulie doesn't want to see you, tell Daria and their aunt that you're just passing through on your way to your mom's and you want them to know that they're in your thoughts and prayers. Stop and buy them a fruit salad or something. You know, bring them food. Make it seem like you're being a good, hospitable Southerner."

"Okay," I breathed. "I think I can do that."

Travis made me promise to text him with an update, and then I ended the call.

Thirty minutes later, I pulled into Aunt Ruth's driveway with a bag of bagels and donuts in the passenger's seat, and a calm settled over me. I had to do this. I had to let him know he wasn't alone.

I parked behind an enormous SUV. It looked like it might actually seat all of Paulie's siblings, which was saying something. A row of Christian bumper stickers adorned the back window. One read, *This fish won't fry! Will you?* with the Christian fish symbol dancing in orange flames. Who threw around the insinuation of Hell like that? It told me everything I needed to know about Paulie's parents.

When I rang the doorbell, all of the peace inside me shattered into a pounding, jangling mess. I considered ding-dong ditching, but before I could dash away, the front door swung open. Aunt Ruth and I stared at each other for a few long seconds. Then she stepped out onto the porch and gave me a hug. Tears prickled my eyes. It was so good to see her.

"I'm glad you're here," Aunt Ruth said quietly.

"You all right?" I whispered, and she shrugged.

I handed over the bagels and donuts, and she chuckled a little. "Thanks, Joel. This is really sweet."

I wanted to ask her how the crosswords were going and a million other questions. It was like seeing family after being away for a long time, even though we hardly knew each other.

"I'm not sure I should be here. But when I heard what happened, I had to stop by. I don't know if he'll want to see me."

She cupped my cheek gently. "I don't know if he'll want to see you either. Only one way to find out, though." She led me into the living room.

The shades were drawn, and it was dark inside. The TV flickered in the background, but the sound was turned down low, and no one seemed to be watching it. Daria, looking thin and pale, sat in the middle of the couch with a man and a woman on either side of her. She had chopped her long, sweeping blonde hair into a ragged, uneven bob, and the pinched, meek woman on her right kept smoothing down the flyaways. The man was holding Daria's hand, and he exuded hardness and constraint. These were obviously Paulie and Daria's parents, but I could see none of Paulie in either of them.

Both of them turned their eyes on me when I entered the room, and palpable protectiveness gathered around Daria, who glanced up at me and smiled. I leaned down and kissed her forehead.

"Been worried about you, Peanut," I said against the top of her head, and she flashed me a wry smile as I pulled away. She was so young. Too young to be filled with this type of pain.

"Daria, you should introduce us to your friend," their mother said. I smiled tightly at her, but then turned away from them. The only other person I wanted to see was sitting off in the corner by himself.

Paulie had his legs curled up to his chest in the recliner, and his eyes were as wide as silver dollars as they tracked me across the room.

I took a step toward him, and he shot out of his chair, which rocked on its own, like it was powered by a ghost, for a number of heavy seconds.

"Excuse me," he said weakly and to no one at all as he escaped to the kitchen.

I followed him, and as I left the room, Daria was explaining to her parents that though she loved me, I was not exactly her friend. I was Paul's.

Paulie stood rigid at the sink, his back to me and his hands covering his face like a sad game of peek-a-boo. It was oddly reminiscent of our breakup. Maybe all things momentous happened in the kitchen.

I didn't want to invade his space or push him into reacting, but the sweep of his neck made my mouth dry. My hands itched to brush through his hair, which he'd grown longer since we'd broken up, to feel its silky threads slip through my fingers. Instead, I lifted a hand to touch his shoulder, and he spun sharply and blindly stepped against my body.

My breath left my lungs on a gasp, and I enfolded him in my arms. He wasn't hugging me back—his hands still covered his face, so they weren't wrapped around me—but he was crowding his body against mine. It was bliss holding him again, and if nothing else, I would savor this. He sucked in a shuddering breath that whistled through the fingers still clasped over his face.

He was hiding from me, but that was fine. I could handle him hiding, or even rejection, but I would never forgive myself if I didn't make it absolutely clear to him that he was not alone.

"You're such a bastard for coming here," he said, his words muffled by his hands. I pulled my arms away to give him space, but he only burrowed harder into my body.

I put my cheek at his temple, so I could press my words close to his ear.

"I know. And I have no expectations. But I wanted you to know that there was someone, out of all of the billions of people skipping around the earth, who was here for *you*, Paulie."

He nodded and sniffled a little. I couldn't stop myself from breathing him in. He smelled like oranges, and my throat tightened up with a mix of joy and longing.

"I've missed hearing my name," he whispered. He dropped his hands, and ground his forehead into my sternum.

"What do you mean?" I ran a hand lightly over his shoulder blades, trying to keep it platonic. But it was pure pain not being able to kiss his neck or sweep my hands down his spine.

"They all call me *Paul*. Hearing you say my name like that makes me feel like myself for the first time in weeks." I couldn't stop myself from caressing the hollow behind the sharp angle of his jaw. Paulie laughed and groaned. "I can't believe I just said that. It sounded like bad rom-com writing."

"It's okay," I said. "I don't watch rom coms, so I can't judge."

"I'm not sure how I should feel about you being here, Joel."

"I understand, and I can leave if you want me to. I just needed to make sure you were okay. When I found out your parents were here, I got worried about you. Worried they'd make you feel bad or unwanted. And, baby, you're not alone. There are lots of people—not just me—who care about you and love you exactly as you are, exactly how you were meant to be, and your parents' opinions mean diddly-squat." He smiled slightly, so I kept talking. "I'm here for you and Aunt Ruth and Daria, but I'm here *because* of you. Because I want to do whatever you need. I can hold your hand, or I can bluster off. I can clean, or keep you company. I can learn to cook tater tot casserole. I can get you out of the house or talk to your sperm and egg donors in there. We can even give them a queer little show together. I want to be whatever you need."

"I don't know what I need, but I don't want you to leave."

Joy rushed through me. He might not have needed me, or trusted me, or loved me anymore, but he wanted me there, and those words set about healing the piece of me that had broken the moment I'd lost him.

"Then I'll stay," I said. "I'll be here for however long you want me."

Paulie finally wrapped his arms around my waist, and I gave in to the temptation to slip my hands into his hair. I held him and closed my eyes to try to remember it, to try to score the feeling of him into my memory, so I could look back on it later and have something left.

Someone cleared their throat and startled us apart, but when I glanced up and only saw Paulie's dad, I reeled Paulie back in and wrapped one arm around his shoulders, anchoring us together. I wasn't going to stop hugging him when he needed a hug just because the person who'd abandoned him at fourteen coughed at us.

Getting caught canoodling in the kitchen by our fathers was becoming quite the habit, but I refused to be embarrassed. Paulie's father refilled his coffee mug, and then stopped directly in front of us. He focused on me, turning his body so Paulie wasn't in his direct line of sight, like Paulie wasn't standing there at all, and held out a hand for me to shake.

I shook his father's hand with my other. "Hello, sir. I'm Joel Smith."

"I'm Gerald. It's nice to meet you, Joel."

"That's kind of you to say so," I retorted, too quickly for it to come off as anything but bitchy.

"I'm sure Paul here has done a fine job poisoning the well against us, but I can assure you we live by a 'hate the sin, love the sinner' philosophy."

Paulie flinched, and I squeezed his shoulder.

"How big of you." I honestly couldn't believe the acid in my voice. Cattiness was not my normal confrontation style, but something about this man brought it out in me. The implication that Paulie had unrightfully told me tales about his family practically washed my vision red. And the fact that this man had not once looked at his oldest son since walking into the kitchen made me itch to throw something. Like a punch.

After an awkward silence settled, I asked, quietly and gently, "How does that philosophy translate to pushing two of your children so far away that they haven't seen you in over five years? How does it translate to throwing your son out of his home before he is old enough to 'sin' in the way you despise so much? Explain that to me."

"Joel," Paulie breathed and grabbed my arm. And I would have quit the conversation if that man hadn't aimed a cold sneer at his son.

"Paul was old enough to know what he was *and* what he was giving up. He wasn't going to change," his father said.

"Exactly! He can't change. We don't have a choice. We're born like—"

"No!" His dad cut me off with a gesture. "I don't believe that. People *can* change. They can *choose*. They can be celibate. They can try to be normal. Paul had the will to do neither, but he would have always been welcome at home if he had been willing to *try*."

"He was fourteen," I said softly. I wasn't angry anymore—well, maybe I was a little—but, mostly, I was just so incredibly sad that a man's beliefs could poison him so much.

"If you're the ex-boyfriend, then what are you doing here?" he asked, his arms crossed and chin hitched, like he was looking down on me.

"I'm here for the people I care about—Daria, Aunt Ruth, and Paulie. They've been there for me when I needed them. Like family."

"How can you be family? You're not even permanent enough to be the current boyfriend."

Paulie, who had been mostly frozen for the majority of this exchange, came to life. He took a step toward his father, and the man actually fell back.

"Well see, *Dad*, that's the thing with queer kids who are disowned by their parents. We get to pick our own family. And you're right. It's not always permanent. You taught me that," Paulie said softly. "We're all here for Daria, though. So let's table this."

His father evidently had enough feeling left in his heart to look embarrassed, and I felt pretty ashamed as well.

Paulie blew out a shaky breath. "I need some air."

He walked straight outside. I followed behind him and found him climbing into my truck.

As soon as I sat down in the driver's seat, Paulie wrapped his fingers around my wrist. "Joel, oh my God, I said such horrible things to you at the Yard. Fuck, I'm so sorry."

I touched the hand griping my arm, feeling the bony knuckles beneath my fingers. "It's okay, baby." I cringed at the endearment, but he didn't seem to have noticed. "I don't care about any of that."

"I can't believe I did that to you, and I said it all in front of people." He buried his face in his hands again. I scooted closer to him on my bench seat, my legs tangling up in the gearshift, and pried his fingers loose. As soon as his face was revealed to me, full of pain and sadness but still so breathtaking, I cupped his cheeks and let the stubble tickle my palms.

"Listen to me, Paulie McPherson. I deserved what you said, so it's fine."

He covered my hands with his so fiercely it made me jump. "No, you didn't! I know I made you think you're not worthy of good things, like respect or love, because Travis gave me an earful about it! I should never have said any of it, and I have no excuse except that I missed you and I was so mad at you."

"Everything that you said was true, Paulie. Even what you said at the Lumberyard that night. And they were things I needed to hear," I said. "I was so screwed up over Diego that I lost sight of the wonderful gift in front of me. I lost sight of you."

"We both said horrible things to each other." Paulie's gaze dropped to my mouth, and my throat went dry. I nodded, and it took all my self-control not to kiss him silly.

"What happened with Daria?" I asked instead. He flinched out of my hands, our moment broken.

"She took a bunch of pills, but they weren't really the right kind, so they just made her sick. I don't think she wanted to die. She's training to be an RN for fuck's sake. If she wanted to kill herself using pills, she would know which kinds actually work. Can you drive somewhere, please? I need to get away from the house."

I drove us through Emporia and out to the burning prairie, and Paulie told me about Daria, from her refusal to take the antidepressants and anxiety meds to her dropping all her classes. He told me how she'd started sleeping through the day and only left the house to get drunk or high with some guy she'd been seeing. He described, in terrifying detail, the way she had cut every one of those stolen pictures of her siblings and parents into confetti. She had been drowning, he said, and they'd had no idea how to stop it. They hadn't realized the severity of her situation until it had almost been too late.

The smell of smoke lingered like memories around us, an ever-present reminder of the smoldering hills. I pulled over in an abandoned farmhouse's driveway at the crest of a hill so I could look at Paulie while he talked.

"She's so lost, Joel. Her self-worth is all fucked up, and it's twisted together with what happened between her and my parents. And I don't know what to do to help her. I'm so scared and so mad. And it hurts that now my parents are here, she seems a little better. It's like Aunt Ruth and I weren't good enough."

"No, baby, you can't think that. She's sick and you've been there with your love and support from the beginning. She's going to need a lot of help, though, and it can't all come from you. It's not fair to put that pressure on yourself. She'll need counseling and the right medicine."

"I know. I'm just bitter about my parents even being here, but it's what Daria wants. She wants to reconnect with the family, even though she doesn't plan to get completely reimmersed in Quiverfull. She wants to keep me and Aunt Ruth, basically. It's so complicated. I hate seeing my parents, and if it were for any other reason than Daria, I would be *so* gone. Dad will hardly look at me, and Mom has said zero words to me. It's like I don't exist. Like I never existed."

Paulie's eyes were dry, but the wrenching in his voice made tears fill mine.

"You exist to me." I ran my fingers through that beautiful brown-black hair. "There isn't a single person in the entire world who is more important to me than you."

Paulie traced his fingertips lightly over the bridge of my nose and the arch of my eyebrows. Then he reached behind him and tugged my emergency blanket from underneath my suitcase. He hopped out of my truck, but I didn't follow because I was still reeling from his hands whispering over my face. It was like he'd touched that dark, deep place inside me where my fears and insecurities flourished, but his hands had said I was still worthwhile, even with the wounds. Eventually, I stepped out of my truck and felt blind and new.

Down the hill, flames licked over old bluestem and new blooming wildflowers like waves lapping at the shore. I made my way around to the truck bed to find Paulie sitting on the blanket. He was leaning back on his hands, his legs dangling off the tailgate, his lithe body stretched out for my eyes to eat up. He tilted his head and closed his eyes against the sun and smoke when I approached. Light-gray wisps swirled around our heads like shadows in a crystal ball.

I propped my hip against the tailgate but didn't climb up next to him. I would be too tempted to touch him.

He smiled, his eyes still closed. "I've heard people say that losing someone is like losing a piece of themselves. It didn't feel like that when I lost you, Joel. But it did feel like the best part of me was stranded and alone. Like you're the only one who can see it. I don't believe in that 'you complete me' bullshit, but I think part of me calls out for you, and it hurts so much not to hear an answer."

His words tore me up. Tore open my misery at losing him, at being so stupid.

"Paulie, I'm so ridiculously in love with you." I didn't look at him, scared of what I would see. Instead, I gazed out over the rejuvenating fire and wished I were close enough to feel the heat. "I know that we might not be able to move forward, and you probably don't want to start over. But I have missed you for every second of every day. Maybe I haven't lost a piece of myself either, but I do know that you hold all the broken bits of me together. When you had the flu, you said that I was never going to keep you, but you were wrong. Even if we aren't together, you stick." I finally turned to him. His eyes were a little shiny. I stepped between his legs, and he rested his forehead on my shoulder. "I want you, in every way. I want to hear your laughter and see your smiling face every morning. I want to hold your hand when life sucks. I want to be your boyfriend, and I want to be your friend. *But* . . . I will be whatever you need, whatever it is that you want. If you don't want me at all anymore, that's okay. I understand. But please say that I don't have to face another day with you hating me."

Tears slipped out of my eyes, and I was so embarrassed. I didn't hide, though. If I could help it, I would never hide from him again. I didn't know what it was about loving him that made me ralph and cry, but I couldn't help but think it was a good thing. That it made this thing between us real.

He nudged his head against mine and whispered, "It hurt to have your contempt turned on me. It still hurts."

I pulled back so I could see his eyes, but he dropped his gaze.

"I'm so sorry. I don't know what else I can say to make it better. I've thought a lot about what you said, though. About Diego. I do love him. I always will, and I'll never regret the time I had with him. But when I look back on my relationship with him, I realized something. We were both naïve and so young, and to be honest, I'm not positive that we were good for each other. I wasn't mature enough, or understanding enough, and he was always terrified. I hated the closet, and he wasn't ready to come out of it. I loved him in this childish way. It's like if you sat a bowl of Kraft Mac & Cheese and a plate of homemade lasagna in front of me. As a child, I would have always chosen the macaroni and cheese. And it's really good, but it's not nutritious and has all kinds of preservatives and food coloring in it."

"You're not making any sense, Joel." He had tears in his eyes, but he still smiled at me kindly. I nearly choked on my need to kiss him.

"What I'm saying is that you're the lasagna, Paulie."

"Oh." He turned his head and stared down at the controlled burn far below us. "So your love for me is adult?" he said, with a tiny leer.

"Yes, and it's healthy. And maybe I've grown enough to be the right man for you," I said seriously. "It's okay if you don't feel the same way. I want you to be happy. And I'll do whatever I need to do to make you happy, even if that is backing off."

"Do you want to back off?"

"Fuck no. I want to spend my life with you."

Paulie twined his fingers with mine, and it was like my heart was made of butter, because simply holding his hands completely melted me. I stood between his legs, our fingers linked, and we watched the fire eating up the prairie, and the men and women buzzing around to keep it on path.

He rubbed his thumb in a circle over my palm and said, "I love this time of year. During the controlled burns, you know? It's like everyone has pushed the reset button. The fire destroys everything, but the prairie grows back greener and healthier."

"I like that idea," I whispered and pressed my forehead against his, our breath mingling together.

"Me too, buttercup. Me too."

chapter twenty-three

eventually, Paulie and I had to return home. He was too anxious being away from Daria for very long. When we walked back through the door of Aunt Ruth's house, Paulie laced his hand in mine, and my heart soared. Aunt Ruth glanced up from her crossword puzzle and laughed when she saw our hands. I smiled at her laughter because that face with the bright eyes and joy was the echo of Paulie's. His mom, who was also sitting on the sofa, wouldn't look at us.

"Where's Daria?" Paulie asked.

"She's taking a nap right now. She has an appointment with her counselor in a couple hours, and she's moping," Aunt Ruth explained.

"I'll drive her," Paulie said, and his mother's eyes finally snapped up. She opened her mouth, like she was about to object.

"I think that's a good idea," Aunt Ruth interrupted. His mom dropped her gaze back down to her lap, and an angry smile twitched across Paulie's face.

"Where's your dad?" I asked Paulie once we were out of earshot.

"He has to work from a distance, and he's too proud to ask Aunt Ruth for her wi-fi password." He barked out a mirthless laugh. "She hasn't offered it either, so he's been going to the public library." He opened up the coat closet and asked, "Unicorns, angry kittens, or teenagers holding hands on a farm?"

What the hell? "Uh, unicorns, I guess."

"I knew you'd make the right choice, sweetheart." He turned around holding a one-thousand-piece Lisa Frank puzzle.

We worked on the puzzle at the kitchen table until it was time for Paulie to take Daria to her counseling appointment. They left with very little fanfare; though the way Daria folded her hand in his when they were heading to the door induced another one of Paulie's brilliant smiles.

When Paulie's dad got back to the house, Aunt Ruth was sitting with me while I worked on the puzzle. She was reading a romance novel with a mostly naked dude on the cover. Paulie's dad eyed both of us and huffed an insulting laugh before joining his wife in the living room to pray over our souls or do taxes or something.

"I borrowed this from the library just so I could be reading a book with a cover I knew would piss him off. Does that make me a bad person?" Aunt Ruth said without even glancing up from her novel.

"Well, I'm pretty sure that's why Paulie wanted to do the rainbow unicorn puzzle too."

"Peas in a pod, me and Paulie. I've always said so."

"Are they staying in a hotel?" I whispered.

"No. An air mattress in the living room. Having more kids than they can afford has made them cheap," she said, loud enough that they certainly heard it.

I snorted, and Aunt Ruth flashed me a self-satisfied smile. I was a little in awe of Aunt Ruth. She'd offered her home to an estranged brother, who disapproved of her, because it was what the daughter-of-her-heart needed. I probably couldn't have been that good of a person.

By the time Paulie and Daria returned home, it was well past dinnertime, but they arrived touting McDonald's drinks, so they must have stopped on the way home. Daria looked exhausted but dry-eyed. She gave everyone a hug and said she was going to bed.

"Door open, Peanut," Aunt Ruth said. Daria just nodded and retreated to her room.

We were all left eyeing each other warily. Paulie ran a soft hand through my hair and sat beside me at the kitchen table. Paulie's parents were also at the table, having eaten dinner in the space not covered in puzzle. After they'd eaten, oddly enough, they hadn't moved back to the living room. Paulie's dad was reading from a devotional, and his mom timidly helped me with the puzzle. Once Paulie sat down though, the atmosphere tightened. We all worked in uncomfortable silence for about an hour, and then Paulie yawned.

"Come on, Joel, let's go to bed." He stood up and regarded me expectantly. I panicked and tried talking in sotto voice, pretending no one could hear us.

"I don't have to . . . I mean, we could get the trundle bed or . . . I could sleep on the couch."

"In the same room with my parents? I don't think so. Come on."

"Seriously, Paulie," I whispered. "It's fine. I could sleep on the floor in your room."

"What, baby?" Paulie said, not masking his ringing voice at all. "Don't you want to go to bed with me?" He smiled, and I could have died. His dad stood up abruptly and left the room, and his mom inspected her lap like it held all of life's answers. Her face was as red as mine felt. Aunt Ruth was watching our drama with a smile.

I narrowed my eyes at him. "I've got to get my bag out of my truck."

"I'll follow." Paulie's smile was unrepentant.

As soon as the cool night air hit me, I spun to face him. "You're evil, Paulie!"

He laughed. "I couldn't resist."

"I *could* sleep on the floor. You know that, right? There's no pressure here."

"Joel Smith," he said, suddenly serious. "Just come to bed with me. I want you to."

"Well okay."

He smiled at me and turned toward the front door. I hurried to catch up with him. When we got to Paulie's room, he fell back on the bed, fully clothed and body completely liquid. I dropped my bag with a thud and stared at him. It was like I had never seen a man before. Or a bed. He was just so unrightfully beautiful.

His brow furrowed. "Come here."

I couldn't make my feet move. He could gut me so easily. *This* might not be forever. He might want me *now*, while I was convenient and warm and here, but what if he changed his mind once this was over? And while I probably deserved to be used and discarded for everything I had done to him, I wasn't sure I could handle losing him again so soon.

"Paulie, I love you. And I'm good for cuddling or holding you, but if we're going to do more than that, I need to know it's real. I know . . . I know that's not fair. I fucked our relationship up in the first place. But I don't think I can be with you that way and then give you up. It would ruin me."

"Come here," he repeated, so I crawled next to him on the bed. We didn't touch, and I couldn't take my eyes off of him. "We're starting over, yeah?"

I nodded, and he placed a palm against the punching of my heart.

"So are you a top or a bottom?" he asked. I started to smile, but he didn't give me enough time to respond. "Because I like both."

"Oh, do you?" I teased.

"Yep. I'm versatile." He winked at me.

"Well, I'll let you fuck me if you buy me a drink. But you have to be good at it," I bantered back, parroting the same pickup line I'd used on Travis all those years ago.

He giggled. "Good at topping or good at buying drinks?"

A laugh burst out of me. "Topping!"

"Well, I've only topped with two guys, but both seemed to enjoy it."

My laughter died. Pain lanced through me like someone had taken a hot knife to my side, and my throat tightened on the need to cry or scream. The need to release something. The thought of him fucking Alex was excruciating. Some of the pain must have shown on my face because Paulie made an injured little moan in the back of his throat.

"Joel, I'm sorry," he choked and tugged me toward him. I fell into his arms. It was awkward and ungainly, and I didn't remember ever being so uncoordinated with him before. From the beginning it had been easy, as if we'd moved together like gears. But this fumbling felt right too. Perfect, even.

"I'm vers, too," I gasped against his neck. "I prefer to bottom, but I've topped with a couple of guys. The last time I topped, I freaked out. See, my high school boyfriend died in a car accident, and it fucked me up. But I'm better now. Well, not *better*. But I'm trying to be better." Paulie tipped my chin up and smiled at me, and it felt like a forgiveness of sorts. "All I know, Paulie, is that I love you, and I want to be with you in every way that you'll have me. Any way you'll have me."

Leaning slowly forward, Paulie brushed his soft, smiling lips across my mouth. It was the first time we'd kissed since I showed up on the doorstep this afternoon, and I was suddenly overwhelmed by the changes a day could make. I moaned, and it was much too loud and ragged for the soft intensity of his kiss. He didn't pull back though. He pushed against me, and I opened to him, tongue caressing his, tasting the sweetness of the Dr Pepper he'd drunk earlier and *him*. God, just *him*. I curled my fingers around the back of his head and held him loosely, stroking the long hair on top and letting the short sides tickle my fingertips. The smell of oranges and a new scent, slightly chemical, like fancy shampoo, wafted over us.

"I could kiss you for ages," he said, his lips brushing mine. I closed my eyes and pressed into his kiss, but I could still see him behind my eyelids—those dark eyes and curly lashes, the five-o'clock shadow, the strong jaw and delicate nose, the adorable gap between his front teeth. He was there in my mind's eye, and he always would be.

Soon we were clutching each other with more purpose, more intention, and the clothing trapping us just upped the excitement. I ran a shaking hand down the slope of his neck and shoulder. "You're so beautiful," I breathed against the sandpaper of his jaw. He sat up, almost clocking my chin, and ripped his shirt off before falling back beside me. I cupped his cheek with one hand, my thumb rubbing over his scruff. With the other hand, I rediscovered the plains and valleys of his body—the hills of his ribs and the soft depression of his stomach. I passed a gentle flick over his nipple piercing, which was a different barbell now, this one gold against the rose of his nipple. Then I coaxed his mouth open with my lips, wanting to take care of him and love on him and show him precisely how precious he was to me.

"Clothes," he murmured.

"Hmmm?" I was distracted by the warm, salty-sweet taste of his mouth.

"You have too many on."

I was wearing a button-up, which seemed to frustrate Paulie. He pawed at the buttons of one of my cuffs, his breath more uneven with each pass of my free hand down his spine. Finally, he whined, "Joel, take your shirt off." I drew back to see his face as I tugged my shirt and undershirt off, and his eyes were full of need. He groaned, and I preened a little.

"Oh, fuck you, you hot bastard," growled Paulie. "I hate you. Do you know how hard it was to stop thinking about you? It was impossible." He made an aggressive grab for my waist, but I slipped out of his hands, wanting us to go slow. I slid against him, our stomachs and chests slipping together.

We lay there forever, just kissing and touching and shirtless. I kissed the words *I love you* into his mouth over and over until he whispered, "Shhh. It's okay," against my lips.

Paulie helped me out of my clothes and shed his own. I felt combustible, like kindling in need of a match, desperate for him to burn me up. He lay down beside me and yanked the covers over us.

"What do you want, sweetheart?" he asked, his hands cupping my face and his lips clinging to mine. He kept our hips separated by a clean foot of space.

"I don't know," I whimpered. I was so overwhelmed. I just . . . just wanted him. Wanted his desire and to be taken care of. Wanted him to believe me when I said I loved him, and wanted to pour it all out for him until he was full of whatever he needed—love or faith or strength. I needed *him*. He nipped the flesh of my shoulder. I gasped. "What do you want?"

He shook his head, and I shrugged helplessly, both of us stuck in limbo, scared to go further, but unable to stop. There was so much pain and past between us.

"Tell me, baby. Tell me. Whatever you want."

He rubbed his forehead into my neck. "I want to be in control. Is that okay?"

"Of course." I hugged him because I understood. Even though we were naked and hard and I was already dripping a little bit of pre-come, the hug was chaste and full of comfort. He shivered against me and pressed his lips to my neck. Eventually, we separated because Paulie started to inch down, and I certainly wasn't going to stop him, but I felt oddly bereft when his warmth left me.

He didn't take me in his mouth. Instead, he peppered kisses across my stomach and the inside of my legs. I pushed the blanket down so I could see his face.

"I've been thinking about this since we broke up," he said as he gripped my thigh and pushed it up toward my chest, opening me up to him. A little choking sound escaped me. He rested his cheek on my other thigh. "I've dreamed about what I would do if I ever got you back in bed, what I would do to ensure you never wanted anyone but me." He pushed his nose into my groin and inhaled, which was enough to totally scramble my brain, but I had to say something.

"Sex isn't the only reason I want you. I love everything about you."

Sex was pretty much dominating my brain waves at the moment, though. The smell of musk and sweat and citrus was floating around us, and my breath was leaving me in huffs.

"That's good to know, buttercup. But I've *dreamed* about this. About how good I can make you feel."

He gripped my thigh harder and pressed it flush against my stomach. When his head dipped down, I realized what he was about to do, and my whole body jolted before his mouth even found its target. His tongue swirled around my hole, and the noise I made was so loud and indecent, I flushed from embarrassment.

"Shhh," he laughed against my skin. Then he licked me, wet and dreamy and soft, and I bit my lip so hard I tasted blood. I couldn't believe it was this good. Like nothing I had ever experienced, so decadent and focused.

He speared me with his tongue, and we both groaned. I fisted the sheets and tried not to rub against his face like a needy animal. His tongue worked the tight ring of muscle, and I couldn't even hear my moans over the ringing in my ears and the rush of blood through my body. The tension in me coiled, slow and intense—I was about to shoot like a prepubescent.

"Paulie!" I gasped. The warning must have been clear, because he sat back, and we both looked at my cock, as if it were about to perform for us. It was dribbling a steady stream into my belly button. He scooted forward to lick it up, tongue slipping in my navel, and my dick pulsed. I had to grip its base to stop the spiral.

Paulie scrambled off of the bed, fast and awkward, his thin limbs flailing. He dug through his bedside table to find lube and a condom, and then fell behind me and pulled me against his chest, like we were spooning. I tried to turn toward him, but he held me with a hand on my hip. His fingers found my entrance again, slipping inside with a pinch. I winced, and he said, "I'm sorry, darling. Too fast?"

I shook my head and tried to relax. He added a little more lube and leaned over my shoulder to kiss my cheek. I craned my neck because I needed his mouth against mine, and I could taste myself on his lips and tongue. He fed it back to me in the sweetest, dirtiest, most tender kiss ever. It was so intimate, my flavor in our kiss, and it touched something deep inside me. Made me weak and twitchy with need.

Paulie slid his lips along my jaw, sank his teeth into my earlobe, and my head fell loosely against his shoulder. He fingered me open for so long that by the time he slipped on a condom, I was sweating and biting the pillow to stifle my begging.

He gripped my hip with one hand and wrapped the other underneath me, resting his thumb in my jugular notch and pressing his palm against my hot skin. Then he slid into me slowly, his heartbeat pattering against my shoulder blade, and waited for my body to stop fighting him. When he was finally fully seated, he breathed, "Oh fuck, Joel," and I trembled.

"Move!" I begged.

He swiveled his hips, and his cock slid over that hot bundle of nerves. I cried out, and then moved my fist to my mouth to muffle the next sound. Paulie batted my arm away and cupped his hand over my lips.

He had never done that to me before, and it startled me as much as it turned me on. He thrust into me hard, and I moaned against his hand, tasting salt and soap. He grunted, sounding so masculine and hot, I nearly lost it right then.

After several minutes, Paulie whipped his hand off my mouth. He ran his palms over my torso and legs, along the sweep of my spine and up into my hair, like he needed to touch every piece of me, to paint me with his hands, all while thrusting into me relentlessly, zipping against my prostate with every surge inside.

I couldn't control my gasps or moans. My begging. The cries pouring out of me like rushing water, wild and without reason. My heart was going to be a pulpy mess by the end of this—it was slamming so hard against my ribs I could feel it in my toes.

He ran a light fingertip along the ridge of muscle where his body pinned me open.

"Oh God, that's sexy, Joel," he panted as his lube-sticky fingers brushed against my stretched rim. He slid his hand back to my front and rolled his palm over the head of my penis.

"Close, Paulie!" I warned, and slid my hand on top of his, trying to slow him down or speed him up or just anchor myself before I tore apart.

"Shhh. Not yet, sweetheart. Please." He dragged his hand off my cock and took mine with it. "Want it to last. Don't want it to end." I groaned but nodded, even though I knew there was little that would be able to stop the train a-rolling when it finally left the station.

He nudged me until I tipped over onto my stomach. Then he pinned my hand and rolled into me like a wave, all liquid movements and insistent push and pull. Sweat poured off of me, a drop of it sliding from the back of my neck down the ditch of my spine. Paulie licked the droplet, and that move, so innocuous but so incredible, made my body tighten like a fist around him. It ripped a surprised cry from him, and then he laughed. I smiled and felt an answering grin against my shoulder blade.

I managed to stop the steady rise of my orgasm and just receive the love he was giving me, letting myself fall melted and open around him. He kissed my neck and then bit it gently, latching his teeth in like he planned to stay there for a while. I closed my eyes, thankful that I got to experience him like this again—loving and demanding and in control of my body. He was all around me. The scent of him on the sheets below me. The flavor of his kiss still zinging around my mouth like the best aftertaste in the world. His weight on my back. His tenderness in every touch and caress.

Finally, fuck, *finally*, the tension in my spine became too insistent, and I involuntarily clenched around him again. We both gasped, and Paulie shifted slightly on his next thrust. He came in differently, the head of his cock brushing hard over my prostate, and I shouted.

"Oh shit," he sobbed, and his rhythm fell to pieces. Knowing he was about to spill was the most incandescent, overwhelming, wretchedly wonderful feeling. He reached underneath me and fisted my cock, and we both came, slow and spiraling, like we were leaves falling from the top of a building, the wind buffeting us and urging us together in sweet, strong pulses.

Just like all intense bouts of pleasure, ultimately the aftershocks faded and my body relaxed into the bed, crushing Paulie's wet hand against my stomach. His cock was still deliciously hard inside me. *Perfect.* It was so perfect, and I wanted him there forever, but he eventually withdrew and stripped the condom.

I turned in Paulie's arms, and he whimpered against my chest. He pressed his cock against my hip—he was still rock-hard—and tilted his head back to kiss me, his mouth urgent and wet.

"Did you come?" I worried I had read his shuddering body wrong, but he nodded, albeit desperately. He pushed his cock against me a second time, like the slight pressure gave him relief. "Again?" I whispered. The fact he was still hard after coming in my ass made a new sweat break out along my spine. It was so fucking hot.

Paulie moaned into my mouth and begged, "Please, Joel," his voice gravelly and frantic. I scooped up as much jizz as I could from my stomach and used it to wet his cock in slow, brutal pumps. His whole body stiffened and bowed backward. I licked into his mouth with tender, soothing kisses until he cried out my name and came again, his semen bathing my hand and mixing with the spunk already gumming up my body hair.

Paulie's next breath was an embarrassed laugh, followed swiftly by a sob.

Tears ripped through his body, and I was at a complete loss. I held him against my chest and tried not to bump him with my sticky hand. After about a minute, I decided to wipe the come off on the sheet and touch him as much as possible, to try to comfort him before he told me it was a mistake and I needed to get the fuck out of his bed.

"Should I leave?" I whispered, but Paulie clutched me harder. He cried and burrowed into me. So maybe these tears weren't regret. *God, please let them not be regret.* Maybe it was just a release of the pain and stress in his life. Maybe he needed to let it all go and finally felt safe enough to do it, like the sex had scratched away a veneer of control, and all of his fears and hopes and insecurities were too close to the surface to keep down.

"It's okay, baby," I whispered into his hair. "Let it all out. I'm right here. I'm not going anywhere." He nodded into my shoulder and pressed an open-mouthed kiss to my neck, like a blessing.

I wasn't sure if I should hold him up, be stoic, and keep it together, or if I should join him. Let him not feel so alone in his pain and anger and sadness. Lend him my tears and cry for *him* for a change, rather than myself.

So I did a little of both. I held him and murmured *You're okay*s and *I love you, baby*s. And I cried. Not big shuddery sobs like him, but quietly redemptive tears. And it wasn't because I felt even an ounce of the hurt or confusion or anxiety he did. This wasn't my moment. No, I pulled from the muscle memory of pain—that hot little coal that throbbed so close to the surface of my emotions. So easily accessible, but a part of myself I had hidden away from everyone. Well, not anymore.

I could hold him and be strong, and cry for his pain and be strong. And love him forever.

Much later, when the crickets were singing from their hidey-holes and the near-silence settled over us like smoke, Paulie's tears stopped and his arms and legs grew heavy against mine.

"I'm sorry. I'm a mess." He sounded so young, though I knew very few people who had been through as much as him.

"Go to sleep, Paulie. I'll be here when you wake up."

He sighed against my neck, and within minutes, dropped to sleep.

I tried to ignore the gluey dryness of our come sticking us together, but I just couldn't. Paulie didn't stir when I rolled out of bed. His skin seemed too pale, the circles under his eyes more pronounced, like maybe he hadn't been sleeping much. I was absurdly proud I'd made him pass out so easily. He obviously needed the rest.

Tenderness bloomed in my heart as I watched him, and I could have stood there forever. But that would have been creepy, so I threw on my sweats and a T-shirt and made a quick trip to the bathroom. I took a fast shower, and got a washrag warm for Paulie. When I stepped out of the bathroom a few minutes later, an errant light from the kitchen grabbed my attention.

I expected to find the refrigerator slightly ajar or the stove light accidently left on, but instead I almost tripped over Paulie's mother examining a photograph on the fridge with a keychain penlight. Thank God I'd slipped on clothes, rather than just my boxers. We eyed each other warily for a beat, but then my gaze slid to the picture in her hand. It was a candid shot of Paulie and Daria, but Paulie was certainly the focal point.

The picture had been taken at Christmas, after I'd fled my mom's house and showed up here like a beggar. Aunt Ruth had said, *"One for all eternity,"* and snapped the photo before Daria and Paulie could fully prepare. In it, Paulie was looking toward the camera, but not exactly at it. His eyes were full of laughter and light, and I would gladly spend the rest of my life chasing that expression on his face. Daria had her head on his shoulder, but her chin was tipped down so her hair fell like a curtain over most of her face. They looked like the models in stock photos that come with picture frames, but with more animation in their eyes.

I glanced at Paulie's mother, but for the life of me, I couldn't remember her name. Meryl? Or Maureen? Maybe Martha? *Fuck it.* It was easier to cope with what they had done to Paulie if I didn't think of them as whole people with names. But Paulie's mom had real tears in her eyes, and her hands were trembling.

"I hope I didn't wake you," she whispered, and I shook my head.

"You know," I said. "Daria stole photos when she ran away. Aunt Ruth and Paulie didn't know she had them."

"I heard. I hadn't even noticed they were missing." She stared at the kitchen floor, and the thin beam from her penlight illuminated her face in ghostly shadow.

"You could do the same, you know? Take that picture. No one would have to know. Like mother, like daughter."

"It's such a good picture of him." The waver in her voice broke my heart. "I wish I knew what he was looking at." She laughed a little, like that was a silly thing to care about, but I didn't laugh at all.

"He's looking at me," I said softly. "We were throwing pretzels at each other."

She finally met my eyes, and I was surprised to see a genuine smile.

"You won't tell anyone if I take this?" she asked. I started to shake my head, but then she said, "Not even Paul?"

I hesitated. "I don't know if I can lie to him. Not if he asks me outright."

She started to put the picture back, but her hands shook so badly she dropped the magnet.

"Oh for fuck's sake! Just keep it. I'll lie if I have to," I whispered furiously. It wasn't the truth, but I suddenly needed her to take that photo. And I had zero qualms about lying to *her*.

"It's better if he doesn't know," she said. "I understand that might seem odd, but it's not fair to him. I don't want to give him false hope. He won't ever be welcome home. It kills me every day, but our views on him and his . . . his, well, sexual choices, I suppose, aren't going to change."

"Ma'am, you keep that picture then, and I'll keep my mouth shut. I'm not a very religious person, but I pray that one day your love for your own son will outweigh your hate for something you don't fully understand."

Tears spilled onto her cheeks, and I groaned. I could deal with Paulie's tears, but I had no intention of comforting this woman.

"My love for him is why I don't want him to know. He's happier here, freer here, with Ruth, and with you, than he would have been with us. I have no delusions about that, dear." She wiped her eyes and nose with the sleeve of her robe. A loud snore from the living room startled us, and without another glance at me, Paulie's mom slipped out of the kitchen, photo in hand, and I returned to Paulie's room.

I hoped she was right. I wanted him to be happy. To be free. I wanted him to look back on his life with Aunt Ruth and, God willing, his life with me, and see that it had been good, see that he had been loved and accepted and beautiful. There would never be any going back with Paulie's parents, not unless they recanted their whole religious-superiority act. And, frankly, they'd lost their chance. But I would be here to show him that he was worthy of love and commitment and every good thing life had to offer.

When I crawled back in bed, Paulie was awake. I rolled him onto his back and used the damp cloth to clean him up, even though it wasn't warm anymore.

"Are you okay, baby?" I asked.

"There's been a lot of stress the last couple of weeks," he hedged.

"I'm sorry if I added to it."

"No. You coming here kept me together, Joel. And then held me when I fell apart."

And maybe that was the crux of love—holding the broken pieces together so the other person could feel whole again.

"I think I needed that," Paulie continued. "The sex. The crying. I'm such a dork, but I feel like I can handle everything now. You know, seeing my parents and all this stuff with Daria. I'm terrified, and mad, and so hurt. But I don't feel like I'm barely hanging on anymore."

He rolled into my side, rested his head on my shoulder, slung an arm across my middle, and covered my thigh with his. It felt achingly familiar.

"You weren't here when I woke up. It frightened me. I thought I had dreamed everything."

"No way, Paulie. Can't get rid of me that easy."

"Good. I don't want to."

"Truly?"

Even though I had tried not to dwell on it, I was very aware that I had put myself out on a wire today, and I was still a little raw. I knew he wanted me, and thought he needed me. I was past the fear that he would suddenly kick me out of bed or yell, *Psyche!* But that childish, insecure part of me that had never heard the words from Diego really wanted to hear Paulie say them. *Again.* Because I was ready for them now.

"Of course, truly. You and me, Joel? We're better than good. You get that, right? I'm never letting you go. You're trapped," he said playfully.

He pushed up and peered down at my face, his arms caging me in. I traced his lips lightly with my fingertips. When he kissed me, we were both smiling.

"Love you," he murmured against my lips.

I pressed my palm against his pounding heart and, as if it were the first time ever, said, "I love you too."

EPILOGUE

One Year Later

Paulie scooted closer to me in the truck bed. The smell of smoke and burning prairie drifted over us. If I sat up, I'd see the bright flash of controlled flames licking down the hill, but I was content to look up at the black sky and listen for the sounds of night animals and feel Paulie's warmth seep into my bones. We weren't completely meshed together yet, but it would happen soon enough.

We had spent the day pretending to be able to afford foreclosure properties in the area, traveling to each one and talking about how we would change the yard and all the things we wanted out of a home. Soon, we would need to head back to Aunt Ruth's to let her new obnoxious Pomeranian outside to go to the bathroom. According to Aunt Ruth, we were the cutest dog-sitters in the world. Paulie had replied that we were just the cheapest.

For now, I was happy to lie next to Paulie and pretend that we could mine all of our dreams and desires out of life, and they would come out whole and shiny. I wanted to move here, to this land that rushed through my blood singing *home, home, home* every time we crested that first limestone hill.

Townsend, Nebraska, would never be home again. Salina, where my parents were about to get remarried, felt good to me, comfortable even, but it didn't make my heart light and heavy at the same time. It didn't make me want to settle down. Not like the Flint Hills.

Paulie and I had a month until graduation, and he was already enrolled in the one-year master's program for accounting at Farm College. But Elkville was not home either, and it would take me a hell of a lot longer than one year to get my advanced degree. I didn't really want to be stuck in Elkville for years to come; luckily, I had options. Dr. Yamato wanted me to stay at Farm College and continue working on the prairie newspaper project while I got my master's degree, but she had also written me a glowing letter of recommendation for the graduate program at Emporia State.

Paulie said, "You know, we could do it. I could get my master's degree and CPA in a year at Farm College, and you could start school at Emporia State at the same time. It would only be a year of long distance. Then I'll be done, and we can find a place together. Out here, closer to both of our families. I'd love to see Daria and Aunt Ruth more often."

I reached across the middle distance between us and touched his cheek. "I want to live here in the Flint Hills. It feels right to me. But I don't want to spend a year away from you."

"I know, but it would only be a year. And we'd still see each other. We'd talk on the phone. Skype."

I had a couple of weeks to make a decision, and I was scared to make the wrong one.

Paulie must have seen a flash of distress in my eyes, because he rolled on top of me and said, "We'll figure it out. No matter what, we'll make it work, buttercup."

He kissed me, dirty and determined, and I groaned into his mouth. We were in the middle of nowhere. Not a vehicle or house or railcar for miles. I wanted him here under the dark sky with the crackle of a controlled burn as our soundtrack, the scent of smoke clinging to his naked skin.

We had the house to ourselves, so we should go back there. It would be safer. Aunt Ruth had gone with Daria to visit her and Paulie's siblings and parents in Missouri. Daria had been invited to a couple of family activities—a picnic and a trip to the zoo—but she was staying at a hotel with Aunt Ruth.

Daria was doing better, and she was nurturing a fledgling relationship with their parents and other siblings. She was back in school, taking her meds, going to counseling, and had sworn off dating for the time being. She was also attending church and seemed to find comfort there, even though it put Paulie on edge. He was convinced she would come home one day from the nondenominational church she went to in Emporia and tell him she didn't support his *lifestyle*. But I knew that would never happen.

"Want to go home?" I asked. Paulie was grinding on me now, and it was going to get messy if I didn't put a stop to it.

"Nope," he said against my neck.

Oh well. I'd tried.

I slipped my hands under his clothes and over the dimples above his ass. He gasped. I smiled and inhaled against his shoulder. The smell of citrus mingled with the sweet smoke in the air, and I was damn hungry. When I moved no further than trailing blunt nails over his spine, he sat up and pinned my hands over my head.

"You gonna fuck me, big guy, or what?" he asked, laughter lacing his voice.

"Is that what you want, baby?"

"You know it is." He took his shirt off, and the light from the moon bathed his skin in silver.

"You're so beautiful," I said. And it was the truth. He was gorgeous, all dark hair and pale skin and liquid spine. His eyes were too shadowed to read, but the white flash of his smile was clearly visible.

He helped me strip, and before I could second-guess myself, I had the packets of lube Paulie always kept in his pocket dribbling over my fingers so I could work him open.

When he finally straddled me and took me inside his body, my heart felt so full I could have cried. Being inside of him was a revelation. *Every time.* From the first time when I almost ruined it all to now, every time was a miracle. I felt alive and loved and in awe that Paulie trusted me. He moved above me like a dancer, rolling his hips and moaning into the open air.

I pulled him forward so I could kiss the gasps from his mouth. He tasted like light and happiness and sex, and I loved him so much. I tried to tell him, but it mostly came out as garbled consonants. He smiled, and his silly gap against the blood-red of his lips made the muscles in my back clench in need.

"Close," I whispered.

He moved my hand from his cheek to his cock, which was smooth and hot and dripping at the tip. I pumped him in time with his hip rolls, and he made greedy rumbles in the back of his throat.

"I love you," I managed to choke out. It was like I'd pulled a trigger. *Bang*. He busted apart, his come scalding my chest and his sobs ripping through the spring air. I followed him over, and it was so easy. Like laying your head on a soft pillow at the end of a long day or breathing in clean air. Perfect and necessary.

Once his breath returned to him, he laughed, and since I was still inside him, I could feel it echo through my body. My come dripped out around my cock, which was a sensation Paulie and I both probably enjoyed more than we should. He sat forward a little, and I slipped out. When he laughed again, this time with "I love you, too" tacked on, it was full of joy and completion, and the sound wavered through the night air like music. Like chimes, maybe, but earthier and deeper.

I imagined the coyotes calling back, *You're home and we're here and it's good.*

"We *are* good," I said.

And even though Paulie couldn't hear the monologue running through my head, he threaded his fingers into my hair and said, "Damn right, Joel. We're the best."

Dear Reader,

Thank you for reading Erin McLellan's *Controlled Burn*!

We know your time is precious and you have many, many entertainment options, so it means a lot that you've chosen to spend your time reading. We really hope you enjoyed it.

We'd be honored if you'd consider posting a review—good or bad—on sites like **Amazon, Barnes & Noble, Kobo, Goodreads, Twitter, Facebook, Tumblr,** and your blog or website. We'd also be honored if you told your friends and family about this book. Word of mouth is a book's lifeblood!

For more information on upcoming releases, author interviews, blog tours, contests, giveaways, and more, please sign up for our weekly, spam-free newsletter and visit us around the web:

Newsletter: tinyurl.com/RiptideSignup
Twitter: twitter.com/RiptideBooks
Facebook: facebook.com/RiptidePublishing
Goodreads: tinyurl.com/RiptideOnGoodreads
Tumblr: riptidepublishing.tumblr.com

Thank you so much for Reading the Rainbow!

RiptidePublishing.com

ACKNOWLEDGMENTS

A huge thanks to the whole team at Riptide Publishing, especially Caz Galloway, for making me a better writer, and Sarah Lyons, for helping me see this story more clearly.

Many thanks to my beta readers: Meredith, Ashley, Dustin, Brent, Dillon, Megan, and Hayley. Without your support, enthusiasm, and feedback, I would never have had the guts to put this story out there. I owe you all endless rounds of drinks. Also, my sincerest thanks to my friends who have sent encouragement and answered questions about Oklahoma colloquialisms.

An enormous hug and kiss to my parents. Your love and support has always been a cornerstone in my life. In many ways, this story is a love letter to your birthplace: the Flint Hills. And to my sisters—I couldn't ask for better friends.

And finally, thank you, Justin. You convinced me to give this writing thing a shot, and you help make it possible every day. For that and for many other reasons, you'll always be my favorite.

about the
AUTHOR

Erin McLellan writes contemporary romance with characters that are complex, goodhearted, and sometimes a little quirky. She likes her stories to have a sexy spark and a happily ever after.

Erin has a bachelor's degree in creative writing from Oklahoma State University and a master's degree in library and information studies from the University of Oklahoma. A former public librarian, Erin still enjoys being surrounded by books and readers, but now she hopes to find her stories on the shelves as well.

Originally from Oklahoma, she currently lives in Alaska with her husband and spends her time dreaming up love stories set in the Great Plains. She is a lover of chocolate, college sports, antiquing, Dr Pepper, and binge-worthy TV shows.

To learn more about Erin and to sign up for her newsletter, please visit her website at: erinmclellan.com.

You can also find Erin on:

Twitter: twitter.com/emclellanwrites

Instagram: instagram.com/erinmclellanwrites

Pinterest: pinterest.com/erinmclellanwri

Enjoy more stories like
Controlled Burn
at RiptidePublishing.com!

Dead Ringer
ISBN: 978-1-62649-338-4

Heels Over Head
ISBN: 978-1-62649-567-8

Earn Bonus Bucks!

Earn 1 Bonus Buck for each dollar you spend. Find out how at
RiptidePublishing.com/news/bonus-bucks.

Win Free Ebooks for a Year!

Pre-order coming soon titles directly through our site and you'll
receive one entry into a drawing for a chance to win free books for
a year! Get the details at RiptidePublishing.com/contests.

48029654R00151

Made in the USA
Middletown, DE
08 September 2017